Staying True

By Suzie Carr

Edited by Trish McDermott

Also by Suzie Carr:
The Fiche Room
Tangerine Twist
Two Feet off The Ground
Inner Secrets
A New Leash on Life
The Muse

Keep up on Suzie's latest news and projects:
www.curveswelcome.com

Follow Suzie on Twitter:
@girl_novelist

Cover photography by Trisha McDermott

For you, Grampa. Bless your sweet soul.

Acknowledgements

Many thanks to everyone who had a part in this book, particularly Joanna Darrell and Cassie Davis for your insights, support, and trust. This story would not have been possible without your contributions. Also, to Bethany Meservey and Felicia Haggerty for your advice, generosity and incredible gift to see what my eyes didn't see. I'd like to thank JG for helping me to brainstorm the title of this book. I will never forget the day you tossed out those two words, *staying true*. They clicked and became the central force in telling this story. I also want to give enormous thanks to my editor, photographer and best friend, Trisha McDermott, for your inspiration, intelligence, and patience. I am also grateful to my Grampa for your wisdom and advice. Thank you for teaching me some of life's most valuable lessons and for encouraging me many years ago to go write a book. This one's for you! And lastly, I'd like to thank my special love, for putting up with my crazy addiction to the written word.

Chapter One
Ruby

I never set out to be 'that girl.' You know, that girl who lived out of her car, borrowed money from her grampa, or fell in love with a married woman.

Yet, there I was, all of that and more.

I curled up next to her, admiring the way her hair fell in gentle waves over her tanned shoulders and spilled onto the mattress. I should've run away. I should've torn myself from her, gotten dressed, picked up my pocketbook and gone to the other room at the other end of the hallway. Instead, I swept my leg around hers and inhaled her delicate scent. My inner voice screamed at me to back away. I ignored it. I justified that we deserved this moment, that we could control our emotions, and that we could frolic in freedom within this wind tunnel and then fly away from it all at will, like free birds.

Chasing freedom in a wind tunnel played tricks and created illusions though. Just like in life, our desires tossed us around and landed us in these unimaginable places where we risked all for the sake of love.

* *

Many Months Earlier

For several years, I worked as a masseuse at an upscale spa. Then, one Thursday morning, I walked into work, and my bosses fired me.

I loved being a masseuse. I loved my bosses. I loved my coworkers. So this hurt.

The spa, with all of its richly-textured walls, amber-hued lighting and museum-quality art, comforted me. My bosses never failed to spoil us with pastries, bonuses, and flattery. They grew this little hair shop into a full-scale, destination spa, and welcomed us all into their business, mentoring us, educating us, and creating many opportunities to grow.

I considered them my family, and never expected they'd turn their backs on one of their own.

Then one day Mrs. Jean Nuay entered. She was a regular pain in the butt. She always complained about stale bread, sour fruit, old coffee and the cold air. Usually, I could calm her down and bring a smile to her face by the time she left her visit. Not this particular day. I could not please the bitch.

The session started on this day just as any of them did. She questioned if I washed the linens and my hands. She insisted on Bach music and fresh sage to be lit. Once I got started on her shoulders, she barked out orders on how I should slow down, speed up, dig in, and lighten up. She tossed out gripes, smacked my hand away when I hit a nerve, even cussed when I told her I ran out of her favorite massage oil. Then, she brought up my predecessor, the infamous Lilly who picked up and moved to Hawaii one day and left everyone sad and shocked. She said, "Lilly massaged so much better than you."

Bells rang in my head. Then, things got fuzzy. I dug into her shoulders so deeply that she screamed out and called me a bitch.

Well, I snapped. I flung a towel at her and walked out on her.

She rushed out with a towel around her body screaming at me. I headed for the break room, passing my two bosses. Then, I heard a gasp and some giggling. I sneaked a peek over my shoulder at a naked Mrs. Nuay bent over, red-faced, squirming for the towel that had fallen to her stubby feet.

My bosses scurried to her side, wrapping her in the towel and hugging her like a child rescued from raging waters.

"If you don't fire that Ruby girl, I'll be sure to file a complaint with the Better Business Bureau," she said.

My boss, Betsy, turned to me and asked me to go home for the day.

"But, I have a full appointment load."

"I know, honey," she said. "We think it is best."

I walked out of the spa that day feeling justified in my reaction, confident my bosses had my back on this. They just needed to calm down and digest the disaster. The next day, I'd go in and explain my side of the story. Simple as that.

So, there I stood the very next morning, not at all prepared to have to defend myself.

"Ruby, we need to let you go," Betsy said.

"But she bordered on abusing me," I said.

Betsy cradled her arms around her chest. "She's threatened us. We can't take that kind of chance."

I turned to Janet, my other boss. "But, she was out of line. She cursed at me. She whacked my hand. She insulted me. She was wrong."

Janet avoided me, shuffling her eyes down to the floor.

"We can't risk our spa over this," Betsy said.

Just like that, because some snobby lady threatened them, they turned their backs on me and tossed me into the wild.

I should've stepped back from them, smiled and been straight on my way out of their spa, leaving with a shred of dignity. Their blessing didn't cross my mind. My rent did. My utilities did. My car repairs did.

Anger overthrew my sense of sanity. I tossed their hot waxing machine off its trolley table, and it splattered all over their granite floor, and on the bottom half of Betsy's Paul Mitchell apron.

I ran out on them. I swept past the clients with foils in their hair, past the product displays, and past my friends, Marcy and Rachel, at the receptionist desk.

A moment later, I climbed into my bright yellow Camaro with its new tires and transmission, and settled into its black leather seat. The needle on the gas gauge teetered on the empty line. I had five dollars and eighty-three cents in my pocketbook. I had drained my bank account reserves on repairs just the other day. Now I didn't even have enough gas to break away from this neighborhood. I sat for several minutes staring at the willow tree in front of me. A bird sat lonesome on a drooping branch. She chirped in vain, probably hoping for a friend to join her, but instead remained alone amidst a flurry of sad weeping willows. We were one in the same, both hanging around in a big world to fend for ourselves.

Fear sucked. I would never choose fear over a friend. Ever.

Marcy opened the spa door and walked toward my car. Her wild, curly hair fought with the strong summer wind. She lit a cigarette mid-gallop and flipped off a truck that sped by her and beeped the horn.

I lowered my window.

"Are you okay?" She hugged herself in the breeze. Her cigarette dangled from her long fingers.

"No need to worry about me." I shouldered a smile. "I'm free now. I hated my long days and strict schedule, anyway. I needed this change."

Her face brightened. "You are so much better off."

"Yes." I smiled to mirror hers. "I am."

"We should celebrate." She took a long drag. "Rachel and I will take you out."

Rachel and Marcy were the only couple I knew who could work and live happily together. I could never stand to be around someone every hour of the day like that.

I smiled up at her. "Sure, give me a call."

She kissed my cheek. "You got it, friend." Then, she ran off.

A few nights later, I sat in a booth at the lounge of the Gateway Suites, across from Rachel and Marcy. They treated me to a Cobb salad and a glass of Merlot.

Our waitress walked past carrying a tray full of fresh burgers and golden french fries over one shoulder. She smiled and rushed past. Lots of men with graying hair huddled around cocktail tables, one elbow bracing their overweight bodies, the other cradling the neck of a beer bottle or glass of whiskey. The stress they carried right between their husky shoulder blades hurt me.

"Janet and Betsy feel so bad," Marcy said, forking a mouthful of brown rice between her chubby lips.

"They said they didn't have a choice," Rachel said.

"That's because they live in fear." I stabbed my romaine lettuce. "It's better for me. I have time to read now and get through some cleaning. I can catch up on lots of things now."

Marcy pointed her fork at me. "I envy you. And not just because of your long, wavy blonde mane." She winked.

I arched my eye at her. "My hair is a mess. I need a trim and a highlight." I tossed it over my shoulders and shrugged, then fought with a cucumber. "The timing of getting fired couldn't have been any worse."

"So, what are you going to do now?" Rachel asked, flipping her long red hair over her shoulder.

"You should reinvent yourself." Marcy sat up tall. "Go out there into the world and spread your wings. Freestyle it for a while."

"Freestyle it?" I swirled my glass of Merlot and inhaled its oaky aroma.

"Yeah, just freelance your services. Be like one of those "ten-minute massage" girls in the middle of the mall. Take a client when you want one and walk away when you don't."

I considered this and loved the idea. I continued to consider this idea even later on as I entered my apartment. Why not?

Freestyle masseuse. It had a nice ring to it.

I flipped through my mail and landed on my electricity bill. I panicked when I saw how much the bill had increased over the past sweltering month.

Fuck freestyle anything. I needed a job.

The next day I dressed up in a pretty sundress, curled my hair in big waves, dabbed on some bronzer and lip gloss and started hitting the streets.

I filled up my gas tank with the little I had left on my credit card and drove around all day, completing applications in countless reception areas across the greater Providence area. How could I explain why I left my previous place of employment? Not one good reason came to mind. So, I settled on the vague 'seeking a better opportunity.'

Well, twenty three spas later, an empty tank of gas, and a maxed-out credit card, I panicked again. What if no one called me?

I pondered a Plan B. When I lived with my Grampa, I would walk dogs for ten dollars. I could walk dogs if I had to. I could walk three or four at a time. I could make up flyers and pass them out to people in my neighborhood. Better yet, I'd be better off in a wealthy neighborhood. I could charge more and walk two dogs at a time instead.

I could do this.

I chopped a tomato and salted it. "I could definitely do this if I wanted." I bit into the sweet and salty fruit and contemplated my future.

Who was I kidding? I didn't want to walk dogs.

I wanted to massage.

Days passed without a ring. I checked my phone every five minutes just in case by chance I had missed a call. I paced my living room. I broke out into yoga poses. I rearranged my couch and end tables. Then on the fourth day, I walked into my kitchen, and my phone rang. Marcy. I flung the phone at the couch and stomped back off to the kitchen to make some tea.

I filled my teapot and pulled out my box of green tea. "Freestyle masseuse or dog walker?"

I loved the idea of saving worthy people from demise, of taking their wilted souls and of bringing them back to life. I'd love to offer this kind of relief to hard-working people who never considered treating themselves to such luxury because they couldn't afford to take the time to indulge.

But what if they could?

I poured some honey into my teacup.

Success in life didn't come from taking, but from giving people something of value, something intangible that would leave them spellbound.

No one needed hour-long massage therapy to benefit. A ten-minute massage could offer equal value. I could charge a fraction. I could work on volume instead. Who needed a spa with a waterfall, marble, and custom drapery? I just needed a portable chair and some willing clients.

I took to the streets the next day and considered this more. I sat on a park bench in downtown Providence and people-watched. Potential massage clients lurked everywhere. Turn a busy street corner, and faces swollen from too many tears stared back. People needed to unwind. They needed to have their knots kneaded out of their bodies before the stress wreaked havoc on their health.

The world overflowed with stressed-out people in need of my services. They carried boulders on their backs, worrying about deadlines and client satisfaction and all of that yucky stuff business people worried about.

I could open up a portable massage business right here in the middle of town. I could start off working corporate wellness fairs, ushering people to my portable chair where I worked out the kinks in their necks. In ten minutes, I could potentially earn the same amount of tips I earned from the rich spa snobs after kneading them for an hour. These ten-minute clients would breathe sighs of relief and ease out of the chair with relaxation dancing on their faces. My job would be to sweep in and dislodge them from this misery and leave them refreshed in just ten short minutes.

I could add real value to people's lives.

Right there on that park bench under the hot, sizzling summer air, I determined my future.

I would become the ten-minute masseuse.

I would seek adventure. I would run from routine. I would charge towards change. I would blossom under the glow of fun. I would breathe energy into this life.

I understood that freedom could never be captured. I couldn't run up to freedom, grab it and constrain it. I had to go with the flow of it. I had to be willing to view the world from a different perspective, like from the inside of a raindrop hanging on the tip of a leaf. Life's surprises happened in places like this, places where no one else had thought to venture.

* *

I arrived at my grampa's apartment at dinnertime. He spooned chicken noodle soup into a bowl. I walked up to him and kissed his cheek. "Smells heavenly."

"You know back when you were a little girl, I used to cook this for you, and you used to hate it."

I grabbed a bowl from his cupboard. "I'd love some now, though."

He handed me his bowl, and I sat down with it at the kitchen table. He joined me a moment later. "So to what do I owe the pleasure?"

I would ease into the real reason behind this visit soon enough. "I just wanted to catch up."

He slurped some soup, wiped his mouth with a napkin, and squinted. "Well, I'm stuck on my latest story. But, it'll come to me." He bit into a peanut butter cracker. "I've been watching television instead."

He looked so feeble, so bored with his present life. This apartment swiped away his humor, his agility, his smile, at times. The oldness of the place had settled into his bones and stole his active spirit.

"Do you remember when we used to watch *The Price is Right* together?" I asked.

His eyes brightened.

"And *Wheel of Fortune*?" I asked.

"Yes, and *Wheel of Fortune,*" he said.

Some soup dribbled down his chin. I wiped it.

"I used to love that old console television. It took up the entire living room."

The color returned to his cheeks. "Yes it did, dear."

We ate our soup reminiscing about the days at our old house, the bed and breakfast called The Rafters. By the time we finished, he sat back and drew a relaxed sigh, one that sparked some life.

"Grampa," I said, reaching out for his hand. "I need to ask you a favor."

"Anything, dear."

I bowed my head and squeezed his hand. "Can I borrow some money?"

He braced his hands on the table and lifted himself off with a groan. He shuffled over to his cabinet and took out a coffee container. "Just one of the several places I keep some loose cash," he said. He shuffled back to me and handed me the container. "You take what you need."

I reached into it and took three hundred dollars.

"I'll pay you back."

"I taught you well," he said cradling my shoulder. "I'm not worried."

* *

For my first order of business, I purchased a portable massage chair with the money I borrowed. Then, I drove around to office parks asking to speak with human resource managers about the benefits of ten-minute massages. They met me with a polite ambivalence, leading to a string of excuses of why they would have to pass.

I lasted two weeks on the streets before agreeing to meet up with Rachel and Marcy again at the Gateway Suites Lounge. "They have the best happy hour specials here," Marcy said, stuffing a chicken wing in her mouth.

"I'm in trouble," I admitted. "In deep trouble." I toyed with the candle on the table, waving my finger over the flame, teasing it to grow taller.

"You're going to end up ruining your supple skin if you keep frowning like that," Marcy said, warning me with a pointed finger.

Rachel put down her beer. "If it's any consolation, the girl they hired to replace you sucks. I had her massage my back. A two year old could've done better."

Our waitress popped over to our table and cleared our pile of plates. Her exquisite makeup and willowy top softened her masculine features. Her dark hair shot out in all these spastic directions like she'd just gelled up her hair and stepped in front of a high-powered fan. Her makeup accentuated her sharp cheekbones and strong jaw, reminding me of a pretty mannequin in the window of Neiman Marcus. "You girls want another round?" Her voice carried a low tone.

"I'm good," I said.

"We'll all take one more," Rachel said. "My treat."

The three of us drank two more drinks a piece that night, and my head buzzed. I scanned the room. "You know, look at all of these stressed-out people in here. I bet I could rake in quite a bit of money with ten-minute massages."

"You could set up your portable chair right over there in the corner, near the chicken wings and nachos. People could not miss you," Marcy said.

"I'm serious. Look at that table." I tilted toward a group of three men in deep debate. "I could waltz up to them, squeeze into their conversation with a smile, and challenge one of them to say no to my hands."

The three men bantered, each of their voices wrestling to be heard over the other's.

"I'll give you twenty bucks," Rachel said.

I zeroed in on the shortest of the three men. I stood. Then, a tall, striking woman, with hair the color of milk chocolate and legs that traveled on forever beneath her business suit, brushed past us.

She charged over to the bar and ordered a drink. Our waitress grabbed a glass and poured her a shot. The business suit lady gulped it back and exhaled. She dropped her face in her hands before lifting and drawing another exaggerated breath. Our waitress delivered her another shot, and she gulped that one back in another toss.

I could work magic with her.

"Ladies, a new client just walked in." I straightened my t-shirt and plopped a mint into my mouth. I studied her like a leopard on the prowl. "Watch and learn."

I scaled over the floor, mesmerized by my new challenge and soaring on the confidence of my wonderful buzz. As I approached, she asked our waitress, "Shawna, can I get another one of these, please?"

Shawna nodded and poured her another. She downed it, wiped her mouth with her fingers and pointed her tiger eyes at me.

I eyed the empty barstool next to her. "Mind if I have a seat?" I asked.

She cocked her head, and a few layers of her soft hair bounced on her shoulder. "Fine with me. I'll be leaving in a moment anyway." She flagged down Shawna again, with a snap of her fingers. "Can I get my total?"

Shawna nodded and headed to the register.

"Bad day?" I asked.

She swept her eyes clear past me. "I don't feel much like chatting right now."

"You look like you could stand to punch something."

She watched Shawna calculate her check. "I could stand to. Yes."

"I've got a pretty strong arm that you're welcome to hit." I flexed my bicep and cradled it close to my side.

She scrutinized it.

"Well, go on. Get it over with. Punch me if it'll make you smile."

At last, her cheeks relaxed, her lips wrestled into a slight curl, and the blazing spokes of her eyes softened and rolled. Her chest pulsed in and out, flapping, attempting to stifle her giggle until she could no longer contain it. "Put your arm down. You look ridiculous."

I dropped my arm and eased onto the stool next to hers. "Got you to smile, didn't I?"

She shook her head. "What if I did hit you?"

I latched onto her tiger eyes. "Dare I say, it was worth the risk?"

She cocked her head and smiled, then Shawna returned with her check. "Here you go, boss."

"Boss?" I asked. "You manage this place?"

"I'm one of the many managers of the hotel, yes."

"Is that why you are all business-suited-up, looking for a good punch?"

She shook her head and fought a new smile. "Do you want a drink?"

I lingered on her playful gaze. "I'll take an iced-tea."

"Can you get her an iced-tea?" she asked Shawna.

"And for you?" Shawna asked her.

"I'm heading out."

I tapped the counter. "Oh come on," I said. "Have an iced-tea with me."

She opened her mouth to protest, then closed it. She did this three times, and each time she scoffed a little louder. "Fine. Two iced-teas please."

I saddled into her gaze. I would win this bet with Rachel. "You know," I said, traveling my glance over to her backside. "You've got a gigantic thing sitting between your shoulder blades."

Her eyes flew open. She jumped off of the stool. "Get it off! Please, get it off!" She all-out whacked herself, spinning, screaming, bending over at the hips and flinging her hair every which way.

I died laughing. I rolled off of my stool, clutching my tummy, losing my breath, tears streaming down my cheeks, as I watched this beautiful girl freak out over a supposed creature on her back.

"Why are you laughing?" She spun around in circles still whacking herself.

I just balled over again unable to speak.

Panic stretched across her face, and she ran up to the table of the three men and subdued her panic long enough to ask the heaviest one to check out her back. The man searched, even ran his fingers across her blades, shaking his head, apologizing that he couldn't see anything. That's when she glared at me. Those spokes of her tiger eyes lashed out, daring me to flex my arm again.

So, I did. I flexed it and braced myself for impact, ready to ingest the pain all for the sake of building rapport and trust and earning my first twenty dollars of the night. A girl's got to do what a girl's got to do, right?

She marched over to me and whispered. "How dare you fuck with me?"

"I'm not fucking with you."

"You're fucking with me."

We eyed each other.

"Can I put my arm down?" I asked.

She sighed. "Look. Whatever game you're playing, you're playing alone."

I reached down for her wrist. "Please, let me explain."

She pulled her wrist back. "Please do."

"You do have something between your shoulders."

Panic sprawled across her face again.

"Relax. You don't have a hairy spider there."

She shivered.

"You're carrying a huge tension ball right across your shoulders."

She squinted. "How would you know that?"

I slid behind her, grabbed her shoulders, and kneaded the muscles around her blades. "I'm intuitive. See right here? You've got this big knot that's digging on your nerves. If you don't get rid of it, it's going to keep bugging you, and you're going to keep running into barrooms downing shots to numb it." I kept kneading, and she didn't fight it. She bobbed her head forward. "Give me ten minutes, and I'll fix you up. I'll relax you with my special touch," I whispered.

She stiffened and pulled away. "I'm not paying for whatever kind of weird service you're offering."

"What do you think I'm offering you?" My face flushed.

"Do you always go up to strangers and start massaging their necks?"

"Well, kind of. Yes." I shrunk.

"Well, I'm not like that." She cradled her pocketbook. "I've got to go."

She stormed past me, leaving me dizzy with her musky scent.

"You're not like what?" I yelled after her.

"A whore," she yelled back then marched out of the lounge.

I tossed my hands up in the air in defeat. I scanned the room and everyone looked at me like I was a serial rapist vying for my next victim. I scoffed and turned on my heel and stormed out of the lounge, saying back over my shoulder, "What are you all looking at anyway? I'm not a whore, either."

I turned and walked out of the door to the outside. My friends followed.

"Hey," Shawna yelled. "Are one of you girls going to pay the bill?"

Rachel lit a cigarette. "I'm not going back in there."

I rolled my eyes and stretched out my hand. "My twenty, please."

She placed it in my hand, and I charged back in.

Shawna handed me the check. "That'll be forty two dollars and seventy-five cents, please."

"Are you freaking kidding me?"

She raised up her hands. "I just pass the stuff out."

I tossed her the cash. "Do I look like a whore to you?"

She laughed and plucked up the money. “Those baby blue eyes of yours have far too much of a twinkle in them for you to be a whore.”

“Thanks.” I placed the strap of my pocketbook back on my shoulder. “Sorry I caused a little scene.”

She waved me off. “She’s stressed and brought you into her tailspin. I wouldn’t worry.”

“So is she really your boss?”

She smiled. “Yep. The best, too. She takes her job seriously, unlike the other bozos in this place.”

“I could’ve helped her with that stress. I’m a professional masseuse.”

“A professional masseuse, huh?” She twirled her silver stud earring, staring off to the side before landing back on me. “Give me your card, and I’ll tell her. Maybe next time, you’ll catch her in a better mood and you can do your job.”

I handed her a business card.

“Ten-Minute Masseuse?”

I smiled. “It’s my specialty.”

She took it and placed it in her pocket. “I’ll make sure she gets it.” She turned and walked away, tossing a towel over her shoulder.

Chapter Two
Nadia

Something about this brazen blonde girl from the lounge intrigued me. Her long, creamy blonde hair and her petite, tight body turned me into a bumbling idiot. The skin on my neck and shoulders still tingled from her touch.

Talk about a red flag.

That playful, carefree attitude of hers sure teased that part of me that had been locked away far too long.

Whatever magic she possessed, I wanted more of it.

I imagined her to be the type to wear flip flops to a wedding and sunbathe nude on her rooftop. This liberal quality excited me. It seemed rooted in something pure and natural. I could imagine her chilling out to the sounds of Bach by a roaring fire while snuggling under a blanket her grandmother crocheted. Everything about her spelled comfort, mystery, and intrigue.

I poured myself a full glass of Merlot and headed out to my hotel deck. I stared up at the starry sky, muted by the light pollution of downtown Providence. Horns beeped below and the heartbeat of cars rocked the otherwise peaceful night. I drew a thoughtful sip, swirling the dry wine around my tongue. My nerves rippled at the slightest thought of her long golden hair, flirty eyes, and soothing touch.

I reached into the pocket of my terry cloth bathrobe and pulled out my harmonica. I placed it between my lips and blew into it, playing a sweet, wailing melody that stilled my restless heart. The lights of the city twinkled and played on that part of my soul that craved light, beauty, and joy.

I gulped the last of my Merlot then jumped into the shower. I turned on the water and stepped into the shower, bowing my head under the spray. I soaped up, lathering bubbles around my skin imagining her hands massaging the bubbles into great mounds of foam.

I circled my nipples and imagined her dewy lips wrapped around one of them, sucking, pulling, and flicking it with her rosy tongue. My body rose up in delightful tucks at her imagined touch, softness, tenderness, caressing those parts of my heart and soul that craved love. In need of a loving touch, a touch that harmonized and spoiled me, I closed my eyes and sealed into this steamy moment. I drifted away from reality under the massager head of a shower and escaped into the memory of this girl, this pure and pristine flower child of a girl. I succumbed to the ultimate point of ecstasy, bucking, groaning, and panting in absolute pleasure.

* *

When I first met my wife Jessica, I feared I'd never be able to blend into her world. She was wild, uninhibited, and the star of the show. I assumed that blending into her life would be like blending into a car wash. How right I was. Car washes could be really fun when you close your eyes and let them take you for a ride.

The first time I saw her work her magic, my heart galloped along with her wild beat.

I discovered her by accident. My friends, Janie and Roxanne, wanted to celebrate their upcoming wedding with fun, so they begged me to throw them the most spectacular bachelorette party. At first, I planned to take them to dinner with a few of our close friends, and then surprise them with a fun trip to Manhattan where we'd lose ourselves in cocktails, dance, and enjoy whatever else the night tossed at us. Then Jessica fell into my lap, literally.

I had been lounging on the grass on the quad reading my calculus textbook. The sun trickled through the leaves and danced on the pages, making it difficult to focus on equations and variables. I dug my mind into polynomials and tried to figure out how they could ultimately fit into my life when a Frisbee smacked my head. Jessica stopped just mere inches from my face to retrieve it. A tease whispered on her lips as they curled up into a smile that I surmised she used on many occasions to jumpstart hearts.

I asked her, "Where did you learn that graceful move?"

She responded, "I'm a dancer. It comes with the territory."

To this I asked, "A dancer? As in ballet?"

"As in Burlesque," she said, then jumped to her feet and strode away. She looked over her shoulder and winked, then ran towards the coeds waiting for her return.

The idea to hire a Burlesque dancer had never occurred to me until that moment. After this girl walked away, I wanted her. I wanted her to be the one who would add value and mystique and thrill to my friends' bachelorette party. For the days that followed, I sought out this girl. I spied on her playing Frisbee under a canopy of sunny skies.

My bravery arrived when her Frisbee once again landed in my lap. Her eyes lit up as if in the presence of someone beautiful. This warmed me straight through to my core.

The night of the bachelorette party, she stood amidst a circle of gorgeous women, swinging her hips and bending in all the right places. She epitomized the beauty of a Burlesque dancer. Her smile, the flirty crinkle around her eyes, the subtle snarl of her nose as she captured the stage, stole my breath. Her hair bounced up and down along with the rest of her God-given, prized features. She knew just how to land in front of people and tease them into submission.

Jessica stole the show, blinding us bachelorettes to anything not golden-brown, not hot to the touch, not doused in gritty skin and sex. Before long, all of us swooned together in one massive wave of euphoria, sweat, and womanly lust. We swayed to a universal melody, lacing our fingers, tracing them along each other's curves, mesmerized as if under a spell where beginnings and endings blurred into one ever-flowing vessel of rippling highs and lows. Legs pretzeled against legs and arms caressed hips and guided them in a fluid dance, bringing us to the root of ecstasy right there at the base of this grandiose entertainment force known as Jessica.

As I clung to the body of a blonde girl with wide hips, Jessica and I locked eyes and shared a liberating moment. Swooned by the flirt in her eye, I transformed into an empowered woman under the strobe lights. Turned on by this drug, this nirvana, I changed. I was no longer Nadia Chase, the boring girl with mousey hair and eyes set just a bit too far apart. I was Nadia, the girl who could morph into someone capable of bringing myself to orgasm on a dance floor.

Jessica turned life into a party. Everyone loved her. My parents couldn't invite her for enough homemade pasta dinners. My sister, Sasha, debated with her on everything, which meant she admired her. My friends hated whenever she didn't tag along for our happy hours. My college clubs demanded she join us. Jessica knew how to stir up life and get it rolling in no other direction than that of fun. Smiles followed her. Laughter erupted around her. Sweet alcohol flowed in her presence like a cascading waterfall.

I adored her. Life couldn't get any better.

Then one night, we were sitting in her car staring out over the horizon at a full moon, and she just started bawling. I begged her to tell me why. She just buried her face in her hands and bawled more. Finally, after an hour or so of coaxing, she admitted that she had a confession to make. She told me about Robby, her boyfriend. “I love him, but not like I love you,” she said under the cascade of fresh tears. “I broke it off with him last night, and he didn’t take it well. He begged me to stay friends. You know how that goes.” She pouted and unleashed more tears. I just hugged her and reassured her she did the right thing. She agreed.

“I just feel guilty for hurting him and for keeping him a secret from you. I just didn’t know how to bring him up to you and you to him.”

“I understand,” I said, cradling her against me, so happy to be on this end of the confession instead of Robby’s. I pitied the poor guy. I would’ve wanted to jump off a cliff if she ended this joy ride for me.

After that confession we grew even closer. She referred to me as her anchor. People treated her like a celebrity of sorts. Small films contracted her to work with them. She appeared in commercials for local cable channels. She even hung out with some of the players for the local professional women’s basketball team because one of them opened up a Burlesque club, and Jessica headlined it. People flocked to get a sight of her, my girlfriend, the woman who would whisper into my ear, “You look beautiful, my Butterfly.” I would melt at this nickname each time.

Activity filled every moment of her day, and to keep that smile blazing like it did, she relied on me to take care of the “business” end of things: to pick out her clothes, to prepare nutritious snacks and meals, and to motivate her to exercise and rest in between her wild romps at the clubs.

Without me, she would have fallen victim to the abuse of such a demanding life. She needed me. I loved being needed. Being needed by her was my elixir. It breathed life into my day.

Jessica treated me like a princess. She treated me to Tiffany jewelry, to gorgeous artwork, to romantic dinners, and to a life where she wanted to show off my knack for things like public speaking at social events, for negotiation skills, and for my sense of style.

We shared a sweet spot for each other. This sweet spot swaddled us in the kind of love where no words needed to be spoken. Back in the early days, I would look into Jessica's eyes and get lost in them. This woman loved me so much more than Sasha's fiancé loved her. This woman placed me on a pedestal higher than the one my father placed my mother on. I became that woman she looked at and whispered into the deepest recesses of a winter's night, "You're the love of my life."

I loved this moment of our relationship. I would've done anything to keep it intact. Whatever she wanted, I would've done. In our early days I learned that Jessica loved to drink. Alcohol livened up her spirit like nothing else. She smiled, laughed, and added charm to a room when sipping on alcohol.

She claimed to have her drinking under control. As we started to become more serious, I'd ask her straight out why she needed to drink so much. She laughed this off saying she didn't need it. She just enjoyed the taste like I enjoyed the taste of coffee. She laid out a deal. "You stop drinking coffee, and I'll start drinking orange juice instead of alcohol."

So, I gave up coffee and suffered mega headaches for weeks. I didn't mind. Jessica drank orange juice instead of beer. She still wore her radiant smile and joked about the funny things that happened the night before while she danced at a party with strangers. My Jessica was still Jessica without the alcohol.

Shortly after, we got married. We hosted a huge wedding filled with family and friends who supported us and our love.

For our honeymoon, we trekked to the mountains. We set out like two wild spirits on the verge of something incredible. We drove through valleys and up mountainsides singing Billy Joel and Eric Clapton songs, hooting and laughing. The sun shined all over our life. I had everything. I couldn't imagine living without her by my side.

This rosy, cheerful halo hung around us for the first year of our marriage. I had stepped into a life others only dreamed about living. My wife and I hosted parties, vacationed on yachts, enjoyed season tickets to the Giants thanks to an adoring fan, ate at fancy restaurants, and lived a life full of laughter and spontaneity.

On our anniversary, we drove to the mountains. We laughed and joked the entire ride up to our mountain getaway. A smile as natural and beautiful as the wind blanketed me in a peace I didn't want to share with anyone. I owned it. I was whole. Life danced with me.

Then, as we unpacked the trunk of our car, reality hit me like a bomb. I reached down for the containers of orange juice which were sandwiched in a crate between a gallon of milk and water. I cradled the crate, even though Jessica insisted she should carry it because of the weight. "It's a good workout," I said, swinging the crate from the trunk and wrestling my way towards balance. Well, my balance caved and the crate tumbled out of my arms and smashed onto the concrete driveway. Milk and orange juice exploded and spilled into a gooey mess at my feet. Jessica dropped to her knees fighting to control the carnage that ensued. Her face sunk as the orange juice and milk spilled from the crushed containers onto the gravel. She gasped like someone had punctured a life-giving bubble, like someone had murdered her child, like someone had reached down from the mountaintop and yanked her heart right out of her chest. I'd never seen a grown woman cry like this.

My life changed in that moment. That pivotal moment would forever be etched in my history as that moment when my wife plucked the keys from my front pocket, climbed into the front seat and drove away muttering, "I can't do this trip without my juice."

I stood under a ripped veil, as I watched our sedan hug the curved driveway and settle into the steep decline. Jessica wasn't talking about orange juice. My wife, the woman everyone loved, was a woman unable to house a smile without first dousing her liver with alcohol.

I decided standing on that mountaintop that I would help her. I would blend-to-mend if that's what it took. That's what married people did. She'd do it for me. Whatever it took, we'd get through this. No one would have to know. No one would ever know. I would guard this with everything I had in me. This would be our secret. We'd deal with it quietly. Yes. That's how I planned it. A quiet descent from a new hell into the arms of safety, of protection, of peace. I'd sweep away the perils that laced into our life and polish it best as I could.

Jessica eventually turned the car around and came back for me. We decided on that mountaintop that she'd check into rehab.

Throughout those first two weeks as a sober person, her spirit crashed. Her dancing suffered. Her mood swings were unbearable. I missed her smile and her laugh. "Life is boring without alcohol," she said to me one night as we sat by the fire sipping tea. "It's like I have nothing to say, nothing to look forward to. Life isn't fun anymore."

This new side of her depressed me. I wanted the old Jessica back. "You'll get through this."

She stared at her tea. "I hate tea."

I placed mine down, too. "So do I."

"Let's just have wine." She scooted up to me. "Please. I promise. I won't go overboard."

I eyed her.

"Was I ever obnoxious? Did I ever pass out?"

I shook my head.

"Did I ever slur my words and embarrass you?"

She never did. She controlled herself, always. I took her hand in mine. "Please let me continue to help you."

She nodded, looking so sad that I wanted to hug her. Instead, she climbed to her feet with her tea in hand. "I'm going to toss this, then go to bed."

The next day, Jessica came home full of smiles and laughter. She swung me around with romantic flair under our living room chandelier. "Have I told you lately how beautiful you are?" she whispered.

I loved this side of her. I missed this side of her. So I chose to ignore the faint smell of alcohol on her breath and just let her lead me to our bedroom where she made passionate love to me under the comfort of our four-hundred thread count Egyptian cotton sheets, thanks to another fan.

So, I blended to mend.

Jessica didn't fall all over herself, walk around with bloodshot eyes, or crack obnoxious jokes. No, Jessica smiled, laughed, and remained in control. Truth of the matter, drinking kept that smile dancing on her face. Why would I ever take that away from her? The day she started passing out and slurring her words like a fool would be the day I would call her on her secret and insist she enter rehab again.

About two months after our first anniversary, my brother-in-law hired me as his regional hotel sales manager. I got to travel all over the east coast and stay at the different hotel chains. Jessica and I both hated being apart, although, I did enjoy traveling on the open road, just me against a brave, new world. For the first time ever, I ate alone in a restaurant, read a book in the stillness of the night, and cuddled up in a bath filled with soapy fragrances all by myself. I was me, not Jessica's wife, not Cal and Marg Chase's daughter, not Sasha's sister, but Nadia Chase, an independent woman with a purpose all of her own now.

This tickled me, which also scared me.

Each time I had to travel, Jessica spoiled me. She'd pack my luggage for me and place love notes in between my undies. She'd also call ahead and order flowers and candies to be waiting for me upon my arrival.

She was the perfect wife, and I loved being the center of her world.

Aside from her secret drinking, our life sparkled just like a gem.

Then, one night Jessica didn't return home.

By the morning, the unthinkable happened. I got a call from her.

"I'm going to need you to come and get me."

"Where are you?"

"I'm at the county jailhouse."

My blood ran cold.

"What did you do?"

"They say I killed someone."

I couldn't find my tongue. "They say?"

"The police."

I couldn't draw a breath without first punching my chest. "And you didn't, right?"

She didn't answer.

"Jessica?"

"It was an accident."

I dropped to my knees. "What did you do?"

"I crashed my car into this other car. I didn't set out to kill anybody."

I bit the inside of my cheek to dull the stab to my heart. "Were you drunk?"

"Fuck, Nadia. What the fuck?"

She was still drunk. I hung up and ran to the bathroom and vomited.

I didn't go to Jessica's rescue. She arrived home with her club owner friend who posted bail for her. She walked straight to the kitchen and cracked open a bottle of wine.

I treaded out of the front door and drove to the inn down the street. I booked a room, ordered room service, and drank a bottle of very expensive wine before calling my brother-in-law and telling him I'd be taking a few days off to get over a flu. Then, I braved the call to a defense attorney.

My darling wife fucked up our lives for eternity. She went out for happy hour with some friends and hopped in her car after drinking twelve beers and three shots. About five miles from our home, she crossed the center lane and smacked headfirst into a car traveling in the opposite direction, killing the woman who was driving her eighty-year-old friend back home after a dinner to celebrate her birthday.

My wife was not only a drunk, but she was now also a murderer.

* *

I couldn't figure out how people didn't see the news report when it aired. After they splashed Jessica's picture all over the television the days after her arrest, I braced for the phone calls from friends, from family, from work.

Part of me just wanted to get the criticism over with. I wanted people to start the judgments and just let them coat me in a few hundred layers of embarrassment so I could start the process of dealing with this ugly fiasco.

Not even my parents called me. I hovered over the call button many times in those first few days to call them, but stopped myself. How do you tell your parents your wife is a drunk and a murderer?

Sasha called me three days in and asked if Jessica and I wanted to go out with her to see her husband's friend play acoustic guitar in a pub in the city. She had no clue Jessica had just killed a woman. "I'm sick with the flu still," I said to her.

"You sound strange. Do you need me to bring you something?" she asked.

My chest crushed my lungs when I attempted a deep enough breath to clear room for words. "I'm fine," I managed. "I just need a few more days to rest."

I hung up and cradled my head in my arms, rocking back and forth.

Chapter Three
Ruby

I loved the word fuck. I loved how that four-letter word tickled the tip of my tongue as it dove free. Those four little letters wielded such power. Nothing could get in its way once it leapt from the tongue.

I wished my mother would've said the word fuck more often and meant it. Maybe she would've amounted to more in life than someone who served as a punching bag to a man with a dick for morals.

I sounded angry still. I hated that after two decades he could still offend me, still get under my skin and scratch at it. No matter how much you cleansed a soiled past, the stench still emanated through from time to time.

As a kid, I hated the yelling, the fighting, and the frightening nights I'd spent huddled under layers upon layers of blankets to muffle the sound of my stepfather taking out his frustration on her. The mornings after were especially difficult because I expected to find her crying, but instead found her doting on him like he was the fucking king of the new world order, like he hadn't impressed upon her milky skin the lashings from his belt, like he hadn't covered her legs in purple. She'd prance around the kitchen with her spatula, singing happy songs, wearing her blue belle apron, and stopping mid flip of the eggs to pour the bastard more coffee and to kiss my forehead.

She allowed him to treat her like a doormat, and I hated that about her. Relationships sucked. I promised myself back then that I would never grow up to be a wife. I planned a much more untethered life. I would live in a cute apartment with lots of plants and sprinkle potpourri throughout so it would smell fresh and flowery. I would hang out with fun friends and host movie nights and feed them buttered popcorn and ice cream. I'd also open my apartment to shelter cats and maybe a ferret. I would commit to no one but me.

Back when I was a kid living under their rules, I'd whisper to my mother after my stepfather planted himself in front of the television, "Are you all right?" She'd shush me and tell me to stop talking such nonsense. She'd remind me that mommies and step daddies argued at times. They said silly things to each other and made up.

Silly things. Huh.

My mother lived to please that man. She stood in high heels far too pointy to be comfortable and wore skirts far too tight. She also catered to this man's ideals before her own, before mine even.

I would never be like her.

My best friend Catherine admired her mother. I could see why. Her mother didn't fake her way through life. Her mother smelled like spring rain and walked with a bounce in her step that told me she didn't spend her nights fighting off a rough man's fists. I even heard her lecture to Catherine's dad a few times, and her dad chuckled and surrendered right away. She exerted the upper hand, and I admired her for that. I wanted to be Catherine's mom one day. Pretty, lovely, and unrestricted to speak her mind in any way she deemed right. I just wouldn't get married. That never added joy as far as I could see.

Misery had killed my mother's spirit. Freedom never tickled her soul.

When my mother died in a freak accident from falling down a flight of stairs while carrying a basket of laundry— a basket of my stepfather's laundry, no less—I took comfort in Catherine's mom's arms. My Aunt Sherry told me to go sleep at Catherine's house for a few nights while she figured out what to do. So I did. I ran. I ran across the street so fast my feet barely hit the pavement. When she opened the front door, she scooped me in her arms and squeezed me telling me everything was going to be all right.

I prayed to my mother for many nights after that, whispering to her restless soul in the darkness of Catherine's room. I asked her over and over again why she didn't just pick up and leave with me. I wanted her to answer me. I wanted her to sweep into those dark nights, pick me up in her arms, and carry me away with her to a place where daisies and dandelions grew wildly and the sun never failed to shine. I didn't want to live with Catherine and spend the rest of my days slumbering in a sleeping bag on her floor under her Mickey Mouse lamp. I wanted a life with my mommy where we each slept through the night in beds all our own, dreaming with smiles on our faces and never waking to hear the sounds of fists or muffled screams. I wanted to wake up and cook pancakes and eggs with her, sing songs together, laugh and dance around the kitchen in our aprons, never fearing that the big, bad man would steal the joy away from under our feet.

I wanted this life. I prayed and begged God to help me out.

Help me out he did.

My grampa showed up at Catherine's house two weeks after my mother fell down the stairs. I hadn't seen him in three years. I still recognized his sweet, twinkling eyes, the roundness of his nose, and his Old Spice smell.

He came to rescue me, to take me away to live with him at his bed and breakfast in western Massachusetts. The Rafters was a huge barn, turned into eight private bedrooms and bathrooms. He ran the place alone, cooking breakfasts for his guests, taking them on tours of surrounding historical areas, and serving them home-baked cookies every night by a roaring fire.

Peace and simplicity couldn't even begin to describe the beauty. The Rafters, with its endless supply of muffins, cookies and comforting fires, filled in the voids and empty nooks of my heart.

This man taught me to open up my arms to life by spoiling me with an overabundance of warmth, spirit, and love.

His love and lessons smoothed over the hurt of being left alone in this world at such a young age. A few months into my new life, I started to see the shimmer of sunlight on the edge of leaves again. I inhaled the garden-fresh breeze that blew across the rolling fields outside of my bedroom window. This renewed air tickled my lungs and cleansed my hurt. By the time I blew out my birthday candles at nine years old, daily life at The Rafters had shaped and molded me, filling me with wonder.

As I approached ten and met new school friends, I began to grow lonely for my mother. My friends talked about how their mothers sewed clothes, sang songs, and read books with them. I'd see them sitting down to dinner with their families, a mom on one end of the table and a father at the other end, and a jealousy would rip through me. I loved my grampa, but I missed my mom. When I brought her up, his wrinkles creased more. So, I rarely spoke of her.

Then Grace came into my life much like a warm spring breeze whispering in after a bitter winter. Her tender smile, her tall and regal walk, and her soft command created an arc over our life. She had walked up to my grampa and asked if he had any rooms available for three nights. He peeked up from his *Boston Globe* with a glow in his eye, rubbed his bristly chin, and told her only if she didn't mind sharing her room with Tommy, our tabby cat.

I, being of almost eleven by then, jumped to her rescue and told her Tommy could stay with me if she'd prefer.

I'd never seen eyes sparkle like diamonds before. Hers did. "Well, all right then," she said, cradling her gentle arm around my shoulder, "Tommy can stay with you then."

Grace rose early in the morning, just like Grampa and me. The first morning, she opened the front door and stepped outside onto the porch without eating breakfast. Grampa grabbed her and objected. "Indulge me, will you? Please eat a muffin, at least."

He teased with her and she teased back. By nighttime when I returned home from school, they were still sitting in the same spots as they were when I left. Grace's leg crossed and touched Grampa's and Grampa's hand rested on the small of her wrist. The two wore peaceful smiles and tipped their heads to me as I passed them by without anything more than a hidden smile on my face. I traveled all the way to the kitchen and broke into a giggle.

On her third night, with Tommy tucked under my arm as I strolled into the kitchen for some milk and cookies, I spied on them. Soft music played on the turntable and Grampa embraced her as they danced. Grace's silver hair was swept up in a gentle twist. She wore a pretty, rose-colored dress with small eyelets at the hemline. They giggled as they circled around the room. My grampa loved her. I'd never seen anything more beautiful in my life.

For two years, Grace visited us on the weekends. We'd spend the time hiking through the trails out back by the river, fishing, or stopping along the side of the road to watch the horses graze in the yellowed grass. Grace added color to our life. She helped me read, taught me to sing soprano notes, and showed me how to bake a proper meat pie. She simplified my life, purified it, and filled in all of its empty pockets with sunshine and laughter.

My grampa adored her. He made her things all the time—flower pots, garden accessories, wooden shutters for the kitchen with painted flowers. He beamed when she entered the room and gushed over her. He fluffed her pillows and offered her the best seat at the table, the one overlooking the rolling, dandelion fields.

Grampa praised her delicious apple pies every Sunday and the flowers that she would dress up our house with every spring. Life balanced itself out for both of us and we finally tasted long-lasting, sweet joy.

He whispered to me one night while we did dishes and she watched the news, “I’m going to ask her to marry me.”

I squealed. Then we jumped around together in circles, hushing our giggles.

I imagined things like her styling my hair for prom one day and painting my nails with her bright red nail polish.

Later that night before we all went to sleep, I pointed to a new pile of books I found in the attic. “Maybe we can read one together?”

She gazed at them and stretched her eyes. “Wow, that’s quite a stack.” She walked over to them and traced her finger along their spines. “I can’t tonight.”

“Okay,” I said. “Tomorrow!”

Her smile sat on her face like a wilted rose. She nodded and walked down the hallway.

She woke up the next day and left the house early.

Later, she called Grampa and told him she left our laundry in the washing machine.

“Okay, sweetheart. I’ll be sure to take the clothes out and put them in the dryer.”

I was peeling an apple and admiring my grampa’s bright smile.

“Oh, on your way home can you pick up some fresh blueberries from the market?” he asked her.

All of a sudden, his face grew a set of deep wrinkles. "I see." He turned his back to me. "California?" He nodded. "Why?" He walked down the hallway, and I could hear only his quiet, muffled voice.

When he returned a while later he told me she left for good. He bit his lower lip and washed the dishes in the sink.

"What did you do to her?"

"Ruby, dear, she left on her own."

I searched his stressed eyes. "I don't believe you."

He slammed a plate against the kitchen sink and it broke. "It happens."

"You ruined everything," I said. "Everything." The tears erupted.

"He wiped his hands on his jeans and grabbed my shoulders. "Listen to me. No one ruined anything." He paused. "Ladies like Grace aren't meant to be tied down." His eyes softened and a smile reappeared on his face. "She can't stay tethered to this place."

"But, I loved her," I said.

He hugged me. "I did too."

I eyed the pile of books on the shelf and suspected I had pushed too hard. I hugged my grampa tighter, hoping my love would be enough to keep him smiling until we could find him someone new, someone I wouldn't chase off next time around.

Those days seemed so long ago.

What did I worry about now? Silly things like whether the apples at the farmer's market were really organic and whether my teeth were white enough.

Speaking of, I loved discovering natural remedies for things. I used to spend a fortune on teeth whitening products that never worked as magically as the boxes claimed they would. Now, I whitened my teeth every other week using regular household items. I dug out the peroxide from under my bathroom cabinet and doused my strawberry with it. I pressed my fork into it, smashing it. Then I dumped a teaspoon of baking powder on it all to form a pasty mixture. I dipped my toothbrush into the whitening concoction when my cell rang. A number I didn't recognize. I got a little excited. Perhaps it was one of the jobs I applied to a few weeks prior wanting to interview me.

"Hello, Ruby speaking."

Silence.

I checked my teeth in the mirror waiting on the caller's response, then picked up the dental floss. "Hello, anyone there?"

"Hi Ruby," a woman said, stretching out her voice full and wide. "This is Nadia Chase, the uptight woman from the lounge." She chuckled. "Shawna, your waitress, gave me your card."

I adored her name. Nadia. It sounded so eloquent. I tossed the dental floss back down. "I see Shawna convinced you that I wasn't a whore." I accentuated this last word so she could hear how ridiculous it sounded. I stared at my reflection, at my ripe nipples.

"I acted foolishly that night." She spoke slowly, deliberately. "I let my emotions go unchecked over something that happened earlier and you just happened to be in the line of fire. I felt really—"

"Ridiculous?"

Silence.

"I suppose I could've stomped a little less." She laughed. "I hope you don't mind that I called to explain."

I loved her sexy tone. "Apology accepted."

"Well, technically I haven't apologized, yet." Her voice teased.

"Well, you should. You can't leave a girl hanging back like that screaming out words like whore in the middle of a hotel lounge." I stirred the toothpaste into the whitening paste. "So, as far as I see it, now you owe me."

"Yes. Absolutely, yes." She marched her words out. "I owe you a beer next time you're around."

I wanted her to agree to a massage. "Is that all?"

She cleared her throat. "Hm. What more did you have in mind?"

I loved her charge. "No potato skins or wings?"

She whispered a laugh and my tummy rolled.

"So why did you run anyway?"

"I just had a bad day."

Her raspy vulnerability pulled on me. "I could've helped you very easily."

"I just didn't know where you were going with it all. It's not every day I sit in the lounge of the hotel I help manage and have a girl place her hands on my skin."

"So you thought I was coming on to you?"

Silence.

She cleared her throat. "We're getting off topic here. I just wanted to call and apologize for running off and calling you a whore. That's it."

Too much hesitation teetered on the edge of her words. "If you say so."

"What is it that you want Miss Ten-Minute Masseuse?" Nadia asked.

My endorphins flew. "I want ten minutes with you."

She chuckled. "Ten minutes?"

"Ten minutes."

"Tomorrow night? Same place? Same time?" she asked.

"Shall I bring my massage chair?"

"Just bring your pretty little self," she whispered before hanging up.

I stared at my reflection and a silly grin stretched across my face. I loved guarded, strong and intense women. They didn't cling or wrap their possessive ideals around my life.

This could be fun.

* *

That next morning, I ran out of the door to pick up my grampa for Sunday mass. I dashed down the side steps and rushed past my landlord's door. Just as I cleared the front landing, he popped his head out to pick up his *Providence Journal*. He waved to me and asked, "Got a second?"

I owed my rent payment a week ago. My mind whirled trying to find an excuse to bolt. "I've got to run. My grampa is probably pacing his front window. I'm already late."

He formed his lips into a silent whistle. "Okay, I guess I'll just catch up with you when you return?"

"Yes," I said with confidence. "Yes, we'll catch up then." I skipped off wishing him a cheery day and undoubtedly leaving him to question why he ever rented his top-floor attic apartment to me in the first place.

His wife hated me. She always flagged me down with squinty eyes. Whenever we crossed paths, she'd plop her hands on her pregnant belly and complain about life's expenses and how money didn't grow on trees. They owned an upscale house with a top-floor attic apartment across the street from a gorgeous tree farm and she acted like she slept on a park bench every night. She hated me. Of course it didn't help that her husband, my tall, scrawny, ruffled-looking landlord, always groped me over with his wandering eyes. She caught him every time. I pretended never to notice and would always end the awkward moment with a friendly tap on her shoulder.

I climbed into my car and contemplated my next move. Beg grampa for a loan again or cancel on him and go beg for some money on a street corner, doling out ten dollar massages?

I started the engine of my pride and joy, my yellow Camaro. Grampa bought her for me the day I graduated high school. She idled, purring like a kitty. I opened my console and pulled out my dust wipes and wiped down the dashboard. Then, I pulled up a few pieces of lint from the passenger seat and tossed them out of the window. I adjusted my rearview mirror and noticed the trail of grime leaking down my back window. I climbed out, opened up my trunk, pulled out the Windex and paper towels and wiped the stains from the overnight storm. Just like always, once I started cleaning one part of the car, everything looked dirty to me. So, I tore off more paper towels and started wiping the smudges from the bumper and then the trunk and then the side windows.

Before I knew it, half an hour had passed. Poor Grampa had probably already eaten his blueberry muffin and was standing in his front door waiting on me.

When I finally arrived, my grampa swiped his hand across the polished dashboard, approving with a smile. I loved that he noticed. I did it for him. We ended up enjoying our Sunday mass and breakfast that day just as we did every week.

He talked to everyone who walked by our table. He started with a smile, and then he would comment on something a person wore or on the child a mother cradled in her arms.

My grampa loved to talk. That man could converse with an ant all day if it would stay put on his fingertip and listen. The women at the senior center treated him like a king because of it. They liked to joke around with him. Once he told me one of the ladies placed a whoopee cushion down on his chair and when he sat down on it, she choked with laughter over it all. The ladies always complimented him, calling him a gentleman and raving on and on about his handsome face and gorgeous thick hair. They begged me to keep bringing him by so they could continue to enjoy him. My grampa would grumble as we shuffled away and tell me that these ladies would soon drive him to drink, and then two seconds later he'd wink and laugh. The man adored these ladies and all of their attention.

I loved people of his generation. They got life. They'd lived it. They carried in their aged brains the answers to those questions most of us young people sought. My Grampa turned eighty-five this year, and he understood life more than anyone else I knew. This man had seen more in his lifetime in terms of advances in technology and in basic human comfort products than any other generation that came before him or after him.

"You should have seen the time I first saw an airplane," he said time and again. "I couldn't have been more than twelve, maybe, I don't know. This thing, it just swooped over my head one day when I was out collecting firewood. I dropped to my knees." He always lowered himself when he told this part of the story. "I didn't know what it was. For all I know it could've been a giant bird or something. My instinct told me to shoot it. Just get my shotgun and shoot the darn thing down and figure out what it was later." He always waited for a reaction at this point. I always giggled.

Nothing in my lifetime had ever lifted me with such awe and intrigue as this airplane did for my grampa.

Now, here was a man who had lived a serious life and yet still maintained daily doses of laughter. Most people were miserable and whiny and self-absorbed in their plights as they interacted with the harsh world around them. Not Grampa. To this day, I had only seen the man lose his cool once and that was when he broke his plate in the sink the day Grace left us.

He had lost lots in his life—colossal losses that would drive most men to drink massive quantities of alcohol, to walk around the streets carrying justified chips on their shoulders, and to sink into pity from time to time.

Not him. He had witnessed the death of three daughters, the death of his beloved wife, the loss of his beloved girlfriend, the demises of too many family doggies to count, and then inheriting me.

Chapter Four
Ruby

I always attracted clingy women who tipped the balance between lust and going overboard by wrapping themselves around me like a chain, choking all the life out of us before we even got started. I suspected Nadia catered to her busy, important life too much to cling.

I looked up at the clock. I had two hours before I would meet her.

I crossed my legs over each other and inhaled, raising my arms way over head and taking in the fresh air blowing in from the open window. I saw her pretty face, her soft lips, her adorable cheeks, her smooth skin, and that long, soft hair, flipping over her golden shoulders.

My heart fluttered.

I stood, in a meditative pose, stretching tall and wide and peeking through my window at a tree against a blue horizon. Nadia's face popped into my mind again, sending my heart on a pulsating journey. I refocused on the leaves. They waved and flapped, dancing with the wind.

I bent over at my waist and stretched my hamstrings. The energy flowed. I clued in to the subtle, sensual tickles dancing inside of me. My mind wandered to Nadia's long legs, imagining her toned calves and thighs balanced by a pretty pair of undies on top and freshly painted red toenails on the bottom.

What a tango we could leap into.

I loved the lure of the dance; the initial eye ballet, the gentle graze of the skin, the intense heartbeat, the delicious flutters, and the gentle guide into that first soulful, mind-blowing kiss.

I would get this girl to dance. It had been two years since my last twirl. A girl needs to twirl. I deserved this.

Nadia

I arrived at the lounge first. It smelled like chicken wings and garlic. A few stragglers sat alone at the bar huddling over beers and whiskeys, picking at pretzels and staring up at the game on the overhead screens. I joined them. I loved blending into this scene to get a customer's perspective. I sat inconspicuously in the same spot as the night we first met. Shawna strolled up to me and cleared the last customers' drink and napkins. She wore her hair in a low, side ponytail.

She wiped the counter. Her green eye shadow complemented her olive eyes and soft rosy lipstick. Shawna was a transgender woman who outshone most women I knew. She brushed me off whenever I'd tell her this. "You're just trying to raise my confidence," she'd say and quickstep away unable to accept the compliment. Her jawline didn't curve like most women. Instead it squared off with her neck, pitching sharply, as if positioning to fight off the stubble she worked so hard at trying to hide through brutal IPL Laser treatment sessions. Despite this, her cheekbones defined her face with such beauty, sometimes I stared, mesmerized by her.

"Hey, so how did it go?" she asked.

"How did what go?"

"I'm assuming you called that girl Ruby, right?" she asked.

"I did."

She arched one of her green shaded eyes at me. "That's it? I did?" She mimicked me. "You've been sitting at this bar telling me your Jessica woes, and you aren't going to elaborate on this?"

I didn't want to jump into a silly conversation about how this girl's beauty, sweet fragrance and innocent smile lit my nerves on fire. "I apologized. The end."

Shawna looked past me and chuckled. "That's not the end, my friend."

I stiffened. I couldn't even see her yet, but I felt Ruby. The room came to life behind me. The air freshened. The lights radiated more brightly as if smiling at me. I turned and watched as she pranced her way over to the bar. She headed to me with her eyes aglow, her bounce bright, her skin the perfect tone of ivory with a splash of rose.

My breath cut short. My body turned to mush.

She walked straight into my personal zone. "Thank you so much for calling me," she whispered and embraced me. She smelled as fresh as daisies.

I patted her back, taking up pleasure in her golden waves. "Not a problem." *Not a problem? WTF?*

She slid back and wandered her soft blue eyes around my face. "You know what I'm going to make happen?"

"I can only imagine," I muttered.

"I'm going to get you to smile." Ruby's voice was warm and amusing.

I purposely remained impassive. "Oh really?"

She climbed on the bar stool next to mine. "Women look prettier when they smile." She flipped her hair over her shoulder, then rolled out a softer, sexier smile.

My mouth dropped, thrown by her candid attitude. I blushed and hid from it by guiding a stray lock of my hair behind my ear. I warmed up to a small smile.

She flashed me a quick wink, sending my heart stampeding out of control.

Shawna arrived just in time. "Hey, pretty lady. What'll it be?"

Ruby looked to me. "Let's have something sweet. What do you say?"

I wouldn't want to disappoint her at this point. "I heard Shawna here mixes up a delicious mango martini."

Ruby slapped the counter. "Well, all right then. Shawna, two mango martinis please."

Shawna cocked her head. "Great choice. Looks like we're going to have some fun tonight." She sashayed away.

"Shawna sure is different from most people," Ruby said, taking a napkin from the holder and wiping her part of the bar. "She seems, oh I don't know…" She continued wiping the bar, reaching out in front of me now, brushing my leg with hers as she leaned in.

I recited a silent prayer that she wouldn't say anything derogatory about Shawna. I'd fought to defend her too many times to ignorant people, and I sure hoped this pretty little thing would not be another of those cases. "She seems kind of sweet?" I asked, offering Ruby the path better taken.

She stopped wiping, and remained close, close enough that I could practically taste her cherry lipstick. She gazed up at Shawna who blended our mango martinis and joked with another customer about the recent Sox game. "I wasn't going to say that."

I protected Shawna. Regulars in this lounge knew better. We all protected her. We all loved her. Every once in a while, we'd get people, usually men, whispering and staring at her with curious eyes, trying to figure her out, jabbing each other's sides and egging each other on to crack on her. None of us stood for it. "Then what?"

"She's more than sweet. She floats around this place in love with what she does. Look at her." Ruby tilted her head and a piece of her hair fell down onto my arm. "She is choosing to spend her time laughing and making new friends rather than sitting behind a desk stuffing her nose in a computer screen all day long. She walks with a sense of freedom."

Shawna was far from free. She put up a good front for sure. "She certainly does live her life according to her own set of rules."

"I admire her for that. I also admire her hair. What I would give to have shine and fullness like that."

"Some people are just blessed by mother nature I suppose," I said, floating on the coattails of her openness and innocence.

Shawna returned with our drinks. "Careful with these. They hit you quickly." She placed them down and strolled away.

We sipped our fruity martinis in silence watching the Sox play Baltimore on the overhead flat screen. "I hate baseball," I admitted.

Ruby peeked up at me out of the corner of her eye. "I can't even look at you now that you said that."

"Is that so?" I watched her lips pucker around the thin straw, as she tugged at the martini. She was too beautiful in this setting, wrapping those glossy lips around the straw, hugging it, nurturing it, masking her playful grip.

She stopped sucking and wiped her lips with her fingertip. I could just imagine how soft those lips would feel. I twitched a bit. So I stood, crossing my arms over my chest now, slightly intrigued and slightly disturbed at my buckling knees.

Ruby studied me. "You are pretty even when you're uptight."

"I'm not uptight." I struggled to smile to prove her wrong.

"Darling, you're so stressed that the air can't move around you." Her soft eyes landed on mine and bathed me in warmth.

"I need to use the ladies room." I ran away, rushing past the bar and pushing open the bathroom door. I walked over to the sink and squared off at myself. My hair wilted just below my shoulders and my brown eyes drooped. Where did those dark circles come from? I wiped away some smudged mascara and tried on a smile. It looked plastic. I didn't even know her, yet, she already drove me to obsess. I would finish my drink and leave.

I walked back out to the bar, sat down, sucked down my drink and suffered a brain freeze. My temples pounded and my head verged on exploding. I grabbed the sides of my head and sank into the bar, whimpering.

Ruby curled up around my back like a stole. She whisked my hair between her fingers and draped it over my right shoulder. Then she leaned in. Her breath blew hotly against my neck. "Just stay right where you are. I'll take good care of you."

Shawna crept up as Ruby's silky hands cradled the top of my shoulders. I waved Shawna away and she retreated in a flash.

Ruby whispered into my ear. "Do me a favor."

"Hmm?"

"Close your eyes."

"Okay." I half-closed them.

She reached over my shoulder to peek a glance. "All the way."

I did as commanded. "Fine."

She kneaded her strong fingers into my tense neck. I moaned. "Oh God, that feels so good."

"Hmm. I bet it does." Her voice spun out, ripe and succulent.

I quivered with each of her kneads. I dropped my head and sank into the pleasure, not caring about curious bystanders. She squeezed my shoulder blades and I moaned. "I'm sorry. These moans are just slipping out."

"Oh, darling, it's okay. Who cares? Enjoy the moment."

I could just imagine how mushy I would become if hot oil and naked skin were involved. I quivered again, and moisture pooled between my legs for the first time in ages. "You don't have to keep going if your hands are tired." I sat taller.

"Shhh."

She caressed my shoulders in long, sweeping grips and I just couldn't contain the pleasure. I exhaled like she'd given me an orgasm right there in the middle of the lounge. Like a kitty she purred her words, leaning in close and releasing her earthy, fresh scent at my cheek. "I could do this for a long time."

How could I argue? I relaxed again and let her refreshing spirit take me on a journey far away from Jessica and from lawyer's bills. I slid right into this sweet spot and let her take me away. I zoned out of the bar, hooked on this mystical ride and imagined lying in a hut somewhere on the coast of Indonesia, a warm breeze blowing through my hair, the curtains waving, while her fingertips flirted with my bare skin. In this dreamy state, she stood behind me, massaging my back, taking in my curves, nibbling on her lower lip. Her hair, blonde and spiraled, hung down and tickled my golden shoulders. Light jazz played in the background, filtered in between our breaths, circling around us like a sexy snake, taunting us with its dangerous venom just enough to send us reeling. Her hands traveled down my spine, up my spine, across my shoulders and down to my breast bone where her long fingers stopped just centimeters away from the curve of my breast. She leaned in, cradled her chin in the crook of my neck and paused to draw in a subtle, but noticeable breath. Her chest pressed up against my back and pulsed. Soon, my heartbeat caught up in hers and in sync we connected as one. Her spirit cradled me, protected me, anchored me to this moment, a moment when I embraced this most raw and vulnerable state where I let go.

I allowed myself to ride on the tailwind of someone so pristine and detached from drama.

Then, her hands left my skin and I heard her talking, talking to someone. I tried to open my eyes but they were too tired, too relaxed. So I bowed my head and listened to her coax another voice to pass her two glasses of water. Then, I heard more voices, the sound of ice being scooped up, the sound of men yelling about baseball. As if tossed in a pool of frigid water, I woke and jumped up.

"Where did you go?" Shawna asked, tripping over giggles.

Ruby caught on to her giggles, too. And, ultimately, so did I. I let the laughter roll, releasing years of frustration, enjoying the lightness of my tension-free shoulders.

Somewhere in between giggling and catching my breath, I'd released myself from my own prison. I could've skipped around the lounge in a happy dance. Instead, I grabbed Ruby by the shoulders, pulled her in, and laid a generous kiss on her surprised lips. She giggled under my kiss and then softened in a sweet, lingering reciprocated touch of her own. I pulled back first and looked away embarrassed. "I'm so sorry. That was totally inappropriate."

She wrapped her hand around my wrist.

I locked onto her teasing, pale blue eyes. "Nothing wrong with a girl expressing herself, now is there?"

I fumbled to match her eloquence and confidence. I could only shrug and shake my head like a fool. "I better get back to my room and make some phone calls." I couldn't stop gazing into her eyes. I needed to pull away from this. "How much for this session?"

She hesitated on my words with a pull on her lower lip and a contemplative stare. I melted. "How about a beer next time you're in town?"

"A beer?" I asked.

"You do drink beer don't you?"

I was married. I couldn't do this. "No I don't." I reached into my pocketbook and pulled out a twenty. I handed it to her. "Is this enough?"

She eyed the twenty like it was a dead rat. Then she cocked her head, reached out for it and folded it between her pretty fingers. "If that's how you want to pay me, then, that's how you want to pay me. Can't argue with a woman who knows what she wants, now can I?"

This time I pulled in my lower lip, resisting the urge to take back my beer resignation. Logic spun me back around again. I pictured a long, drawn-out talk months into our beer dates where I'd have to tell her I was married and obviously a terrible wife for flirting with the notion that I should be kissing and drinking beer with someone other than Jessica. "That's me. A woman who knows what she wants."

"Suit yourself." Ruby shrugged and then walked away swinging her hips far too deliberately for me to look away. She turned back and caught me staring and winked.

Chapter Five
Ruby

I left the lounge confused and caring too much about why Nadia treated me like a service representative. That twenty dollar bill insulted me. But why? I achieved my goal. I massaged her, and I earned twenty dollars.

I walked through the garden patio admiring the ferns and the pretty, festive lights overhead, vying to recover my balance. This woman affected me like no other. I wanted her to like me. I wanted her invite that night to have meant more than a service call.

I strolled past the gift store and admired a leather satchel with gold plated buckles, trying to cool myself and get a grip. I would not tangle into this mess. Nope. I would not. I was fun. I was spontaneous. I lived on the edge. I headed straight for the pool.

Guests had long since left the chaise lounges and warm water. So, I tore off my clothes and dove in. I swam laps, then rolled over to my back and floated, watching as my nipples bobbed. Cameras surrounded all corners of the pool, and I willed for Nadia to be watching. I wanted her to see me as the free-spirited girl I was and not a desperate fool vying for her attention.

While opening up into great strides racing from one end of the pool to the other, my mind continued to wander. Nadia Chase's moans played on my heart, as did the way her skin flecked in the glow of the dim lights.

I flapped my feet and paddled to the far end of the pool fighting off these images. I would not obsess. I focused on my feet and how the cool water refreshed them with each splash. I inhaled the familiar chlorinated scent and basked in the humidity that marked so many of my childhood days with my childhood friend, Catherine, at the community pool.

I wondered what my life would've amounted to had she and I remained friends. Would we be long-distance friends who called each other on the weekends? Would she have invited me to her wedding and baby's christening and asked me to stand in as godmother? Would she have approved of Nadia?

Nadia. She was tricky. She had softened beneath my fingertips one minute and the next had pulled the thick curtain over herself and shut me out. No one acted with such intensity one moment and severe restraint the next unless something scared her.

Her mystery intrigued me. I didn't like this. I needed to act more unaffected, more poised, more undeterred by her. Instead she sat in my brain like a statue, taking up space she didn't deserve. She garnered my thoughts.

I swam backwards towards the pool ladder, flapping my feet, escaping into the chlorine and cool water.

I climbed out of the pool and headed over to my pile of clothes. I picked up the twenty I earned from Nadia and shoved it into my jeans, got dressed, and walked out of the pool area with dripping hair.

Several minutes later, my car guzzled up the twenty dollars in gas and left me dry. When I returned home, all of my possessions blocked my front door. Things weren't even in boxes. They were just tossed on the porch. T-shirts, bras, flip-flops, blankets, and bowls.

I ran down the steps and knocked on my landlord's door. He answered without looking me in the eye. His wife popped up behind him, her frizzy hair and her makeup smeared. She reminded me of someone who partied all night and forgot to wash her face after. She handed my cat to me. "This here's the last of your things."

I took Bentley into my arms. "You're kicking us out?"

"I can't pay my bills on your good looks, honey."

"I have nowhere to go."

"You have a good car right there." She tilted towards the Camaro, all shiny and perfect under the street light before slamming the door.

If I couldn't find a place to live and the money to afford it quickly, I'd have to sell my car. I didn't want to do this because Grampa had worked so hard to buy it for me.

I stood numb with my cat, sweating in the muggy night air.

We spent the night in the car. I curled up in my front seat, and he balled up under a tote bag in my back seat. When we woke up the next morning, my neck was cramped.

* *

I would have to ask Grampa for his help again. Even if he minded, he'd never express it. That man didn't speak one negative word, ever. Even about Grace. And that woman broke his heart. Yet, he still admired her and spoke of her like she was one of the gentlest creatures on the face of the planet. He was so sweet with her, yet he wasn't enough.

He spoke only good words of her, even after he realized she took off with his signed golf clubs from Jack Nicklaus. That day, we had planned to spend the day driving balls in the backfield. The sun had sprinkled golden highlights all over the fields and trees that day. The Rafters looked just like a Van Gogh painting. Bold pink, yellow, and orange strokes had splashed across the sky. I stepped out onto our back patio and breathed in the fresh mountain Massachusetts air waiting on Grampa to come out of the detached barn with his prized clubs, the ones he swore improved his golf swing.

He disappeared into the barn for too long, so I fed the birds, tossing out sunflower seeds and giggling as they pecked the ground like wild savages eating their very last dinner. Just as I emptied another handful to them, Grampa exited the barn empty handed, whistling a Kenny Rogers tune. "Seems I don't have those clubs anymore." He placed his wrinkled hands on his strong hips and looked up at the painted sky with a smile on his face.

"Well where did they go?"

He stretched his eyes out to the horizon, squinting now. "I forgot that I lent them to Grace."

My heart skipped a beat. "So she has to come back then?"

He shook his head. "No. I'm going to let her keep them. She liked them. They'll keep a smile on her face."

I grabbed at his plaid shirt and pulled. "No. You have to get them back. You have to call her and tell her she needs to bring them back to you. Jack signed them for you."

He covered my hand with his and squeezed. He looked down at me with a kindness that could not be easily replicated by many. "She's not coming back."

I shifted forward, desperate to force him to get her to come back to us. I feared the end of ice cream night. I feared that I'd forget how to hem my pants and how to cast on and cast off the knitting needles. I worried I'd forget how to brush my hair so it fell in long waves over my shoulders. I didn't want to have to tell Grampa I had my period and needed maxi pads. What would happen when I needed to get a bra? I panicked and ran into the house, tossing teardrops the size of marbles off my face as I scaled the steps.

My grampa's heavy feet pounded up after me. I reached my room and he caught up to me quickly. His heart raced, his face reddened, his hand scratched his wiry gray hair. "She's happy and we need to be happy for her."

"How are you going to be happy?"

He grasped onto my bony shoulders and spoke to me like an adult. "I could never be happy knowing she wanted something more than this. This farm, this bed and breakfast, this is my life, this is our life. She didn't want this."

"She baked here. She took her showers here. Of course she wanted this." She had swarmed around the kitchen humming songs and took long baths smelling of lilacs. How could he say she didn't want this place?

"She cried a lot because her big spirit craved more than this place."

"She only cried once. Just once." I yelled this. My grampa flinched just as he did that day she cried and tried to hide her tears with big sunglasses. She cried because we had to cancel a trip to California. "And that was all my fault. I ruined the trip. I cried, too."

He arched a wiry eyebrow at me. "You had the flu. We couldn't go."

Reality slammed me. "I irritated her, didn't I?" Of course I did. I didn't need him to answer this. I whined too much when it snowed. I never did my homework properly. I ruined their television nights by begging to watch my silly shows. "She has every right to hate me."

Grampa pulled me in and patted my back, kissing the top of my hair. "Dear, you have it all wrong."

I curled up into his strong arms. "She left because of me."

He drew a deep breath. "I'm never going to lie to you. You know that right?"

I nodded and swallowed my tears. "Tell it to me straight. I can handle it."

"She left because of me." He said this in a voice that was too high, like he just hit his toe with one of the golf clubs.

"I don't believe you." I wiggled away from him, facing him like a grownup. "She laughed all the time around you."

He gazed out past me, across the open field. "She's meant to be on her own."

I turned and looked out over the same pretty field where the dandelions were dancing in the wind and the blue sky cradled piles upon piles of fluffy, white clouds.

"She's meant to travel and explore," he said in a low voice. "That's what I love about her. I would never want to ruin that about her."

"Why is she like that?"

He rubbed his chin with his wrinkled fingers, ushering me over to the bench under my window. We sat and he exhaled, looking like a worn-out sneaker, all rumpled and weathered. "Do you remember those outdoor cats we tried to turn into housecats?"

"Yes. Those cats did not like it here."

"That's right." He raised his eyebrow again. "Do you remember how much they whined and cried?"

"They destroyed our door."

"They wanted out. We were forcing them to live a life they didn't want to live."

"Why were they like that? We offered them everything they needed. I even welcomed them to sleep with me. They could eat whenever they wanted. Drink milk. Play with toys and catnip. What more could a cat dream of?"

"Freedom." He grinned down at me. "They only knew freedom. They were born and raised to roam without limits. This place jailed them."

I frowned. "So this place jailed Grace?"

"Yes. This place jailed her."

"She seemed so happy."

"Most times she did like it. But then there were those times when she hated it," he said, offering me a polite smile but failing to meet my eyes. "She knows this is my life. She knows I crave companionship. She wants to travel and meet new people and live her life out of a suitcase. That's the last thing I want."

He stared up at the sky. I watched him disappear to somewhere up in the clouds. "What do you want?" I asked, pulling him back.

He shrugged, as if to clear his discomfort with this talk. "I want to stay here and cook people eggs and pancakes for breakfast until the day I die. I want a companion who wants that too."

I studied his expression. "You're sure she's not the one?"

"She's like a wild flower that needs lots of room to grow. This life here would suffocate her."

"Aren't you sad?"

"I know she's happy. So, I'll be alright."

"So we need to find you a new girlfriend then?"

"We need to be on the lookout." He grinned, but I saw no twinkle in his eye.

He never dated another one. Grace had stolen the last bit of his love. Even though he would never admit it, a piece of him died that day we sat on my bench and pretended we didn't need fancy golf clubs or Grace's warm spirit to keep us happy.

A part of me died, too. I carried the weight of that day even still. I would never want to get tangled up in some complicated woman's life as a result. Instead I sought solitude and simplicity. Always.

* *

I pulled up in front of my grampa's one-story apartment the next morning for Sunday mass, and sure enough, there he stood, nose pressed up against the glass of the door, waiting on me. He rushed out of his door, locked it, and headed to me before I could fully escape my front seat.

"Wait," I yelled, jumping out of my car. I reached into my back seat and pulled out Bentley.

He halted in the middle of the sidewalk, eyeing Bentley with a flick of caution.

"It's just for a few days." I held Bentley up by his armpits showing off his cute, vulnerable, helpless side. We moved in closer and my grampa blinked as if navigating a tightrope. Bentley didn't exactly shower my grampa with love. Most times he scratched and batted him with his huge claws. "They're exterminating my apartment."

He stepped aside. "Just a few days, you say?"

I couldn't hide my giggle as I passed him. "Just a few days for sure."

I unlocked his front door and placed Bentley on the Berber carpet. Grampa snuck in behind me. "I've still got a litter box in my pantry closet with a bag of litter next to it. I'll get that prepped for him." He rushed past us not waiting for my reply.

I batted a wad of paper around with Bentley as Grampa fixed the litter box in his bathroom. A few minutes later he grazed past me, keeping a firm eye on Bentley, and escaped out of his front door with a quick leap.

Outside on the front walk, I kissed his cheek. He smelled like Irish Spring. He glanced at my thin t-shirt and hatless head. "You're going to catch a sunburn walking around in this heat like that."

"Yes, sir, I know." I reached up to his hat and stole it from him and skipped to the car. "Next time, I'll be more careful," I shouted over my shoulder.

We drove to church in comfortable silence. He stared out of the window as if in awe of the lush green landscape and wild flowers. His mouth hinged open, his eyes stretched, a sweet smile danced on his wrinkled face.

After church we ended up at our favorite spot. I sat across from him in our usual booth. His eyes drooped more than usual and his skin hazed over with a pale hue, deepening his wrinkles. He looked old and tired.

"Are you feeling alright?" I cupped my hands around his cold fingers.

Dazed, he looked down at our entwined hands and bobbed his head as if convincing himself all was well. "I am, dear. I feel fine. Don't you go worrying about me." He stretched his neck over to the kitchen. "Where is Berta with that coffee?"

I clutched his cold hands. "She's coming."

My grampa aged before my eyes. New wrinkles had formed every time I visited him. His voice grew hoarser. His hair turned wirier, and his eyes glazed over more and more. I didn't want him to get old. I wanted him to be that strong man he always had been right up to before he had his prostate cancer and mild stroke last year, and before his eyesight started leaving him.

"So, how's your newest story coming along?" I asked him.

He cleared his throat and opened his mouth to speak. Sometimes it took him a few tries to get the words out. This time, he got it on the first attempt. "Well, I'm having a hard time figuring out what to do with the cat in this one, you see." He laughed and his whole face lit up. The color restored and his eyes brightened. "The lead cat is so darned pesky, I don't know what kind of journey she's going to take me on next."

"What's her name?"

"Dragger." He cleared his throat again and pointed his eyes at me. "You know why?"

I scooted up taller in the booth. "Tell me."

"Because she drags the other cats all over the darned house in search of clues. You see, she's leading the investigation of a string of robberies occurring in the residence." He said this with the seriousness of a person recounting truthful details of a real-life criminal investigation. "She even has the family dog involved in this one."

"The kids are going to love it."

"I'm just a silly old man who likes to tell silly stories," he said. "These kids don't want to hear them. I do think they enjoy the chocolates I toss out to them, though." He winked.

"This one sounds like your best story yet." I doled out encouragement that a year earlier he would've been offering to me instead. Life had turned on us in a flash. For a lifetime he led me, and then suddenly our roles reversed. Out of nowhere the shifting wind came in and toppled the status quo, leaving us grasping onto naked branches and praying the wind would be gentle and keep us close to the roots that defined us.

"My best ones have long been written, dear." He patted my hand, and then looked out through the window at the tourists strolling by. "I think I'm going to try an omelet today instead of my usual."

"Good for you, Grampa. Maybe I'll do the same." I swallowed the angst building in the back of my throat and blinked away the tears that stung my eyes. When Berta arrived I told her, "We're going to try something different today. We'd like two omelets."

"Would you like to go really crazy and add some wheat toast to those orders?" she asked with a happy tune.

"Grampa?"

He looked away from the tourists and back at me, the haze returning to his eyes. "Yes, dear?"

"Want to be different and add wheat toast to this order?"

He nodded to Berta. “Yes, let’s add some variety.”

She jotted this down. Before sweeping away towards the kitchen, she shared a knowing smile with me. We shared this smile every Sunday. We’d been ordering these unique omelets for over a year now, and God bless Berta for pretending we’d just ordered something different.

Things like rolling fields, ripe crops, bountiful fish, and nights in front of a roaring fire with guests at The Rafters used to keep him going. Now, an omelet served as the greatest thrill of the week.

He picked up the newspaper left behind by the last person in the booth. He squinted. “How I miss reading the newspaper.” He tossed it to the side and looked out over the breakfast crowd instead.

I wanted my old grampa back. This one sat prisoner in a sad fog. This one was chained to an existence that trapped him and his big spirit in an old person’s body. This one held all the secrets to living a great life in the reserves of his brain, and I feared I’d be unable to access this information before long.

Why did life treat great people like this? Why did it steal all of their greatest attributes and abilities and sandblast these gifts into a corner in the back of their minds, rendering them incapable of sharing them with others?

Somewhere between those beautiful gray eyes of his still remained the smartest, coolest, most enthusiastic man I’d ever known.

I would reignite that spark in him.

The doctors told me to keep him excited, active, and talking to keep him young and spirited. So, I did. Every Sunday I picked him up at his apartment and took him to Sunday mass where he led me to the first pew, directly in front of the statue of Mother Mary, and insisted that I pray for the entire half hour before mass began. After, we ate our “unique” omelets, and then we got crazy and visited the senior center.

Despite being weak, he still carried his smile around for all to enjoy. The women, some ten years younger, sat next to him and talked his hearing aid off. Some even envied me when Grampa would pay more mind to me than them. They vied for his attention, and my grampa, God love his good soul and wit, would wink at me and roll his eyes, as if saying 'these freaking women are crazy.'

He sipped his coffee, slurping it like a little kid. His eyes puckered with each sip. "This is good stuff today."

I sipped mine with equal thought. "Hmm."

We ate our omelets and drank one more cup of coffee before I braced to ask for his help. I studied the situation. If I asked him for a loan to hold me over, I'd repay it to him along with the other three hundred I still owed him. "Grampa, can I ask you a favor?"

He sat up taller, leaning in with his good ear. "Yes, of course, dear."

His eyes twinkled. He loved being needed. He always did. Loaning me money lifted his spirits and put a glow on his face. "Can I borrow a little more money?"

"Of course." He dipped his head. "I've still got some back in my apartment." He leaned in and whispered. "I keep the rest of it in my purple wool sock."

"Grampa, be careful who you say that to. You don't want someone taking advantage of you."

"Yes, dear." He bowed his head like a child.

I reached out and cupped his cold hands again. "We're going to have fun today, you and me."

He looked up and beamed, showing off his white dentures and beautiful smile. "What are we waiting for then?" He jiggled his hands from mine and slid out of the booth anxious to have some fun.

I lived for these moments. He needed me just as much as I needed him.

* *

Once Bentley and Grampa reunited without claws and scratches, I returned to my apartment with five hundred dollars. Grampa had insisted the money needed spending. “It’s just sitting idle doing nothing anyway,” he had said.

I knocked on queen bee’s door and handed her the money. “This isn’t gonna cut it,” she said. “I’ve already rented the attic apartment.”

“You just kicked me out last night.”

“I’ve got bills to pay.” She slammed the door in my face.

I glanced at my yellow car, my new temporary home, and surrendered to it.

* *

I zoomed down the interstate going eighty on my way to nowhere. The open road scared me a little this day. My heart pinched a little tighter. A strange and uncomfortable pain pulsed at my temples. Suddenly, the horizon stretched out much too far with nothing in the middle to cling to. I treaded alone in this open sea, fighting to stay afloat. All that strength that I started out with vanished and left me panicked, flapping my legs like a duck without a mission, pointing towards some far away land that, for the first time in life, I feared I wouldn’t be able to reach.

I pulled over to the side of the road and sucked air into my lungs, willing it to end this dizzy spell. I turned on the radio and breezed through commercial after commercial in search of a song, a debate, a joke, something that would calm me. I landed on Bette Midler’s “Wind Beneath My Wings.” I pulled over, closed my eyes, placed my hands on the steering wheel and bowed into it, resting my heavy head.

My mother's pretty face flashed before my eyes. She waved that spatula she always danced around the kitchen with. Her bobbed haircut swung in unison. She loved Bette. I could see her, singing along, sashaying her hips, flipping eggs and pancakes, asking me to wipe the table down fast before my stepfather came down for breakfast.

My mother mastered feigning strength among her biggest weaknesses and fears. She put on a good act, appearing in control one second, and the next bowing down to her stupid husband's insults. She clung to a life of misery, for what? For solace? For safety? For comfort?

Then she died along with my dream for us to live life out on the open road, just the two of us, driving down the interstate singing songs loud and eating popcorn and drinking sodas.

The loss of that dream strangled my chest. I pressed harder against the steering wheel. I wondered if my mother's life would've been different had she gone through something like being homeless. Would she have risen to the challenge?

I sat up and stared at that blank horizon again. "I think you would've risen to it, Mom," I whispered. "You just didn't give yourself a chance."

From deep within I started to sob. I continued until the horizon turned into a royal purple and the faint circle of the moon appeared as my guide to carry on with my travels and never settle for comfort, for security, or for someone else's ideals.

* *

A few hours later, I parked along the Blackstone River Park and ate a sandwich that I bought with my grampa's money. I played with my cell, searching my Twitter feed for entertainment. As far as I could tell, I could enjoy this simple pleasure for about another week before my cellphone carrier pulled the plug on me, too.

As I read a quote about living with reckless abandon, my cell rang. It was Nadia. Like a fool, I answered her like I'd been waiting my whole life to hear from her. "Hey, you!"

"Um—hey, you." Her tone was demure. "I was wondering. Um—See here's the thing, er—I could use your services again. Whatever you did the last time worked. So, any chance you'll be available this weekend to give me another one of your ten-minute massages?"

A dizzy stupor rose in me. "See, and you doubted me."

"Hmm," she replied without much commitment. "I've got this terrible kink in my neck and it keeps me up and stresses me out. Nothing is working. Hot water, heating pad, muscle cream, none of it."

A sweet current rushed through me. "So I was right."

"About?"

"You are uptight," I teased.

"Do you always grill your clients like this?"

I laughed. "Client? So you're my client now, huh?"

"If you'll have me?" Nadia's voice pulled on me.

I held the cell away and drew a large breath. "Same place?"

"Well, don't you have a massage studio?"

I looked around at my shiny, black leather interior. "I'm a traveling masseuse."

"So you mean you go to people's houses and such?" She sounded alarmed.

"Wherever they're comfy."

"Isn't that kind of dangerous for someone like you?"

"Someone like me?" I asked.

"You're a sweet, innocent woman. We live in a crazy world filled with people who might enjoy taking advantage of that."

“Oh, I can handle myself,” I said more defensively than I expected.

“I didn’t mean to insinuate that you couldn’t. I’m just curious as to why you’d put yourself in such a vulnerable position?”

“Well, I’m looking for a place,” I answered truthfully. “For now I’m trying to get into corporate settings. Desk massages.”

“How’s that going for you?”

“It’s going just fine. I’ve got a few leads. People seem interested. You know how the business dance goes.”

“Tell me.”

“Oh, well, you know, you pitch the idea. They let it marinate, and meanwhile I offer them a trial period. They perk up and feign a little disinterest even though I can see the wheels in their brains turning, imagining a staff fully relaxed and engaged in their work. It just takes time.” I stopped myself from babbling further.

“Well I’m sure you’ll charm your way into many corporate offices in no time,” she murmured.

“Yes, it’s just a matter of time.”

“Hmm.” Nadia paused. “So let’s say Friday night the lounge again?”

“Friday night it is.”

She cleared her throat. “I’ll see you then.”

“Right. See you then.”

After hanging up, a giddy rush coursed through me. Talk about a sweet distraction.

Chapter Six
Ruby

I contemplated asking Grampa if I could live with him. I didn't want him to view all of his hard work raising me as a failure though. So, I slept in my car for the next three nights. Each morning, I simply entered a new gym and asked if I could take a guest tour. Each one allowed me access to it all, even the showers. For food, I volunteered at soup kitchens. I could handle this homeless thing. No rent. No furniture required. Shower and eat for free.

On the fourth morning, after scrunching up into a ball for six hours, I woke up with another stiff neck and not being able to wriggle my toes. This scared me. I loved my toes.

Placing my pride aside, I called Marcy and Rachel.

Just like loving family, they welcomed me to live in their home with them.

"You can have this room on the left," Rachel said, escorting me down the hallway of her and Marcy's condo. "It's got a nice view of the water."

"I can't thank you enough." I placed my luggage down near the twin bed.

"I changed the sheets so they're nice and fresh for you."

I looked around my new bedroom, a sunny room with tangerine-colored walls and paintings of the sea. I handed her the five hundred dollars I had borrowed from Grampa. "I hope this is enough?"

She placed it back in my hand. "Keep it. When you're working, you can pay us."

That very day I went job searching again. This time, I applied at retail stores, at pet stores, at garden centers, even at the breakfast restaurant where I ate with Grampa on Sundays. I went to the beauty supply shop and applied there, too.

The receptionist wore pink braces on her teeth. She smiled and her mouth looked like bubblegum.

“I love your braces,” I said.

“Thanks, hun.” She scanned over my application. “My younger sister is a breast cancer survivor.”

“Younger?” This girl couldn’t have been more than twenty-five.

“Yup. She just turned twenty-three last month. Her boyfriend discovered the lump, and next thing she had a double mastectomy.” She continued scanning my application as though she just told me that grass grew green.

“Poor thing.”

The girl stopped scanning and just stared at me. Her jaw hung and her pink braces sparkled under the reflection of the overhead fluorescents. “Her new ones are beautiful.” She glanced down at her flat chest and shrugged. “A hell of a lot better than mine.”

“Will she be okay?”

“She’ll be fine.”

“That puts things into perspective.”

“Yep.” She twisted her mouth and studied my history.

I prayed she’d look right over the unemployed part. “I mean just this morning, I stressed about my frizzy hair. How foolish, huh?”

She dropped my application to the counter and picked up a bottle. “Just stick some of this Moroccan oil on it, and it’ll be good as new.” She opened up the lid, squirted a few drops into her palms and massaged them together. Before smoothing onto my hair she sniffed it. "Smells like eucalyptus."

How could she think about shiny hair at a time like this when she sported pink braces and mouthed the words cancer and sister in the same sentence?

"So do I get the job?"

She shrugged and picked up my application again. "Not sure, Ruby." She placed heavy emphasis on my name as she scanned my application. "Why did you leave your last job? You left that blank."

"Looking for a better opportunity," I blurted out.

"Here?" Her lips curled up into a wry smile.

I glanced around at the chaos of hair and nail products. "Well why not?"

"Says here you are a masseuse. You're never going to like it here."

"Of course I will." I leaned into the counter. *Hire me, damn it!*

"A better opportunity, huh?"

Adrenaline pumped through me. "Yes."

She tossed the application back down again. "The boss will never hire you. You've got too many credentials to work here. A masseuse doesn't leave her massage job at a fancy day spa to come work in a supply shop."

I flushed. All of my needs suddenly buried me. I stared her down. *You don't understand. I need this job. I'm taking money from my grampa. I just moved out of my car into someone's spare bedroom. Please.*

She pointed to a bulletin board behind her. "There's a new job posted. The Della Norte Day Spa has an opening for a massage therapist. Walk right in and earn forty-thousand dollars a year with that position. At least that's what the girl said. Apparently the existing masseuse took a job in Florida and is leaving her clientele behind to the next lucky one."

I had already applied to that one and they never called back. I secured my pocketbook strap over my shoulder. "I'd rather work here."

"We're not going to hire you."

My fragile pride unraveled in front of me, leaving me vulnerable to her sarcastic grin. "Then, fine. I'll apply to the spa. Thanks for the tip." I couldn't disguise the anger in my voice.

I walked away and looked back as I exited, unable to leave a mess where I might one day need to return for supplies should I ever get my life back on track. "Sorry about your sister."

"Thanks," she murmured.

I brushed past the window on my way to my car, and through the thick glass, with all the posters claiming the biggest savings, I could still see her pretty pink braces smiling back at me.

* *

When Friday night arrived, I walked into the Gateway Suites lounge with butterflies. Shawna busied herself with mopping the floor behind the bar. She was attractive. Her body rocked, and I envied her thick hair. A sadness haloed around her. An uncertainty. A constant, look-over-the-shoulder-type apprehension.

"She's running late," she said from behind the bar.

I eased onto a stool. "Nadia told you I was meeting her?"

"She tells me everything."

"So you and she are close?"

"You could say that." A playful smile danced on her rosy lips.

"You have a crush on her, don't you?"

"I admire Nadia. That's it," she said with a completely straight face hindered by a blush.

I grinned. "You are totally crushing on her."

She scoffed and rolled her eyes.

"So, why is she so stressed?" I asked.

Her eyes flew open. "You know I can't answer that."

"I won't tell."

Just then, a couple of guys entered and sat at the table next to me. Shawna approached them, and they sneered at her, looking her up and down. Then, the bigger of the two grabbed Shawna's arm. "What are you, a fucking dude?" He laughed along with the bald, fat guy sitting across from him.

Shawna blushed a deep red and tears sprang to her eyes.

Whoa. Hell no are these fools going to bully her with me standing right here. I stood up. I wrapped around the table and grabbed this burly man's arm and dug my fingernails into his skin. His eyes popped. He released his grip on Shawna.

I dug deeper. "Apologize to the lady," I said to him.

Shawna cradled the tray to her chest. "It's okay. No need to cause a scene," she said to me.

I dug my nail again. "Apologize or leave."

"I'm not going to fucking apologize," he said.

His friend stood. "Let's just get out of here."

"What'll it be?" I asked the guy. "More pain?"

He stood up and flung my arm away from him, pushing me against the table. I pushed him right back. He grabbed my shoulders and lurched at me. His friend plucked him off of me.

He glared at me and Shawna. "Freaks." His spit hit my face.

"Go on, get out," I said, pointing to the lounge door. "Take your ignorance and go elsewhere."

He shoved off with a grunt and his friend followed, pulling up his pants over his gut, and waddling away.

I turned to Shawna. Her face burned red. Little blotches popped up all over her chest and arms. I pulled her into my arms and hugged her. "I'm so sorry they were such jerks."

"It never gets easy."

"Next time, dig one of those nails into his arm like I did."

She chuckled. "You're all right."

We shared a friendly grin.

"Thank you for standing up to him for me."

"I'd expect nothing but the same from you. Call it a mutual trust among women."

Shawna sat down on the stool next to me, placing her empty tray in front of us. "People don't generally trust me." She fiddled with the lip of the tray, spinning it now. "You know?"

"No, I don't know," I said, mesmerized by her ability to spin the tray in perfect rotations with just a finger. With that kind of strength and control, she'd heal a lot of people as a masseuse. "People always trust bartenders."

A wistful look swiped across her angular cheeks. "Not bartenders like me."

I leaned in. "Like you? What does that mean?"

She blushed. "You do see that I'm not like you, right?"

I hovered over her question. I didn't know the appropriate response. "You're a beautiful woman stuck in the wrong body. Doesn't give him the right."

"So you're not bothered that I'm transgendered?"

"Are you bothered that I'm a lesbian?"

She swallowed a readymade comeback that I rendered senseless now.

"See, not very comfortable being asked such a question, is it? Yet, here we are justifying ourselves."

She toyed with a napkin, wringing it up tightly. "It's not easy being transgendered."

I had never met a transgendered person before. I had so many questions. They sat on the back of my tongue waiting to pounce. "It's not easy being anything. Yet, here we are, surviving it all."

She offered me a sideways glance. "I bet you've got a lot of questions, don't you?"

You bet I did. I wanted to understand her. I wanted to know when she realized that she wanted to transition. I wanted to know what she looked like under her clothes. Did she still have a penis? Did hair grow on her chest? Did she enjoy wearing lacy undies like I did? Did she trim her hair down there or let it run all wild like men often did? How did she smooth out her Adam's apple? Why hadn't her voice changed to more female? "I would never ask you such personal questions."

"Ask me."

"Really?" I asked.

"Do you have any questions?"

"Abso-freaking-lutely," I said.

She giggled and her cheeks relaxed, balancing on her face like chiseled art, shining to life. "Go ahead and ask me. I'm an open book to you now that you used your fingernails as a loaded weapon for me."

"Really?"

"Abso-freaking-lutely." Her eyes twinkled.

Where did I start? "When did you choose to be a woman?"

She clenched her jaw. It quivered under her teeth grinding. I hit a nerve. This girl needed to talk. "I didn't choose to be a woman."

I scrunched up my face trying to figure this one out. "Huh?"

"I am a woman. I was just born in the wrong body. Since I can remember, I've always felt like a girl inside even though I have a penis. I never felt like a boy."

"Do you get attacked often like you did tonight?"

"It's been a while. We get a lot of regulars in here and everyone is always nice and respectful for the most part. Just every once in a while a drunk jerk comes in and stirs up shit. Most people just accept me here."

"And that's why you love it."

"That's why I love it, Ruby. That's exactly why I love it."

She spun her tray with the tip of her finger. We both took up refuge in its spin. A few stragglers sat at the bar with their backs to us sipping on beers and eating the complimentary peanuts. Candles lit up each table casting a tranquil and serene blanket over the lounge. I glanced to the bartender behind the bar who was wiping down the counter and laughing with a skinny, unshaven guy.

I needed to segue into something more comfortable. "So, anyone special in your life?" My voice crawled out weak and shallow.

"You ask that as if I have a choice in that."

"Why wouldn't you?"

She sat up taller on the edge of her stool. "You have a beautiful view of the world, little miss sunshine." Pain etched across her face.

"I don't follow you."

"I'm stuck mid-transition." Her face blanked. "I'm not exactly girlfriend material. I prefer solitude over the inevitable awkward moment."

"So you hide?"

She cocked her head. “I read a lot of lesbian romance novels and live vicariously through the characters. It’s safe and comforting and all I need. Freedom is a good thing in my case.”

“That’s not freedom.”

She raised her eyebrow. “Maybe not for you. For me, it is.” She popped off of the stool and leaned against the bar. “Enough talk about love. Go ahead and ask me something else. It’s your open invitation. I don’t do this often.”

I gazed into her eyes. In them I saw a softness, an innocence and a desire to connect. “I’ve never met a transgendered person before.”

“So, I’m your first?” A hint of a smile played out on her lips.

“My one and only.” I rolled out a wink and a flirty twirl to my hair.

“Ask me anything.” She studied my twirling finger.

“I just want to know how it all works.”

“How my body works?” she asked with a trace of anxiety.

I wrapped my hand around her wrist and smoothed my voice. “I meant psychologically, not physically.”

She pulled in her bottom lip and bowed her head. “The physical is so much easier to explain.”

“Hey.” I lifted up her chin with my finger. “We can stop.”

“No.” She shook off my comment. “I don’t mind. Not with you. I feel oddly safe with you.”

“Then you wouldn’t mind if I told you I think you’re gorgeous and I’m jealous of your boobs?” I glanced down at her cleavage. “They’re curvier than mine, that’s for sure.”

She smiled. A moment later she looked down at my pathetic boobs. “A pushup bra would do you good, dear.”

I scanned mine. "No doubt." I pointed my eyes back down to her boobs. "They're perky."

She cupped them, tilting her eyes up to the ceiling, thinking about it. "The hormone therapy is finally starting to perk these babies up. That and a pushup bra."

"Hey, Shawna," the other bartender called out to her. "Can I get some help back here?"

"I have to go," she said, standing up.

"So that's it? That's all I get to understand? You have gorgeous boobs from hormones and a pushup bra?"

"I'm such a tease, aren't I?" She curtseyed and flung her hair over her shoulder with melodramatic flair. "Just stay away from my girl crush." She winked.

I tripped over this request. "I can't promise that."

She smiled and messed my hair. "Relax. I'm just kidding. She's not in my league anyway." She laughed and walked away.

"Hey," I yelled out to her. "She's not out of your league."

"Who said anything about me being out of her league?" Amusement flirted on her face. "You twisted that one around. I've got standards to uphold." She flounced away like a drag queen all done up on Pride day.

I had the distinct feeling she and I were going to become great friends.

I sat at the bar and sipped an iced tea while waiting for Nadia. A few minutes later, she arrived wearing dark blue jeans and a delicate brown and blue top. Her cat eyes latched onto mine as she swaggered towards me.

"I'm so sorry. I ran a little late." She doled out an apologetic smile and fell onto the stool beside me. "You do work miracles I hope?"

She smelled like the spring earth, sweet and flowery. My heart raced.

When she waved at Shawna, I imagined nuzzling up to her and getting drunk on her soft skin and beauty.

Shawna walked over. “What’ll it be, boss?”

Nadia looked to my iced tea. “Whatever she’s having.”

Shawna squared off towards the bar with a nod.

I cradled my iced tea glass between my hands, swiping the condensation, searching for my voice. “So,” I said.

She relaxed into an easy smile. “So. Thanks for understanding my lateness. My brother-in-law held me hostage to a phone conference. Once he gets talking, there’s little to do to stop him.”

“Brother-in-law? So this is a family operation?”

She looked ahead, staring at the bottles of liquor. “By marriage.”

Of course. That explained everything. The mystery, the pullback, the guard. “You’re married?”

She turned away from the bottles and back at me. “My sister’s husband.”

I paused longer than customary, mesmerized by the delicate curve of her upper lip.

Shawna returned with her iced tea. “Don’t forget, pottery tomorrow ten a.m., right?”

Nadia cocked her head. “Wouldn’t miss it, my friend.” She squeezed her lemon in the tea, watching Shawna sashay her way back to the customer at the far end of the bar. “We’re creating matching mugs.”

“I love pottery. It’s so earthy, so pretty.”

She sipped her tea. “Can’t leave out fun.”

“The way this place is running you ragged, I’d imagine you need to have some fun.”

"This place is my escape." She ran her fingers through her hair, tossing the front fringe over to the right. "There's a soothing quality about this place, don't you think?"

I scanned around the lounge. Soft lighting, greenery in the corners, and leather chairs added a peaceful element. "If it didn't smell like chicken wings and beer, it'd be a perfect massage room."

"Yes. I guess the chicken wings might detract a little from the whole Chakra thingamajig." She giggled. Her skin glowed when she smiled. "Speaking of," she continued. "Tell me more about this traveling masseuse business. I'm very curious. How does it work? How do people find you?"

I sipped some tea. "Well, it's just getting started."

"What's your plan look like?"

I twitched. "My plan?"

Her eyes bore into mine. "Yes, your plan."

I didn't like her interrogation. I shifted on my stool. "Well, I'm trying to get some contracts with some corporations. Most are a little closed-minded to it. I'm working on it." My face grew hotter by the second. "So, I was thinking until those leads come in, I could pass out my card and travel to people as needed."

She twisted her mouth. "Hmm. Like I said on the phone that sounds dangerous."

Well, we all didn't have families who owned hotels. "It's entrepreneurial."

"Entrepreneurial." Nadia stared off to the bottles in front of us again. Her cheekbones went on forever. Her lips curved as if flirting with the rest of her face. "You know…" she paused, reflecting in a sip. "We've got lots of people walking through our garden patio all day long between business meetings and luncheons and dinners. We also get a lot of foot traffic from local businesses. The garden area serves as a pass thru between the business districts. We don't have a spa on site. We should. A portable massage chair in the right spot could address our clients' needs and not be an expense for us at all."

I liked where she headed with this. "It could be a cash cow," I added.

"Indeed. What would you need, some scented candles and a chair?"

My heart raced, and a smile too big to contain took over my face. "Are you serious?"

"The massage you gave me that time did some major wonders for me. I think we could work something out, don't you?"

My hope rose, and I did my best to keep level. "Yes. Oh my gosh, yes. I have a chair. I just need a relaxing space. I would just need to curtain off a section of the lounge to bring it to life." My words sped up and tumbled out in a mess. I wanted this more than anything. I needed this. "It would be super easy and hardly any stress for you."

Nadia giggled. Her face lit up. Her eyes sparkled. "Okay, let's have a walk around shall we?"

"We shall." I jumped off of my stool and grabbed my pocketbook. I followed her and then I remembered I hadn't yet paid.

Nadia grabbed my wrist and pulled me. "My treat."

She kept her hand on my wrist for a few seconds longer than she needed. When she slid it off, my breath escaped in a gush.

She motioned for Shawna. "I'll be back to settle the bill in a few minutes."

I followed her lead, through the lounge doors and out into the open foyer where large palm trees grew in enormous planters. People checking in lined up at the guest services counter. They all had shoulders and necks that could use my touch. I got so excited.

She waved to bellhops, and they bowed to her. My head buzzed. The potential excited me. People lurked everywhere.

She skirted us through a maze of floor plants and couches. Soon, we landed on the corner of the grand garden patio area that housed a tall banner stand promoting the Gateway Suites Executive Packages. “Right here.” She waved her arms around. “What do you think?”

Joy bubbled up inside of me. I saw a future filled with opportunity. “It could work,” I said in my most reserved voice.

“Well think it over. Then, we can negotiate.”

I stood with my hand on my hip, holding back a series of cartwheels and rolls. “Okay I’ll let you know.”

We stood staring at each other. A warm silence filled the space around us. A woman wearing a name badge sprinted up to Nadia. “We’ve got a situation at the front desk with the guy from Nike. He’s saying they should’ve had an extra conference room. We don’t have that booked. He’s not happy. He prefers to speak to someone in charge.”

She sighed at me. “Can I take a rain check?”

“Of course.” I stepped back and let her pass. “Shall I call you when I decide?”

“I hope you do.” She smiled and walked away.

I looked at my corner. My corner. A knot sat in my throat. My own corner. I swallowed my silly smile and walked back through the maze, through the foyer, and past Nadia at the front desk addressing a man in a dark suit who waved his arms all around him. She looked up at me as I passed and waved. She hung onto my gaze, then winked and returned to the rants of the man.

Chapter Seven
Nadia

When Jessica first landed in jail, I took up pottery with my sister, Sasha. I needed to keep busy. Sasha needed a companion. Pottery cost a lot less than therapy. So, why not? I agreed to attend a girls' night at a local pottery café. A group of us sat around a long table and ate nachos, drank cheap wine, and giggled over our inabilities to paint straight lines. That first night we painted peacock platters. I painted mine with chili pepper red and orange.

The day I went to pick it up at the pottery shop after it had dried in the kiln, I took one look at it and hated it. The orange overtook the chili pepper red. It reminded me of Jessica's orange jumpsuit in prison. I paid the lady for the platter, drove home with it in the trunk of my car, and later smashed it against the patio in my backyard. After sweeping up the mess and tossing away all remnants of it, I wiped my hands clear of ever loving the color orange again. I tore through my house and tossed anything orange into an oversized trash bag and heaved it into the trashcan.

Eventually, I graduated from merely painting pottery to actually crafting it myself. Creating something out of nothing fascinated me. Sasha and I even grew closer, and our conversations evolved into honest ones. She'd fess up that her kids drove her crazy when they whined, and that she hated when Keith traveled and left her alone in their big house without a dog or an alarm system for protection.

My sister and I met up for class every Tuesday when I was in town, which wasn't often anymore. I traveled quite a bit up to our Rhode Island office. I didn't protest against this. I begged for it. My job offered me the greatest excuse to not have to spend my nights visiting my wife in jail.

Jail, what a depressing place. I used to visit Jessica every possible chance I could in the beginning. We'd cry the whole time, shedding tears over our pathetic situation, over the life we lost for the next year or two.

She spent our visits complaining about the food, the rough girls who coerced her to do things for them, the uncomfortable bedding, and the ridiculous rules imposed. I'd sit and console her, trying to get her to see the positive in the negative. I urged her to connect with others, to get involved in working out, to start reading. I wanted her whole again. I wanted to reclaim our special love.

For two long months we endured these painful visits. Then, one day I entered, and a smile had taken over her face. Finally. She told me all about a new job she started in the laundry room. "The girls are so sweet," she said. "They invited me to sit in on their bible study."

I smiled at this. "I can't picture you sitting down reading bible passages with a straight face."

"What choice do I have but to mingle?" Hope sparkled on her face.

I nodded and agreed.

Future visits turned into educational sessions for me. She talked for thirty minutes straight about religion, sins, and forgiveness. Forgiveness entered her heart and lifted her spirits. Soon, though, she couldn't eat a peanut or sip coffee without first offering up a prayer. Once I made the mistake of laughing at this new side of her, and she refused to talk with me.

Just like with alcohol, she couldn't just attend a few bible study classes and call it a day. She had to dive into it with everything she had and let it consume her.

Before jail, we never fought. We laughed and fucked a lot.

Now with jail barging in between us, we cried and fucked ourselves a lot. Me in our bedroom. She in her jail cell.

The logical side of me understood this side of her was temporary, and that just as soon as she completed her jail sentence our life would resume. Good thing because this new sober Jessica was challenging and serious. I never would have sought out this version of her. I would've tossed that Frisbee right back at her and retreated back to my calculus studies.

She refused my help and turned to God instead.

So, I escaped this version of Jessica by working hard.

When I first talked with Sasha and my brother-in-law, Keith, about wanting more time up at the Rhode Island location, they called me crazy. I convinced Keith by convincing my sister. Sasha loved rescuing me. This placed her in the one-up position. I forfeited that position over to her a long time ago because frankly, she smiled more, and we fought less. I didn't need to outshine her to be whole.

I told her that things weren't going well in my marriage, and that I needed some time away. "It's the only thing that will help save my marriage."

"That's just going to tear you more apart," she said.

"Trust me. It will only improve."

Keith handed over the Rhode Island location to me the very next day.

When I did come home to Connecticut, I always got together for pottery with Sasha. This particular night I was shaping a vase into an hourglass. Sasha was molding her wet clay when she asked me, "I have several bags of old clothes I cleared from my closet the other day. You can stop by and pick out the ones you want before I send the bag to Goodwill."

I pinched my clay to mold the lip a bit better than I had it, sinking into it to avoid the sudden stab of anger. “I’m not poor.” I left it at that. Short. To the point.

She folded her clay in on itself, then rolled it on the table. Her palms steamrolled it, pushing it back and forth, with an air of authority to it. “You always take my old clothes.”

“I’m capable of taking care of myself.”

“Sorry,” she said, folding up her mouth in a tight line.

I focused harder on my vase, avoiding her stare. “You know, in the time she’s been in jail, I’ve gotten along just fine.”

“Of course you have.” Her voice pierced too high, mocking me. “Keith pays you extremely well for what you do.”

I pressed too hard on my vase, and the side of it collapsed. I stared at its carnage, a wilted gray mound of now shapeless, useless clay. Growing up I always felt sorry for Sasha and downplayed to her. I hated that I no longer had to downplay. Life did that all on its own now. When did I become the one who needed fixing? “Well what I do is stressful.”

She twisted her mouth. “Yes, I’m sure it is.”

I grabbed my clay and tore it up, mashing it against the table. “I landed a new account for the hotel. The Women’s Expo is going to start hosting their quarterly events in the main conference room.”

“Fantastic,” she said, trying out this new emotion where I, the one who always slid into the backseat so she could possess the front, now pushed her aside and challenged her for the prized shotgun position.

“Yes. I also hired a masseuse to be on hand during peak hours to take care of stressed guests.”

“Keith never mentioned that to me.”

"He doesn't know, yet." I looked up at her. Disbelief spilled into the fine lines around her eyes like she'd just witnessed a UFO landing in the parking lot.

"Keith doesn't like surprises."

"Well, life is full of them. So, maybe that husband of yours just needs to get used to them."

She stopped molding. "Something's different about you. Is everything okay?"

"Oh everything is just fucking lovely." I glanced at her out of the corner of my eye, blowing out a deep breath.

"I don't know how you do it, honestly." She pinched her clay.

My sister thrived on the idea that Jessica wore permanent scars now. "We're fine."

She rolled her eyes. "She fucked up. I don't see it getting fine."

I stood up, pushing against the table. "I'm getting coffee."

"I'll take mine black," she snapped. She could be so curt.

"Fine." I turned and plowed towards to the old man serving it up at the pottery café.

My sister dug at every turn. She loved holding the ace card. This made her feel good about her life, about her husband who I doubted loved her the way she loved him, about her misbehaved kids, and about her lonely existence. I hated that I protected this façade for her by not challenging her on these things. After all of these years, I still protected her by taking on her attempted manipulations.

* *

I met Ruby at her corner the following week. I had arranged for planted trees to be brought in to form a privacy wall. Patina art now hung on both walls of the corner. I purchased a heavy-duty portable massage chair along with a trolley cart that carried some scented candles and plants.

I arrived carrying a tote bag filled with new business cards, a cell phone, and a name badge. Ruby stood behind a man, massaging his neck. His arms dangled by his side, and his face relaxed in the head rest. Ruby massaged his shoulders from behind, digging her hands into his skin. I waited outside the privacy wall, peeking in on her through the leaves. She wore an adorable prairie-style top that showed off her femininity with grace and style. She worked the man's shoulders with great focus, directing each knead with purpose.

My blood flamed. What I would've given to be that man in that moment.

Once the bell dinged, the man paid her the ten dollars for the ten minute massage. Then, she strolled up to me wearing a sassy smile that stole my breath. I didn't recall seeing a woman more beautiful than she in that moment. Everything about her spelled simplicity and beauty.

"You look radiant right now," I said. "You're in your element, I can see."

"It's only noon and I've already made three hundred bucks." She looked ready to twirl. Could she be any more adorable?

"How many people have you massaged today?"

"I lost count. There are so many. Did I tell you how happy you've made me?"

This flattery tugged at my heart. I could only smile.

"Shawna's sending all of the breakfast customers my way. You'd think she was getting commission or something." She leaned against the freestanding register counter and counted this new money the man handed to her.

"Treat Shawna with the respect she deserves, and that girl will bend over backwards for you."

"She tells me you are close." She looked up at me with a coy arch to her eye.

My cell rang. Jessica calling on her lunch break. I dismissed the call and looked back up into Ruby's angel eyes. "We take care of each other."

"She admires you."

I held Ruby's gaze. "We're just friends."

"What a shame for her."

My heart galloped. "She deserves someone less complicated than I am."

"You don't look complicated to me." Ruby eased her sweet voice out and landed on a smirk.

"You don't know me."

We shared a quiet moment.

My body buzzed to a new level. Even my tongue tickled.

"Maybe we need to do something about that," Ruby said.

"Maybe we do," I said, running right over the consequences of employer/employee relations or of my wife for that matter. I didn't do this. I didn't flirt with pretty women.

Shawna rounded the corner and saved me from committing to anything stupid. "Got another one for you." She turned behind her and ushered in a middle-aged lady wearing a taupe suit. "She's the one with the magic touch."

Ruby greeted her with a hug. "Nice to meet you. Come right over here, and I'll take good care of you."

I waved and followed Shawna back to the lounge, leaving her to sprinkle some of her magic dust on someone else for the time being.

* *

I got back to my hotel room by two o'clock that afternoon to refresh for a meeting. Not more than ten minutes into a quick nap, Jessica called again. I groaned, then answered.

"I missed you earlier. Where were you?" she asked.

"Working." My tone was too dry. "It's been so crazy busy," I said with a little more life.

"Everything okay? You don't sound like you."

"I'm just tired." I sat up now and fanned myself with a brochure about Block Island. "I had to sit in on an important meeting." My first lustful lie. "Did you have something important you needed to tell me?"

"Not really. I just wanted to say hi."

That's all we ever said to each other anymore. "Hi," I said, trying out my best light-hearted tone.

"Hmm."

The typical dreaded silence seeped in on us.

"So, did you read the email I sent to you?" she asked.

"Not yet." I rolled my eyes. Fucking bible passages.

"It's a good one. Really opens up the mind."

All of her emails were these long, drawn out passages about the mystery and awe of God. I believed in God, but I didn't want to read about man's interpretation of Him in an email from my wife who spent the better part of her life sinning up on a stage.

"I'll read it. Right now I need to go back to a meeting."

"Okay." she said. "I love you."

"I love you, too." I lingered, feeling guilty. "I really do."

"I know, Butterfly."

"I'll call you later on after the meeting." I hung up and then took a nap.

* *

A few hours later, I visited Shawna. I avoided the foyer area. I didn't want Ruby to think I was checking up on her. I couldn't help but to sneak a peek at her as I snuck around the backside of the lounge. She sat in her chair looking up at the grand lights above with a look of awe and joyful curiosity.

I snuck one last peek and entered the lounge.

I sat at the bar. Shawna fed me three glasses of iced tea within half an hour. "You seem lighter tonight. Doesn't have anything to do with that cute blonde Ruby does it?"

"I'm married. Remember?" I arched my eye at her.

She laughed. "Yeah. Yeah. You're a good girl. I remember." She refilled my glass again.

I chewed on my straw. "Jessica asked me if I read the bible passage she emailed to me."

Shawna plucked a shot glass down from the back counter and poured some Sambuca in it. "Girl, you need this."

I picked it up, eyed it and tossed it back. It burned and tasted horrible. "Another please."

She refilled it and watched as I downed that one too.

"Careful, too many of those and you might do something wild and crazy like get a massage that you won't run away from this time around." She winked and walked away.

An hour later, back in my hotel room, numb from three shots, I decided I wanted to enjoy this great night.

I deserved a great night.

I deserved to relax after all I'd been through over the past year.

I deserved a massage.

People got massages all the time.

I worked hard.

Her hands could certainly help put some of my stress at bay.

It was just a massage.

She was a masseuse.

She massaged people.

I needed a massage.

Fuck it. I called her.

"Have you left the building yet?"

"I was just getting ready to close up for the day."

"Can you take on one more?"

"Depends," she said.

"On?"

"Is it you?"

My insides rolled. "Yes," I whispered.

"Are you coming down now?"

I lingered on her question, telling myself to go down to the foyer, I closed my eyes for reason to set in. I only saw her long blonde hair tickling my back as she leaned over it, pouring her attention onto my skin, into my soul. "I was hoping you'd come up."

Not more than ten minutes later, I paced my hotel room, sobering up and wondering what the hell I had just done. I should cancel. I should not bring a beautiful girl into my hotel room and let her massage me. This was wrong on so many levels. I imagined her soft hands kneading my tired muscles, oil slick between our skin, her lovely, fresh scent sprinkling the air, her petite body all curled up around mine to get a good balance, a good grip.

My head swirled. My inner thighs moistened. A most delicious dance stirred in my tummy.

And then Ruby knocked, and my heart pounded clear out of range.

It's just a massage, I repeated in my head as I stood staring at the door. I envisioned her silhouette on the other side, curvy and well-balanced, her long hair waving around her shoulders and her breasts, and her soft curvy hips, hugging the air.

How would this play out? We'd greet each other with easy smiles, hearts pounding, imaginings of bare skin slicked with oil and gentle breezes filtering through the window? Would we be able to restrain ourselves? Would our self-control disintegrate before us like cotton candy on a wet tongue? Would emotions flow in and rupture the dam of mental fetters and moralities, increasing our heartbeats, causing our breaths to levy against our lungs in a fight to stabilize?

Ruby knocked again.

What the fuck was I thinking?

Chapter Eight
Ruby

Golden accent lamps adorning the outside of each door lit the hallway, adding a cozy, sophisticated vibe. I knocked on her door with a skip in my heart. I shifted my portable massage chair higher up under my arm. I knocked again, staring straight at the peep hole, smiling in case she was staring back at me.

At last, Nadia opened the door.

She curled up against the door looking sexy, teasing me with her cat-like eyes. "Thanks for coming."

I wrestled with my massage chair until it fell to the ground. "The pleasure is all mine."

She stooped down to pick up my chair and handed it back to me. "Please go on in."

I entered. The room smelled of roses and carnations, transporting me to a tropical island where romance and beauty soothed reckless nerves. The suite was bigger than my old attic apartment. A flat screen television hung on the wall above a credenza that housed all the necessary fixings for a relaxing evening: a corkscrew, a crystal ice bucket, two glass tumblers, and a set of napkins folded up like fans. On the TV, a news reporter's hair blew in her face as she stood on the side of the road recounting details of a horrific car crash on Interstate Ninety-Five.

On the opposite end of the room sat a blue suede couch and a matching recliner, complete with a coffee table adorned with *Overture, Rhode Island*

Monthly magazine and the *Providence Journal* undisturbed, still cocooned in its delivery plastic wrap.

A harmonica, black, silver and shiny, gleamed on the arm of the recliner, along with a half-filled glass of red wine. Two cushy slippers snuggled up to the leg of the recliner, and a knitted coffee brown blanket was balled up in the seat.

Her laptop sat unopened on the coffee table alongside a leather portfolio with notes scribbled on the memo pad.

A beautiful oil painting of a wooded pathway going nowhere draped the wall above the blue suede sofa. Fresh flowers sat on an end table on the side of the couch, and they bathed the room in a light summer scent and brightened up the cherry wood furniture.

A small kitchen sat at the far end of the living room. A full-sized, white refrigerator and a full-sized stove filled its small space leaving barely enough room for the small, round table. It held a basket of apples, oranges, and grapes.

Past the living room, a long hallway with a mirrored closet led into a bedroom. A silk robe draped over the edge of a King-sized bed.

I dropped my chair, and my pocketbook followed. I walked into the space mesmerized. I'd never been in a hotel room this extravagant before.

Nadia walked into the kitchen and plucked up an apple. "Hungry?"

I followed her. She leaned against the door opening. Her erect nipples, bare of the shelter of a bra, stood firm against her pink t-shirt. The shirt clung to her taut waist, hugging it and going on forever down to her curved hips. A perfect silhouette. I crawled my eyes back up to meet her amused eyes. I took the apple from her and bit into it.

Sweet juice filled me. "Amazing. Even the apples taste decadent."

Nadia rolled out a soft chuckle, the kind that curled my toes and sent delightful ripples through my system.

I walked out of the kitchen and headed back into the enormous living room.

She strolled over to my pocketbook and picked it up off of the floor. "You should never leave a pocketbook on the floor." She placed the strap over my shoulder, tucking it in close to my neck. Her fingers tickled my skin. "It's very bad luck."

I cradled the strap to my shoulder, watching as she leaned against the credenza, admiring the perfect profile of her perky breasts, her lean waist, and the soft curve of her butt. "I never worry about bad luck."

Nadia bent over and picked up my chair this time. She revealed to me her bare breasts as they dangled behind the curve in her t-shirt. She placed my chair on the couch and paused before it. Her shoulders rose and fell hard, her breath determined and strong.

"So you stay in Rhode Island all by yourself?" I asked.

She placed her hands on her hips and spoke to my chair instead of me. "I do."

"So no girlfriend or boyfriend?" I bit into the apple again.

She rolled her eyes off to the side, towards the television, confusion blanketing every square inch of her face.

"It's not that difficult of a question."

"No, I suppose it's not." She still planted her eyes on the television, twisting her mouth a bit. Then, with a dismissive shake of her head she said, "No, I'm not dating anyone." She crossed her arms over her chest, stretching her long sleek neck and showing off her beautiful skin, not taking her eye off of me.

We stared in silence, our eyes reflecting a rising passion. The room curled in around us, enveloping us in a sweet, private moment where we silently confessed a mutual attraction. I loved independent women. They seemed less crazy, less complicated, and less scary to be around. They knew what they wanted, got it, and called it a day. I admired that— a woman who knew what she wanted. Right then, her eyes bore into mine and told me she wanted more than a massage, more than this nonsense talk about dating and apples. This woman was hungry, and not for fruit.

I cooled us down by pitching a banal statement. "So, you must be some star sister-in-law to have the hotel grant you this sweet place." I looked around the room feigning interest over the artwork and furniture, but could only reflect on how beautiful her nipples looked against the pink of her t-shirt.

"My sister upgraded my room this week."

"Oh?" I dared closer.

"She sometimes digs a little too deeply, and when she does she always swings into savior mode. She goes all extreme, sending me fruit baskets, flowers, and booking me the executive suite when it's available."

I rested on the intensity in her eyes. "I'd get her to piss me off more often. Is she the reason you looked upset that first night I met you?"

Nadia arched her eyes at me and walked over to the credenza. "My sister attempts to overpower me. She needs to stand tall against me. I let her have fun with this most times, but not always. That night you and I first met, she took things a little too far." She opened up the ice bucket and spooned some ice into each glass. "Sangria?" She picked up the full bottle. Her cheeks reddened like little apples of their own. Her lips were dewy and pink.

She caught me staring at them, and a tease played out on her face. So I just kept right on staring.

The wine filled the silence with a refreshing, cascading, flowing sound, adding to the sexy vibe swirling around us. My mind wandered, imagining the two of us bathing underneath a waterfall, clinging to each other's naked bodies, and kissing each other like two famished virgins in need of nourishment.

Nadia handed me my glass. We clanked them together and downed them like water. I handed mine back to her, and she refilled without a question. We drank three glasses just like this. After the fourth and final, I followed her over to the couch. She sat first, in the middle seat. I reciprocated this bold move by sitting close to her, facing her, facing those lovely, perky breasts smiling at me from under the thin cotton.

We lingered over our wine. "So," she said, her lips dark pink and full. "Where was I?"

My head spun, dancing with the vapors of the Sangria. "I'm your massage therapist," I said, my words slurring, my body moving in even closer. "Tell me your worries." I toyed with my hair, enjoying the flirt in her eye.

Our eyes sealed into this moment, exchanging an energy that magnetically pulled me to her. "I don't think you want to hear my worries." She lowered her eyes like a shy damsel, innocent to her power.

"Sure I do," I whispered.

She inhaled. "Well, my family drives me crazy."

I braved my arm against the back of the couch so it rested near her shoulder. "Go on."

"My sister and I pretend to get along, but I don't think she really likes me."

"How can she not like you?"

"You don't have a sister, do you?"

I shook off this question with a quick tilt. “I would’ve loved a sister.”

Nadia resigned to this on a sigh. “She’s got her good side.”

“But…?”

She rubbed her fingers together. “But, she’s also got her not-so-good side.”

“Like how?”

“Well, she can’t handle when something good happens to me.”

I studied the small patch of burden on her face. “So she’s the jealous type.”

Nadia looked at my arm grazing close to her shoulder. “The fact is that we get along better when I’m the one failing and she’s the one rising. She can’t stand as number two, ever. She’s always counted on me to be the number two. It’s like attention breathes life into her, like if she doesn’t have it, she’d die.” She folded her legs underneath her. “I find it easier to just let her step up and take the front stage. I just sort of blend to mend.”

I mirrored her position, folding my legs. Our knees brushed one another’s. “Blend to mend. I love it.”

She smiled, and her eyes sparkled. “Listen to me ramble. I’m sorry. Let’s talk about you.”

I touched her knee. I couldn’t help myself. “I’m enjoying this. Keep talking. Tell me all about this sister of yours.” I wanted to hear it all. I didn’t want her to stop talking.

She plowed right in. “She’s a show-off. That’s why she hated me for a while before I learned that stealing the front stage hurt more than helped me. It set me up for one torture session after another.” She paused and dropped her hand near my leg.

I brushed up against it. She blinked heavily and gulped.

“Go on.”

"So, being a few years younger, I always wanted her attention. I thought if I impressed her she'd let me hang with her friends or invite me to walk to school with her or something, you know?"

"You were feeding the fire."

Nadia tilted her head and gazed into my eyes. "I fed that hungry fire, yes."

Fire sparked in her eyes. The blend of Sangria and soft lighting added to the chemistry igniting around us.

"So, here I was this scrawny ten-year-old kid trying everything to get my sister to congratulate me, take me into her social circle, and introduce me as her friend. I tried everything to make her like me. I bought her little bottles of nail polish and stuffed animals. I made her bed for her. I folded her laundry. I shared my games with her. I let her have the top bunk bed. Still, nothing. She hated me."

I traced my fingers along the couch just inches above her shoulder, wanting so badly to land on her skin. "That is so sad."

"I would try extra hard to impress her with knowing all of the lyrics to hard songs or getting high grades on school tests that most of the kids failed. I just wanted her to look at me and say, 'Hey, great job'."

"She couldn't." I repositioned myself to lean against the couch, closer to her.

"Exactly. The more I bragged, the more she hated me. Then, one day I won a short story contest. I couldn't wait to tell her. I had worked so hard on it. Mine won first place. She couldn't even bring herself to say congratulations." She flipped her hair, and some of it landed near my fingers. "It hurt."

I inched closer to the piece of hair, finally playing with it, rubbing it between my fingertips, intoxicated by the intimacy of the moment. "Keep talking," I whispered.

"She said to me, 'What do you want from me? Do you want me to tell you Mom and Dad view you as the golden child? Do you want to hear how pretty you are? Do you want me to follow you around and do everything you do because only you know how to do it best?' I had hurt her."

I twirled her hair around my index finger. "You didn't mean to."

"Up to that point, I wanted to outshine her thinking she'd respect me more. Yet, my successes turned into her failures."

"But, they were your successes."

"I didn't need to flaunt them in her face. One-upping my own sister proved the worst thing to do. No wonder she hated me so much."

The more I heard Nadia speak, the more my desire to stay in this moment intensified. "Hmm."

She leaned into my hand.

I massaged her hair.

"My sister is vulnerable," she said, sinking into the massage. "She needs to shine. This is what defines her. So, one day when she dressed up for a school dance, I told her she was so much prettier than I was. I'd never seen a smile light up a face like that before. After that she accepted my help in fixing her hair and makeup. Next thing I knew, she invited me to the movies with her friends and even treated me to some popcorn."

"Blend to mend," I said.

"Blend to mend," Nadia murmured, staring at my lips and scrolling up to meet my eyes. "I like when she's happy. She's a better person that way. If I'm not a threat to her, we get along better. However, the minute something good happens, she turns right back into that little ball of jealousy. It drives me crazy."

My fingers continued to get lost in her hair. "You want her to like you, and you're willing to sidestep your glory to make that happen?"

She clicked her tongue. "She needs the glory more than I do."

"It must really eat her alive that you have this cushy job with her husband at the helm, no?"

"Quite the opposite. If I worked for someone else and shined, she wouldn't know what to do with that. At least with me here, she retains a certain level of control. We discuss a lot. I bring her in on decisions. She's a stay-at-home mom with the fringe benefits of power and creativity."

"Do you let her take credit for your ideas?"

Nadia shifted and clenched her jaw. "Ninety-nine percent of the time, yes."

"And the other one percent?"

"That's why we had a fight that night. I hired a different caterer for a big event, and instead of going off on me, which would be much healthier, she turned all inward and sad. I hate it when she does that because she makes me feel guilty for—"

"—for being a success?" I massaged her scalp deeper.

She cupped her hand over mine. "Why am I telling you all of this?"

"Because you need to."

"I didn't realize what a mess I created until now, you know? I just wanted to build a better relationship."

"You like to know you're needed."

She exhaled.

I propped up on my knees. "Turn around, darling. Let me work out this stress." I guided her around and swaddled her in deep massage. "You are so kinked up back here."

Nadia bowed her head and groaned.

"So she married this wealthy guy?"

"Yeah. We met him at a friend's wedding."

"We?"

"He came up to us and he asked me to dance, and when I saw my sister's face drop, I bowed out, feigning a headache. So he asked her to dance, and they hit it off. He's creepy to me."

I softened my touch, leaned in close. "How so?" I whispered.

Her breaths quickened. "He's a player. He's come on to me right in their house with my sister in the next room. I've seen him here taking ladies out. He's wealthy and owns the whole chain of Gateway Suites on the East Coast."

"Does she know?"

"It's hard to miss."

"I'm surprised she wants you working with him."

"I'm gay."

"Well," I said, turning her back around to face me, bubbling with adrenaline. "That makes two of us." I played with a strand of her hair again. She leaned into my touch. So, I twirled the piece around my finger, holding a piece of her captive. Her chest rose and fell in stronger waves, her nipples toying with my eager eyes.

"You're beautiful. Do you know that?" she asked.

My skin tingled. My face flushed. I could easily lean in and kiss her, and I doubted she'd fight me on it. "You're my boss now. And I really like my new job."

Nadia traced her finger against the blue suede of the couch, trailing the curve of my leg. Slowly, seductively, she teased with the suede. "You're right. This is so unprofessional of me to be flirting with you like this."

I expanded my twirl zone so much so that my finger flirted with her cheek. "I am so attracted to you."

"I should look away from you right now." Her seductive clutch tightened. "I'm finding it so hard. Nothing else in this room is as interesting."

I released her soft hair and sat back against the arm of the couch now, crossing my leg over my knee. "I should go, huh?"

"Please don't." She crossed her leg over her knee just like me. Only her foot fidgeted whereas mine lounged midair, relaxed. "You still owe me a massage."

"I do." How I'd get through it, God only knew. I was a horny mess. I needed to refocus. "I need to use your bathroom first."

Nadia blinked then laughed. "Right down the hall on the right."

I rushed towards it. Once inside, I stood staring at myself. I didn't even have to pee.

I scanned her sink which was cluttered with Crest toothpaste, dental floss, Shaper Plus hairspray, Paul Mitchell Sculpting Foam, and a variety of lotions and facial creams. She probably stood at the sink naked, her skin dripping in moisture from a fresh shower, applying her facial cream to her soft skin. This just turned me on more. *I can do this. I've massaged plenty of beautiful women. Just do your job and walk away.*

I walked out of the bathroom. Nadia stood baring the backside of her voluptuous body. She dropped one cloth after the other, and I just stood there watching it all unfold. Slowly, provocatively, she undressed her upper half, and then sank into my chair. I stood in the hallway, drooling, staring, and craving to run my hands all across her sweet, buttery skin.

There Nadia sat, uncovered and unexplored on my chair, the chair I'd carried under my arm. Never did I see this coming, a beautiful half-naked lady waiting on it in her hotel room for me. I stood, ambivalent. I wanted to run to her and take her in my arms. Yet the other side of me argued that I should just stay put right there in front of the bathroom door and avoid the eventual disaster of charging into this innocent massage moment as a hormone-induced junkie wanting to get high.

Her chest pressed against the chair. She relaxed wearing just her silk bottoms. Her golden spine, straight and perfect, waited to be healed. I'd never massaged a half-naked client without a protective blanket before.

I steadied myself and walked in like a professional masseuse should.

"Let me get a blanket for you."

"Don't bother," she said, squirming against the plastic seat. "I figured it would just get in the way, right?"

I lost my breath. "Yes, ma'am."

She snapped up, her breasts danced forward along with her flowing hair. "Ma'am? Really?"

I clicked my tongue. "No?"

"No." She wrapped her hair around her neck and rested back down against the head stirrup.

"Deal." I went into this massage like I did any other. I cradled my hands around her shoulders and worked my touch into her tired, knotted muscles. "You really need this."

Nadia moaned.

My tummy rolled.

I closed my eyes and pretended I was massaging a three-hundred pound bald man. I ripped into her muscles, angling my palms deep into her tissue.

She moaned again.

I opened my eyes and took in the full beauty of her spine, so perfectly arched in all the right places. I breathed in deeply, imagining my lips on her skin, blanketing her in soft kisses along her shoulder blades and down her lovely spine.

I eased Nadia's tension for ten short minutes before surrendering my access to her beautiful skin.

I leaned in and whispered, "How was that?"

"Heavenly."

I slipped my hands off of her. "Be careful in rising. Sometimes people feel dizzy."

I guided her as she rose. She turned to me all sleepy eyed. "Thank you." She reached for her pink t-shirt and pulled it back over her head. "I needed that."

We sat on the couch again, folding in on ourselves.

"What other stories do you have bottled up in that pretty little head of yours?"

She eyed me with great care. "I've told you too much."

"Oh come on, darling. Don't raise your guard now."

She leaned in, so close I could smell the sweet mint on her breath. "Sometimes words get in the way."

Nadia's lips called out to me. On reflex, I placed my finger on them and circled. If I kissed her, I wouldn't be able to stop there. This pulse radiated between us. I needed this job. She just trusted me with all of this personal stuff. If I kissed her it would ruin everything we just shared. I couldn't pull away from her lips, though. They called out to me like a magnetic force, luring me to them. "I should go."

She feathered my lips with her finger now, releasing puffs of sweet air into my zone. "Yeah, it would be a good idea."

I rose, which caused me to move in even closer. "It's the Sangria."

Before I knew it, my lips were on hers. My hands cupped her face, and her hands traveled to my shoulders, pulling me towards her. We breathed as one, her lips brushing against mine in small seductive sweeps, her tongue teasing mine in a dance that twirled me, sent me reeling, soaring, flying high. "I shouldn't be doing this," she whispered.

"Me either," I said, drunk on her.

"There's too much you don't know." She pulled away and jumped up. She raked her hand through her hair. "I'm sorry, I can't."

I caught my breath, steadied my heart with a hand to my chest. "I understand." I stood and smoothed my hair. "We'll just blame it on the wine."

"Yeah." She looked confused.

"Oh, come here." I opened up my arms to her. "We just shared a moment. It's perfectly fine. I get it. It's a line we shouldn't have crossed." I laughed. "It's my first week, and I'm already trying to get into your pants."

Nadia laughed too.

We clung against each other sharing a good laugh. "So, I'm not fired or anything, right?"

She pulled away and held me at arm's length. "We're good." She blinked heavily and nodded. "Tomorrow, when we see each other, we'll share another good laugh and pretend it never happened."

"Well, all right then." I grabbed my pocketbook and chair.

"Okay," she said all professional, escorting me to the door.

"I'll see you tomorrow," I said.

"Until tomorrow." She smiled and closed the door.

I wobbled all the way to the elevator, drunk on a lot more than just Sangria.

* *

I bumped into Shawna on my way out of the lobby area. She looked tired. She limped up to me, dragging her feet.

"You need a massage," I said.

"I'm too tired. I just want to go home and relax in a tub, listen to some jazz, maybe sip some wine and call it a night."

I held the door open for her. "Long day for you?"

"The breakfast girl called out, and so when Nadia called me in a panic, I filled in."

I scanned her heels. "I don't know how you do it."

"I do it because I love this job."

We walked past the valet parkers and out to the far end of the parking lot. "Two shifts, though?"

"You're so naive." She scrambled through her pocketbook for her keys. "That's why I like you so much."

I blocked her with my portable chair. "Naïve?"

"It's not a criticism. Your innocence is a gift."

I narrowed my eyes. "Everyone is not out to get you."

She rolled her eyes. "You haven't lived my life. So you can't toss out bold statements like that." She patted my arm. "Have a good night."

She walked towards her car, limping, as if carrying a lifetime of trouble on her shoulders.

Chapter Nine
Nadia

I adored Ruby. When she left my hotel room, I lounged on my bed and attempted to concentrate on an episode of *King of Queens* where Carrie's father and Doug become best friends. Lost on the show's humor for the first time ever, my mind drifted.

I closed my eyes and imagined her hands on my shoulders again, then her soft lips on mine. My body seared.

I shook my head and sat up. I could not fantasize about her.

I walked over to the window and opened the curtain. The city of Providence lit up below me. People walked on the sidewalks some in pairs, some in groups, their laughter echoing off of the brick buildings. Ruby had long disappeared. Did she go home to a wife? A girlfriend? An empty apartment? Did she have a cat or perhaps an adorable dog that we might one day walk together?

I spun away from the window.

I would not obsess over her. Ruby was simply a fun girl with a killer smile and a knack for buckling me at the knees. God she was something else.

I went back to my bed, slid under the covers and caved into thoughts of her long blonde hair tickling my skin as she leaned over me, seducing me with her charm in a passionate moment that could only be described with words like thrilling, intoxicating, and inescapable.

* *

Jessica called me the next morning. "I've got some good news."

I braced for it. "Tell me."

"The lawyer thinks I'll be released early."

My heart sank. I wasn't ready for her to come home just yet. "How early?"

"Four months."

I sat on the edge of my bed. "Wow."

"Yeah. Wow. Crazy, huh? I've been a good girl, I guess."

The tension shot right back between my shoulder blades. I envisioned our new life, sitting across from one another having nothing in common but our history, pretending to be interested in how we spent our days, wishing in silence for our old times. "That's fantastic."

"We'll get a fresh new start. Finally."

We needed a fresh start. "Yeah, finally."

"You know what the first thing is that I want to do when I get out?"

I clamped onto the hope. "Tell me."

"I want to eat lobster at that restaurant in Mystic where we had our first date."

We had gotten silly drunk on cheap beer that night and ended up pulling off to the side of the road to make out for hours. "Sounds lovely."

"It's almost over."

This wasn't a victory race. "Yeah. Almost there."

Silence hung between us. Someone in the neighboring hotel room turned on the television. I could hear Matt Lauer from the *Today Show* laughing.

"So, have you talked to your sister yet about hiring me?"

"Not yet. I will." They would never hire a convicted felon. I would never ask them to either.

Long pause.

"Jessica? Are you still there?"

"Why haven't you asked her yet?"

"Well, we didn't know how long you'd be incarcerated," I said this with scorn, my anger renewed for what she'd done to us.

"Incarcerated? You make me sound like a—"

"—just drop it."

"I wanted you to be happy with this news. You sound more disappointed than anything."

Didn't I have the right? "So much has changed, you know?"

She exhaled, and her pain curled up around me, choking me. "Maybe if you came to visit me more often, we could deal with all these changes better."

I sat up taller. "We've been over this. My schedule is challenging."

"You choose Rhode Island over me," she said. "I'm not blaming you. I'm just stating the fact. You didn't have to switch locations. Keith would've kept you on in Connecticut, and we both know it."

"You're antagonizing me." She never argued with me before jail.

"I'm just stating the facts. You have distanced yourself on purpose. Admit it."

I would not admit that, even though it was true. "Where is this blame coming from suddenly?"

"You've changed so much. I don't know how to speak with this new version of you."

I liked this new me. I no longer catered to her ideals or sacrificed my happiness for hers. "Yes, of course I've changed." My temples flared. How dare she turn me into the guilty one? "You want to hear exactly how? Do you?"

"Yes. Tell me." Her voice steamed out all smooth and collected.

"I'll tell you how." Fuck her and her new virtuous attitude. "For starters, I fixed the lawnmower last week. Yup, I had to take it apart and put it back together again. I did it by watching a YouTube video. I fixed it all by myself because my wife decided to get drunk and kill someone."

She gasped.

I carried right on with my argument. "So what fucking choice do I have but to change?"

"You're being unreasonable," she whispered like everyone in the state prison could hear us.

"Oh, I'm sorry." I flew up from the bed and paced the room. "Am I embarrassing you?" I had never yelled at her before. Never. This rage needed releasing.

"What do you want me to do?"

I barged right over her question. "You know another unpleasant task I had to do a month ago? I had to get the ladder off the hangers under the deck, place it up against our home, and climb up the steps all the way to the roof holding a hammer and five roof shingles because our home is falling apart, and because I'm the only one here to fix it."

She exhaled. "Why didn't you call Keith?"

"Go crying to him so he and my sister can gloat about how fucked up our lives are?"

"Huh. Nice. Feel better slamming me when I'm already down and out?"

"You put yourself there. Not me."

"Well, go on then. You're on a fucking roll."

"You're a felon Jessica." My chest beat wildly. "A fucking felon."

I flung my phone across the bed and rose, pacing my hotel floor like a tiger pissed to be locked up in this cage.

Slamming her? Huh. Maybe she needed a good slamming. My tongue turned numb. My skin burned. My blood pressure spiked by the second. Tears stung my eyes. The end of what we used to have arrived. It stung, blasting sand and grit in my face and blinding me.

I walked back over to my bed and plucked up the phone. "I'm not going to sugar coat things for you anymore."

She was sniffling.

"Stop crying," I said.

She sniffled some more.

My heart slowed. My breaths rolled out smoother. My mind cleared. "I just don't think it's a good idea for me to beg Sasha and Keith to give you a job. We can find you work someplace else," I said softly.

"You're afraid."

"I'm not afraid."

"You are though. You're worried about what everyone's going to say behind our backs."

"Well of course."

"Why do you care?" she asked.

"Because it matters." I saw a future with her laboring for eight dollars an hour, or resorting to drug sales, or pimping herself out.

She cleared her throat. Sniffed. Clicked her tongue. "There's this long line of women staring at me right now. I'm hogging the phone. Can you just come for a visit soon so we can talk this out face-to-face?"

"Of course," I whispered.

"Until then, Butterfly." Her voice cracked.

Butterfly.

That word transported me back to my old wife, to our happy days, our free days. Peace and familiarity landed softly on the wings of that word.

"Hey," I said. "I love you. I hope you know that."

She breathed out. "I love you too."

* *

Unsatisfied people took risks. Some jumped from airplanes, some dove hundreds of feet underwater, some trekked up dangerous mountain sides in search of justice, youth, and thrill, anything to purge the unsettling rustle of fear and angst and apathy from their systems.

I chose to make a phone call.

When Ruby answered, I said in as sweet a tone as possible, "It's me. Nadia."

"Hello, Nadia." Her voice was quiet and soft.

"I could already use another massage."

"Then, I'm your girl."

"I won't argue with that." The flirt tumbled out before I could stop it. "I come to you a humbled girl in need of help."

She rolled out a sigh that sent my heart into flight. "I hope you do."

"Shall I come down this afternoon?"

"I'd be disappointed if you didn't," she whispered and faded out like a song I didn't want to end.

I cradled the phone to my ear for several long seconds after she hung up, savoring the residual softness of her voice still dancing on my heart, light and airy, a pleasant escape from my reality.

An hour later, I was eating breakfast in the garden patio restaurant when Ruby strolled by wearing a flowing shirt that mirrored her willowy personality. Her blonde waves bounced along her shoulders, and when she spotted me, her cheeks flushed. I waved her over.

"Have you eaten breakfast?" I asked.

"Are you inviting me?"

"Please sit. Have a cup of coffee with me."

She slid into the chair across from me. "So," she said, flipping her hair over her shoulder.

"So."

"About last night, I'm really sorry if I got too personal with the questions."

I cupped my hand over hers. "It's okay. I needed to talk. You're a good listener. I trust you'll keep it between us?"

"It's safe with me."

I drew back my hand. "I felt bad later because I painted an unflattering picture of my sister. She's not that much of a devil."

"I get it." Ruby waved over the waitress. "She's just insecure, and you're just sweet enough to see that."

The waitress arrived. "Coffee for you, too?"

"Yes, ma'am."

Ruby watched her walk away. Peace spread around her, like nothing in the world could penetrate and destroy her positive vibe.

"So, about last night," she said. "I'm sorry if I acted unprofessionally."

I stopped her. "We had a beautiful conversation. You massaged me, and we said goodnight. Nothing unprofessional about that."

She chuckled. "Right."

The waitress returned with a fresh coffee. "Here you go."

Ruby and the waitress chitchatted about the weather, and I sat like a dork admiring her beauty. Her smile mesmerized me with its peace and simplicity. Calmness and serenity haloed her.

In that hotel room I changed into a lotus flower, opening up to her sunshine one petal at a time, blooming to life and feeling desirable, beautiful, and sexy. I would love to cuddle under my blankets with her, sweep her up into my arms, and hold her tight. I could see myself sleeping, not afraid of gentle snoring, wrapping my legs around hers, fondling each other's fingers and kissing them until the night shadows turned bright with sunlight. We'd wake and stretch, blanket each other in soft kisses before we climbed out of bed hand-in-hand, and strolled to the kitchen for coffee and overfilled bowls of Honey Nut Cheerios. I could see myself spoon-feeding her, wiping dribbles of milk from her chin and kissing the tip of her nose.

I could so easily fall for someone like her. Someone fun, sweet, different. Someone not in jail, not an embarrassment, not a person I'd have to defend for the rest of eternity.

When the waitress walked away, she turned to me and raised up her coffee mug. "To our new friendship."

I clinked my mug against hers. "Cheers to that."

We drank our coffee and chatted on about the hotel, and then about local sights in Rhode Island, laughing and bantering until we emptied our mugs.

"I should go," she said, lingering her hand over her pocketbook strap, not committing to plucking it up. "I'm late in opening my massage chair."

"Yeah, I should get to the front desk and see about this convention going on today and tomorrow."

Ruby slid off of the chair. "Don't forget about that massage."

"I'm already thinking about it."

She strutted away, swinging her pocketbook over her shoulder and flinging me one last wave.

I winked.

Ruby blew me a kiss.

What the fuck was I doing?

* *

"I'm an idiot." I handed Shawna the new menu proof from the printer.

She looked it over. "I wouldn't have chosen this particular green shade, but the layout looks clean and fresh."

"I'm not talking about the menu."

She sat on the stool next to me. "Spill it."

"I adore this new massage girl."

Shawna slapped the table. "I knew it."

"This is not a good thing." I stole the menu back from her, needing something to fidget with. "To top it off, Jessica called and told me she's getting early release in four months."

Shawna simply arched her eye in quiet solidarity.

I drummed the menu against the cocktail table. "I don't know if I can do this. She expects me to pick right up where we left off. Of course, she's different now. I have nothing in common with this new Jessica. She's too serious, too sensitive, just way too much. I liked her so much better when she drank."

"Slip her some alcohol every now and again," she said with a wink.

I slapped her with the menu. "Seriously. She obsesses over my every word and reads into everything. I just wish she could be sweet and fun and attentive without the alcohol."

"You mean someone more like Ruby?"

"How screwed up am I, huh? I've been flirting like crazy with her. She massaged me last night in my room."

Shawna backed up. "Whoa." She grimaced. "Did you…?"

"No." I slapped her again with the menu. "God, no. I'm not going to cheat on Jessica."

She narrowed her eyes. "Like she's done to you?"

Jessica didn't technically cheat on me. She had cheated on her boyfriend, Robby, with me. "I swept into her life and confused her."

"I know. You rocked her world." She laughed. "Does Ruby know you're married?"

"It didn't exactly come up in conversation."

"It should." She stood up. "Better to just get it out there in the open for both of your sakes."

I didn't want to tell her. I wanted the dance. I wanted the mystery. "I will."

"Good girl." She patted my arm and grabbed the menu from me. "I've got a bar to get ready."

Chapter Ten
Ruby

What a gig. People loved ten-minute massages.

I could not screw this up. Rachel and Marcy would be accommodating for only so long before they would surely start to get cramped from my dependence on them.

I brought in over seven hundred dollars of business each day in the garden patio at the Gateway Suites. I would get half of that. Not too shabby for one day of work.

As clients filtered in, tired from their business meetings and long flights, I rejuvenated them. They tipped me generously and walked away breezy and redefined. Yesterday Shawna fed me clients all day. I would do the same for her today, and hopefully they'd tip her just as generously because they'd come to her relaxed and happy.

On this morning, so many clients poured through the garden patio that I actually had to take time for a break around lunchtime. I headed over to the lounge to check in on Shawna.

She wore a pretty skirt, low-cut blouse and high heels again. "You are torturing yourself."

"I love heels." She slid an iced-tea in front of me.

"You're so beautiful. I just can't understand why someone hasn't snatched you up yet."

"Honey, look around."

I scanned the cozy lounge. A sea of men blanketed every nook and cranny of it.

"Even you'd be dateless working in this place."

I plopped my face in my hands. "So no interest in men, right?"

"I love me some curves. You can keep the beard stubble."

I laughed and sipped my tea. "So what does that mean? Are you straight or a lesbian?"

"I guess it depends on who's forming the opinion."

I needed to understand. "I'm confused."

"Don't you have massage clients waiting for you?"

"I'm not on a schedule. That's the glory of it all. So, can you stand here for five minutes and explain, please?"

She filled a glass with ice and poured some Sprite into it. She took a good long sip, eyeing me. She emptied it and poured herself another. She gulped that one back too. She went to pour herself a third.

"I'm not judging. I just want to understand."

Her eyes filled, and she twisted her mouth to the side. "I'm just used to people mocking me. No one's ever really asked to get a real answer. I surmise they just want a good laugh. I've been caught in that trap a lot."

I placed my hand over hers. "I'm not going to laugh at you. It kind of hurts me that you think I would."

She stared at me. "I've been through a lot." She bit her lower lip and stared out over the lunch crowd. "The short answer to your question is this – I'm a woman stuck in a man's body. That has nothing to do with my sexual preference. I identify with being a woman more than a man, even though I have the man parts."

I nodded assuring her safe ground. "Go on."

She tilted her head, narrowing her eyes, testing me.

"Go on." I reassured her with a squeeze to her hands.

"I view myself as a lesbian because I've always considered myself a woman, and one who adores women."

I squinted trying to understand.

"And just in case you are questioning this, a transgendered person's sexual orientation has nothing to do with his or her gender identity. The two are unrelated. Trans people are lesbians, gays, bisexuals and straight too."

"So, the women you've been with, how do they identify with you? I mean are they lesbians, bisexuals, straight?"

She exhaled, twirled her glass, and then volleyed it back and forth between her hands. "Ruby, dear, I've experienced sexual encounters with all kinds. As you can see, by my single status, it's not easy for them. If I'm having sex with a woman, she might be viewing me as either a lesbian or straight."

"Why don't you just get an operation?"

She picked up the glass and placed it into the bin behind her with a laugh. "You know what I am growing to love about you?"

I arched my eye waiting.

"I just adore your innocence. You've got no filter, and I surprisingly take no offense to that. Most people I'd want to slap for asking me such an invasive question. It's not invasive coming from you." She leaned back on the bar counter.

"I'm just trying to understand, that's all."

"We can pick up on this later. You should get back to work."

I peeked around the side lounge door to my private oasis and didn't see anyone standing there waiting. "I've got about five more minutes to chat."

She scanned the room. "No one is flagging me down, either."

"Then tell me more."

She studied me, then leaned in and spoke lower. "Surgery is a serious commitment. So much has to happen before that is even considered."

"Like what?"

"I have to go through a period of time where I've been documented as living what's known as the *real-life experience*. This pretty much means fully adopting my gender role as a woman in everyday life."

"Well, that's easy. Aren't you doing that already?"

"It's not as easy as it sounds. I've been living as a female here for about nineteen months now, which is the longest ever for me. Usually in the past, when someone harasses me, I freak out leave town and start over again." She pushed a napkin around in front of me. "It's just not an easy process. I'm lucky here because people are just really cool about it all. This has definitely not been the norm for me."

"So, you've been running around for most of your life?"

"I've lived in ten different cities running away from this decision. I run to get away from the transgender life. It's easier sometimes to just be male, even though sleeping on a bed of sharp nails would hurt less. I don't get the stares, the abuse, the ridicule, or the funny looks that I do as Shawna. You should see when I have to use a public restroom as Shawna. The stares are crazy. Being Shawn is easier in that respect. I don't have to put up with any of that crap. However, I hate being Shawn. So, I always get pulled back into needing to stay true to myself because the urge to live as I am truly intended never goes away. So, I start the process all over again. The psychotherapy, documenting the real life experience, all of it."

"So you haven't been tempted to run this time?"

"This time is different." She scanned the room as if taking it all in for the first time. "This place is home. I belong here." She landed back on me and smiled as peaceful as if she just stepped out of church with me and my grampa.

"You like bartending, don't you?"

"I don't like it." She paused dramatically. "I love it."

"It's not confining being behind that bar all night long?"

"I've never felt freer." She looked away wistful. "I like that people need me here. This place needs me. No place that I've ever worked needed me like this. No one stares funny at me when I dress up extra girly like they did at my office jobs."

"Office job?" I shivered. "I'd rather die."

"Yeah. I earned my master's degree in computer science while I was Shawn."

"What? And you're tending bar? The two are just so different."

"I hated it. So boring, you know? Sitting in front of a computer all day long killed me. Especially when I became Shawna and wore nylons. Those things just dig into the tummy when I'm sitting. I'd end up with gas pains until the wee hours of the night." She flipped her hair over her shoulder and fanned herself. "It's getting stuffy in here just thinking about it."

"What did people say when you went from Shawn to Shawna?"

"They sent me home on my first day dressing up as Shawna. I showed up to work wearing two-inch heels and a pretty, red dress that scooped low in the front and came up to just above my knee. I wore a new wig I had custom-made and strutted into work as me, Shawna. My boss nearly choked on his bagel when he saw me and immediately headed to his phone to call HR. The rep came to me and asked that I follow her down to the administrative offices. They told me I disrupted the workflow and sent me home. Apparently, I had created a wind tunnel so fierce that I supposedly threatened the entire workforce that day, and thus the meltdown of several hundred client accounts. I could come back to the office if I dressed appropriately. So the next day, I didn't show up. I never even sent them a letter of resignation. I just dumped the big project I was working on into their laps and let them figure it out. That's when I left town again and headed here to New England. I liked its quaintness."

"The Gateway Suites shines like a beacon to us in need."

"Sure does." She played with her hair. "I just happened to be driving and crying, something I did often back then, and I glanced over at the Gateway. I needed a place to stay for the night and decided to treat myself to something classier than a motel with cockroaches. After I checked in, I went down to the lounge for a drink. That's when I met Nadia."

"Nadia to the rescue."

She chuckled. "I told her I needed a job. She said they needed someone to serve food. So, I put on an apron that very night and started serving nachos, calamari, potato skins, and mixed drinks to the crowd who didn't care that I wore a wig and high heels. I brought their food to them, and they loved it. So they tipped me generously and chatted with me all night long as they watched football on the big television screens. I found a home that very night."

"I could sit here all day long and listen to your story."

"I've got a table waving to me." She waved back to them. "I've got to get over to them, and you've got to get massaging."

I stood up and reached over the bar for a hug. Her eyes grew big, and she flagged her arms around not knowing what to do with them. I laughed and pulled her into my embrace. She turned red and giggled.

* *

I once dated a girl named Trellis who knew how to bake the best casserole dishes. She also knew how to bake extremely moist cookies. She would hand me a plate of them on every date, letting me know that I played on her mind as she spooned cookie dough onto baking sheets and melted along with the high oven temperature. At first, I thought this was adorable.

By the fourth time of hearing how much I swept into her mind, though, I began to choke on the confines of her tight focus on me. This girl didn't know anything about me, yet, she admitted to me that she dreamed of me taking showers with her, sleeping in her arms, and spending lazy summer days by the poolside reading magazines together.

She had concocted this entire future for us that required I settle in beside her at every waking hour. She knocked on my apartment door for our fifth date to go to the Performing Arts Center to hear Rascall Flatts in concert. I ignored her. I spied on her through the peephole of my door and watched as she practiced her smiling face all while balancing her cookie plate in one of her delicate hands. She propped her other hand on her hip, then changed her mind and dropped it. Next, she fluffed her hair, wiped her teeth with her finger, and smiled again before she broke into her tenth knock. She knocked a total of twenty times before her smile turned upside-down.

I felt sorry for her, but who had time for such a clinger in life? I would never settle down with anyone who baked cookies for fun. I wanted to live, be daring, be bold, and sample life's greatest treasures. I couldn't do that if I lugged around twenty extra pounds from eating cookies every moment she stepped in front of me. She smothered me.

Most girls did. They became obsessed after two dates. They started planning our future together, committing me to endless nights of strolling through city parks hand-in-hand staring up at the moon with love dripping from our bodies. If I held their hand too quickly, love, not lust, rested on their eyes, expecting me to jump into their bed, and ultimately their lives, signing document after document of legal papers announcing me their benefactor, their partner for life, their soul mate.

I just wanted to sip martinis, flirt with no restriction, and allow the euphoric rush of the moment to sweep us up into the heavens. Then, once we landed safely back on the ground, we go our separate ways and agree we had a spectacular, mind-blowing evening together. As soon as strings attached, the fun disappeared. The euphoric ride ended abruptly. The thrill of the chase ceased.

The chase. That's what I loved. Once I caught up to my object of affection, the adrenaline subsided. Most women craved companionship and that lasting bond. Not me. I just wanted to find someone who could have fun and not get all possessive and start prepping wedding vows and selecting table cloths and curtains and color schemes for a shared condo she envisioned after just one kiss.

Women just wanted to nest. I wanted to fly away from that nest. That nest freaked me out with all its confines and trappings.

Now Nadia, that woman's mystery sent me into lustful overdrive.

That morning, I was prepping my booth for the next client when she walked into my massage oasis looking all empowered in her pants suit and smart makeup.

"How's your day?" she asked.

"It's been wonderful." My smile spread quicker than I could control it.

She mirrored it. "Do you have a few minutes to chat?"

"Sure. Let me lock up the register, and I'm all yours."

Nadia walked out of the oasis, hands folded behind her back, standing tall, and taking in the beauty of the place she helped manage.

I fell in behind her, and she led me to an elevator. "I figure we can go up to my office where there's a little more privacy." Her hands remained folded behind her.

We climbed aboard the elevator and took it up three floors to the executive offices. We passed several offices and came to hers, a nice corner one with a big window overlooking the patio area that contained my massage corner. My heart galloped imagining she could see my every move from her perch.

I traced my finger across the edge of the window railing. "We're having our first official meeting, and I didn't even have a chance to prepare." I looked up at her.

Nadia closed the door behind us and closed the window shades to the hallway. She cleared her throat. "This is not a meeting you could've prepared for."

Panic gripped me. "Are you firing me?"

"What?" She laughed. "I'm not going to fire you." She reached into her pocketbook and pulled out a checkbook. She sat down and wrote out the check. "I just forgot to pay you last night for the massage."

This insulted me. Why didn't she just slap me across the face? "You don't have to pay me."

Her red fingernails glistened under the lights as her pen scrolled across the check. "Sure I do. Otherwise I'll be afraid to ask you for another treatment."

Her pen continued to dance across the check, wiping out the romance from the night before. "Don't be ridiculous."

Nadia ripped out the check and handed it to me. "I trust that's enough?"

I glanced down and handed it right back to her. "Fifty dollars?"

"Not enough?"

“I’m not taking your money.” I folded my arms over my chest in silent protest.

“We’re two professionals who understand money must be exchanged for such services.”

She sounded like the president of a company all of a sudden. Where did my sweet, flirty Nadia from the night before go?

“Fine then.”

“Fine.”

“Well, if this is going to be a regular treatment option for you, we should settle on an actual price that is realistic.” I matched her tone.

She stretched her eyes and cocked her head. “Oh, I like this side of you. The professional,” she whispered.

My tummy flipped.

“What would be reasonable?” she asked.

“I charge a dollar a minute.”

“So, if I didn’t want to rip up this check, I still have another forty minutes coming to me?”

Were we negotiating the price of a new car? “You can take it all in one shot or break it up into smaller sessions. Whatever you wish. You’re the boss.” I said this with more hurt than I meant.

Her face softened. “How about a ten-minute treatment right now?” She removed her jacket. “Should I just slip this shirt down a little over my shoulders?”

I walked around to the backside of her. I helped slide the silky cream shirt off of her shoulders. Then, I brushed her hair off to the side. “Just relax.” I would remain professional. I would not cross the line. I would leave with my job intact. She was a client. Just a client at this point.

She bowed her head and softened like putty in my hands. I rubbed her neck with my thumbs, circling it, pressing it, and feathering it. "Feeling better?"

She moaned.

I continued circling her skin with my thumb as I traveled down to her shoulders. I gripped and kneaded them and enjoyed watching the curvature of her spine in the small space between her skin and her silky shirt. I could picture my tongue tracing it up and down and her moaning and melting below me.

Nadia's breathing deepened. It filled the office with a rich melody that I soon fell into sync with. I rubbed her shoulders in wide circles, leaning in closer with each angle until my lips were just shy of her neck. She leaned into my breaths, and soon cupped her hand over mine. "I can't massage you if you're trapping my hand," I whispered.

"I can't help myself if you keep blowing your warm breath on my skin." She looked up at me, seduction playing on her eyes.

I ignored the warning bells ringing in my ears. I bypassed the red flags waving me away from her lips. I couldn't help myself. I leaned down and kissed her. She pressed her lips into mine with a hunger she had kept hidden the night before. I swiveled around to her front and straddled her. I couldn't kiss her hard enough. She raked her fingers through my hair and pulled me to her. My body pulsed against her with each pass of her tongue through my lips. I sealed my hands around her shoulders and rocked against her.

"We have to stop," she whispered into my mouth.

"No," I said, kissing her harder. "Why would you want to stop?"

She pushed back from me and cupped my face in her hands. "I should tell you something." Dread circled the spokes of her eyes.

I knew before she could say it. "You have a girlfriend."

"No," she said, pulling in her lower lip. "I don't have a girlfriend."

"Then what?"

Nadia hesitated, drawing a deep breath. "I've got a wife."

Chapter Eleven
Nadia

We agreed to be friends.

After I explained the whole messy story to Ruby about Jessica, she asked me, "Do you love her?"

"I care about her."

Ruby arched her eye at me. "Do you love her?"

"I don't want her life to be ruined by what she did."

"You're not answering my question." Her eyes bore into mine.

"I don't know." I paused and took in the empathy on Ruby's delicate face. "I'm angry."

She stepped closer to me. Her hair was a mess from my fingers just half an hour prior. "You have every right to be."

"I don't do this," I whispered. "Go around kissing other women. I don't want you to think I'm like that."

"I don't judge." Ruby slipped off her light sweater and swung it over her shoulder. "I'm sure what you're dealing with must be hard."

"So hard." My breath caught. Her eyes were so soft and caring and offered the perfect place to take up refuge. "It's been over a year. I've gotten used to living alone now and getting along without her. We've grown so far apart."

"Do you visit her?" She ran her finger up and down her arm. God how I wished it were my arm.

"At first, I used to visit her daily. It's a terrible place."

"I can just imagine." Ruby hugged herself.

"People stare. I have to talk to her through Plexiglas. Armed guards watch us out of the corners of their eyes. And, we have nothing to talk about anymore. We sit in awkward silence, playing with our fingernails and shifting in our seats a few hundred times. It's awful."

"How often do you go now?"

"I visit her when I go back to Connecticut. That's only every other week or so now."

"I don't know that I'd be able to go in there at all. So kudos to you."

"It's strained our marriage, as you can imagine."

Ruby stretched her eyes. "Relationships are hard enough, right?"

"Even when they're good, they're hard." We lingered on a stare. "She told me to think of her time in jail as a soldier's deployment. We went into this committed to the notion that the time away will strengthen our love." I bowed my head. "I'm looking forward to the day she's released so we can go back to what we used to have with each other."

Ruby counseled me that afternoon, assuring me that my feelings were justified. She swept out of my office with all of her grace, leaving me breathless and even more curious and intrigued.

As the weeks sped by, we spent lots of time together. I liked having her in my life. I liked walking into work and seeing her smiling face. I liked looking down on her from my office and watching her in her element. I liked stopping by and handing her a coffee and embracing each other in a friendly hug. I liked when we met at the end of a long day and enjoyed a drink together at the bar. We'd share laughs, we'd share tales of our day, and we'd share stories. I loved hearing about her grampa. She adored him, and to me that just spoke volumes about her character. "He's my life," she'd say.

My grandparents lived across the country, and I had only seen them five times in my life. We'd meet at various funerals for distant cousins or third generation aunts or uncles. They didn't hug me. They simply nodded, smiled, and carried on their boring conversation about politics and their flights into Connecticut. "I'm actually a little envious of that."

"I owe him everything. He's blessed me over and over again."

"I'd love to meet him one day."

"You're welcome to join us on any Sunday. We go to ten o'clock mass at Saint Mary's in Providence, eat some brunch, and then head over to his senior center for some Wii."

I cringed. "I haven't been involved in a spiritual ceremony since—"

"Since your wedding?"

"Yes. Since my wedding."

Ruby draped her hand over my arm. "Come with us."

"No. I couldn't. I wouldn't want to intrude."

"My grampa would love it. The more the merrier."

"I'm not religious. I wouldn't know what to do. How to act."

"It isn't some wacky place where we perform rituals. We simply walk down the center aisle all the way to the front row, shift to the left, and sit directly in front of the priest's pulpit. That's where Grampa insists we sit."

"I'm a heretic. I don't belong in church."

"It's a shame," she doled out. "My grampa would love you."

That next Sunday, Shawna invited me out to breakfast. I showered and met her in the lobby. She wore a conservative blue dress and flat shoes. A goofy smile spread across her face.

"What are you up to?"

"Just get in the car." She pulled down on the ill-fitted dress. "This thing is giving me a wedge from hell."

"Where are you taking me to breakfast?"

She sighed before dropping into the front seat of her car. "St. Mary's."

My heart leapt. I climbed into the passenger seat. "Did she put you up to this?"

Shawna simply rolled her eyes on the start of the engine and sped off.

A grin, too large to be hidden, etched itself on my face for the entire drive.

* *

We walked into the church. Music filled the large space decorated in stained glass windows and large murals depicting the Stations of the Cross. It smelled like incense and furniture polish. Elderly women with blue-tinted hair and flowery blouses and men in blue blazers and ties tied too tightly sat in pews with their heads bowed. Parents pointed their fingers and glared warnings at their fidgety children. Babies cried. Candles burned. And the sun filtered in through the ceiling slits.

I spotted Ruby and her grandfather in the front row just where she said they'd be. Her blonde mane flowed behind her. Tiny twists on either side pinned her hair back. She wore a baby blue shirt. Her grandfather wore a gray oxford sweater. His hair was steel gray and wiry. He sat still, staring up at the altar.

We walked up the aisle, and Shawna's shoes clacked on the granite floor. She hung her head in reverence. "Why is everyone looking at us?" she muttered.

"No one is looking at us." I scanned the aisles and willed people to stop staring. I even shot a few bold older people dirty looks. "Just keep walking to the front," I said to her.

She groaned and trudged onward.

As we closed in, Ruby turned over her shoulder with a satisfied smile on her face. Her eyes flickered with intensity. I unraveled at the sight of her. My heart thumped. My breath cut short. My legs turned to jelly, and I hardly noticed Shawna's clacking anymore.

Ruby stood and tilted her head in a way much too sexy for a church setting. She waved to us both. I entered the pew, and she wrapped me into her arms. "I knew you would come," she whispered.

"I feel very out of place." My lips flushed up against her ears. She smelled delicate and lively.

"Let me introduce you to Grampa." She squeezed me and pulled away.

I glanced over at him. He continued to sit still, staring ahead, a bit of moisture brimming on his eyelids.

She cradled her hand on his shoulder. "Grampa, meet my friends Nadia and Shawna."

He looked up, stared at me, and then broke into a sprightly smile as if we hadn't seen each other since the days of the Titanic. He climbed to his feet, and with the strength of a twenty-year-old man, he pulled me into his arms and squeezed me. "Nadia. What a lovely name you have." His voice bounced off of the high ceilings. Our pew neighbors smiled and nodded at us.

He pulled away and held my hands in his and swung. He smiled, like all of his youth had just reappeared and we were soaking up the sun on a beach in Malibu amidst a backdrop of sailboats and pelicans. Even his wrinkles faded and his nose and ears shrunk in size compared to his large spirit. He smelled like he'd taken a soak in laundry detergent.

Her grampa motioned to the seat where Ruby had been sitting. "Here, sweet Nadia, you sit next to me."

I sat on command.

"And you can call me John."

"Okay, John," I said, shifting on the hard wooden seat in search of a comfortable spot.

He turned to Shawna and welcomed her with the same lively hug. "Aren't you a beautiful thing," he said.

Shawna's eyes twinkled. "It's a pleasure, sir. Ruby talks so much about you."

"You sit on the other side of me. Come on," he said pulling her across the space in front of him.

"Now listen," he said loudly, shifting from me to Shawna. "Some people call me Aura. Other people call me Jack. And some call me John."

"I can barely remember one name, and you want me to remember three?" Shawna asked, her smile playful.

He laughed so hard he started to cough. His whole face lit up. His eyes watered. His hands trembled when he clapped them in obvious joy over his three names. "I'll let you pick one. Though, I must tell you now, that I love John the most. And you know why?"

"Tell me." Shawna placed her hand over his.

"Well, I'll tell you. It's because that's the name my wife called me. She couldn't pronounce Aura, and Jack didn't sound right to her, so she decided she'd call me John. She just plucked that name right out of thin air."

Ruby tapped my leg. I looked up into her watery blue eyes, and she winked at me. Then, she placed her hand on my leg and just left it there for the entire forty-five minute mass. For the first time in my life, I prayed mass would last forever. I didn't shift. I didn't flinch. I didn't care that I was a married woman sitting in a church pew in between a girl I wanted to wrap myself around and her grampa. Everything just felt right.

"Your grampa is adorable," I whispered.

She flaunted a victorious smile before releasing me with a nod.

Later, we went to breakfast, and he filled us in on everything hockey. I knew nothing of hockey other than a puck, skates, and ice were involved. He recounted games from the seventies, and the star-studded wins thanks to the talents of players he rattled off like I would talk about event planning checklists.

After breakfast, we went to the senior center.

"Watch this," Ruby said, taking my hand in hers and leading me towards the main sitting area where oxygen tanks, mixed nuts, and cans of ginger ale ruled.

As soon as this man walked out of the bathroom and towards his friends, they all brightened. Their cheeks blushed, and their eyes glowed. He was the man of the hour, the celebrity, the one everyone wanted to claim as their friend for the day. He happened to also be the only man in the room.

One lady with a French knot in her hair grabbed his hand and kissed it. Grampa pulled it back. Then another curled up to his side and whispered something in his ear. They shared a giggle, and then, yet, another woman stole him away by handing him the Wii control.

"These women fight for my grampa each week."

We sat and watched him beat this lady in Wii bowling. She blushed and bantered with him, nudging him whenever he knocked a pin down. Ruby rolled her eyes. "Same thing every week. He could have his pick here."

"Yet he chooses none?" I asked.

"These women aren't his type. He likes them younger than this."

When the game ended, the lady insisted on another round, but he turned her down. "I want to play against Nadia or Shawna now."

Ruby pushed me towards him. "Well, go on. Don't keep the young man waiting too long or else he might conjure up a way to beat you."

Did he ever beat me! I tried. I really tried. But this man, he had powers.

He beat a competitive Shawna, too. She whizzed her arm back like she was tossing a full-fledged professional bowling ball down a genuine bowling alley.

Later, we relaxed in a circle of folding chairs, sipping Earl Gray tea. He piped up again, sitting tall in his chair and telling us stories.

"I moved to America when I was nine. We lived on this small farm. There were twelve of us. The farmhouse fit us all perfectly. It sat on two hundred forty acres. We had forty cows, and three horses. We raised chickens and grew all of our own food. We didn't have a grocery store closer than one hundred miles. So, we grew vegetables and canned them in our basement. We'd bury them in sand to keep them cool and preserved."

"Tell them about the fire," Ruby said.

"Oh, the fire." He nodded his head up and down. "There was this big blizzard." His voice bellowed loudly. "Everything was frozen. I went out to the barn to get some tools for a project in the farmhouse, and when I looked up at the roof, I saw a shingle on fire."

"How did it catch fire?" I asked.

"Spark from the chimney. I ran inside and told my parents, and no one believed me."

"How could they not believe you?" Shawna asked, hanging on this man's every word. I wondered if she had ever known someone as sweet and adoring in her life who she could look up to and admire. The way she had clung to his words since church, I highly doubted it.

"I joked all the time," he said, straightening his lips.

"So, what happened?" I leaned in.

"Our house burned to the ground. We tried to save our furniture, but the snow buried it and ruined it. We had to just watch it all burn."

"Where did you go?" Shawna asked.

"We had nowhere to go. Some neighbors took us in and fed us scrumptious pies and spaghetti with meatballs and the yummiest garlic bread I've ever eaten. My parents didn't want to be known as moochers, so we moved. We moved to Massachusetts to a place called The Rafters."

"That's where I grew up," Ruby said. Her smile sat perkily on her pretty face.

"We ran a small farm and sold our grain and chicken and beef to local markets," he continued. "And when my parents died, I took over. I hated farming. Hard work, you know?"

I didn't want to disagree. "I bet."

"So I decided to turn The Rafters into a bed and breakfast. My wife and I ran that place like a couple of expert tour guides. By day I'd take the guests out on adventures—fishing, hiking, typical tourist stuff—and by night, my wife would bake them homemade dinners and pies. One of us would end up playing the piano and singing songs to the guests while they read and relaxed by the roaring fire and ate cookies."

"Heaven," Ruby said. "It was heaven." Her eyes glowed.

"What happened to The Rafters?" I asked.

Ruby shook her head, urging me to cease. So I did.

"Or better yet," I jumped back in. "Tell me something else interesting about your life. Ruby tells me you're quite the story teller."

"Oh, I've got stories. I used to write them as often as I could. But my eyesight." He shook his head. "I like to tell them to the kids at the library. You know they sit there and listen like little angels. I love telling them the story of when I saw my first airplane because they scoot up really close and giggle when I tell them I almost shot the plane down with a shotgun!"

Shawna scooted up like one of those kids. Ruby ducked back and slung an arm around my shoulder. I leaned into her.

"I heard a high-pitched whining. I looked up and saw this thing flying above. It looked like a big bird. I headed towards my front door to get my big rifle. The mailman had been approaching and said, 'That's a plane.' Turned out he was right, and the plane landed in a big farm over to the right from us. Eventually, they started flying from that farm offering people flights for $1.50. The pilot would take people all around town. Fascinating stuff," he said sipping on his tea thoughtfully.

We ended our fun afternoon by bringing him back to his apartment in Ruby's yellow Camaro. He turned to me and Shawna with tired eyes. "You will come back again, I hope?"

We both nodded.

"I'd love to," I said.

He placed his hand on my forearm. "You thought I was going to be some old, cranky guy who farts and blows his nose every two minutes, didn't you?"

I laughed out loud at this. I pinched his cheek. "You're even cuter than your granddaughter. Shh. Don't tell her."

When we walked back down the walkway, Shawna said, "I wish I had someone like him in my life."

"Well, now you do," Ruby said, clutching her hand.

When we arrived back at the parking lot of Saint Mary's where Shawna's car was parked, I didn't want the day to end. "Why don't we all go and grab a bite to eat?"

"I've got all the fixings for a spaghetti dinner if you girls want to take a drive to Jamestown," Ruby said.

I looked to Shawna and sent her my best plea.

She nodded. "Why not?" Then, she further accommodated my plea by suggesting she follow us in her car.

I had Ruby all to myself in the front seat of her yellow Camaro.

* *

Ruby drove with one hand on the steering wheel the other one draped on the console between us. I draped my arm, too, so they brushed up against each other. An electric current buzzed between us, connecting us.

"Nice set of wheels."

"My grampa bought this for me for my high school graduation."

"He's such a sweet man." I nudged her arm to keep the current alive.

"I begged him for it. I researched this car, dreamt of this car, talked nonstop about this car for like a year. And then, he had his friend deliver it to the driveway, and when I stepped out to head over to the field for graduation exercises, it sat there with a big bow on it. I thought I had died and gone to heaven."

"I see you take very good care of it." There was not a speck of dust anywhere.

I glanced at her profile. She pulled in her lower lip. "He sacrificed a lot for me to have this."

"I'm sure he did."

"He's always sacrificed in his life. Especially with his girlfriend. He fell madly in love with Grace, and she left him. She broke his heart. He couldn't even stand to live at The Rafters anymore. So, he sold it, and he's never been the same since."

I didn't know what to say, so I just held her hand.

"I am still angry and devastated. He moved from this beautiful home with rolling fields, streams, and endless activities to his apartment at the senior housing complex. A part of him died that day we moved. It's like his spirit wilted, like his purpose erased, and left him only with a bunch of empty years ahead of him with nothing more to do than play Wii with a bunch of old people."

"Do you hate Grace for it?"

"Grace just wanted her freedom. She couldn't be caged into a relationship. How can I hate a person who is just like me?"

I squeezed her hand, offering my respect. "So you aren't the relationship type?"

"Not at all. I will never end up like Grampa."

How could I argue with that logic? I envied her freedom. "So, your Grampa sounds like he needs to have some fun."

"I don't think Sunday church and brunch are quite working that well anymore. I sometimes worry that he's bored with the routine of it all."

"Well, let's change it for him then."

"So you're willing to do this all over again?" Ruby teased.

"Maybe I am," I said.

Ruby graced me with a sweet, lingering smile. "I'm going to miss you when Jessica gets out of that prison. Do you think she'll let us stay friends?"

Dread fell over me. "Probably not."

"Well, we'll just have to be creative then."

Ten minutes later, we arrived at Ruby's condo. She lived right on the water in Jamestown. We stepped into a pristine white space accented with red window treatments, pillows and frames. "I rent a room from my friends. They're away this weekend visiting friends in Miami."

"I need to use the little girls' room," Shawna said.

"Down at the far end of the hall."

"Might be a few minutes." She ducked past us and ran down the hall.

"She's so sweet. We've got to set her up with someone."

I wagged my finger. "She's already warned me to stay clear of that."

I sat on the arm of the recliner. Ruby snaked around me and wrapped her hands around my shoulders and kneaded them, relaxing me in an instant. "Close your eyes, darling."

I did. I sank into her touch like I was sinking into a warm bath drizzled with soothing oil.

"You were so sweet today," she whispered. "So very sweet." She teased me with a light touch, tickling my senses and bringing my skin to life.

I needed to touch her, to cuddle, to be in her arms. I reached up and tugged on her fingertips. She stopped massaging and leaned her chin against my shoulder. I pulled her fingers to my lips and kissed them, one at a time. Her chest rose and fell against my back. My insides quivered.

"You're a sweet friend," she said before drawing her hand back from my lips. She traced my shoulder, slowly, sensually, staring into my eyes.

Shawna emerged from the bathroom, catching us in this provocative stare. "Listen, we need to go. I'm not feeling well. My stomach is a little queasy."

"I can make you some tea," Ruby offered.

"No, we should go."

I wanted to punch her. I didn't want to leave. "Come on, let us make you some tea."

"Please," Shawna said. "I need to get back to Providence."

What could I do? Look like a total bitch by forcing her to sit and enjoy tea that could quite possibly send her flying back to the bathroom again? "Fine. We shall go, then."

Ruby and I shared a lingering gaze.

When we stepped out into the fresh sea air, I turned to Ruby and waved at her beautiful silhouette. Her hair blew around her, and she looked just like a sea goddess.

"I'll drive," I said. "Give me the keys."

"I'm fine," Shawna said.

"You're fine?"

"Trust me. You'll thank me later for this."

I grabbed her wrist. "You're the one who dragged me to church today."

"That had nothing to do with trying to set you up with her. I wanted to meet her grampa."

"Bullshit."

She stopped walking. "Just be careful. That's all."

"Of course." I nodded and pressed on towards the car.

* *

Two nights later, Ruby called me. "What do you say we play Monopoly?"

"Monopoly?"

"I just saw it in the gift shop and I bought it. What do you say?"

"Do you want to come up to my room to play?" I asked.

"I'll be up in five minutes."

It's just Monopoly, I said to myself as I spritzed the air with perfume, fluffed the pillows, and squirted breath freshener in my mouth.

Moments later, Ruby entered my room, and filled it with her light fragrance. Her hair fell loosely in long waves, and she wore pink lip gloss. I could handle this.

"See?" She lifted the box. "They have the Providence version of it."

"Cute." I followed her towards the living area of the suite. I had already set up a blanket on the floor. "Some wine?"

"Do you even have to ask?" She smiled. She set up the board while I filled our wine glasses.

A few minutes later, we were curled up on the floor flipping dice and getting a little drunk on Merlot.

"So my grampa adored you and Shawna."

I moved my toy car three spaces and landed on the Roll Again square. "He's fascinating." I picked up the dice and rolled again. This time I landed on Go Directly to Jail. "How appropriate."

Ruby picked up the dice. "Sorry about that, darling. We'll get you out soon." She scooted up on her knees and tossed the dice.

"I hope so. I don't ever want to stay long in jail."

Ruby relaxed back down on her folded legs. "How did you react when she first landed in jail?"

I never talked about this. People judged. They sat back on their security blankets with smug faces like I was suddenly beneath them. But not Ruby. Her eyes softened. Her beautiful aura shone brightly. Sweet innocence cascaded around her.

"Do you want to know the first thing I thought about?"

She moved in closer to me, knocking over her growing pile of hundreds. "Tell me."

"I worried that she didn't have hair gel."

Ruby chuckled and tilted her head towards her shoulder. "What else?"

"I remember thinking this poor girl isn't going to be able to use her cellphone to check her Facebook. She lived for updating her Facebook status and checking to see who liked her updates and photos."

She smiled.

"I also worried that she had no pillow to rest her head on at night. She had this favorite pillow she always called True Blue because it never failed her. As long as she could ball it under head at night, she could sleep. The thing was ten years old."

"You couldn't take it in to her?"

"I threw it out in the trash one night. That and all of her clothes, and her shoe collection."

Ruby reached out and touched my cheek. "Remind me never to get on your bad side."

I cupped my hand over hers and closed my eyes. I was pushing the line, but I couldn't resist. Her hand comforted me.

"Tell me more," she said.

"Jessica had so many friends. I worried for her that she'd die of loneliness in jail. She's a pretty girl, so I could only imagine her getting gang raped, bullied, and tossed around like a bag of potatoes."

"Was she ever, you know, raped?" She feathered my cheek with her comforting touch.

"She never told me. And I didn't ask."

"I bet she misses touching and kissing you something terrible."

"It's been a long time."

"Do you miss touching and kissing her?" Ruby asked.

"Before all of this happened, we were very close, very affectionate. Now," I rolled my eyes. "This is going to sounds strange. Now that she's sober, she's just hard to get along with. We just fight all the time now. We both pick on each other about stupid things. When drinking, she let a lot of things slide. Nothing bothered her. Now everything is amplified, she says."

"You liked her better as a drunk?"

I clung to Ruby's caring eyes. "So sad, right? She's far more pleasant when she's drunk. No one realized she had a problem."

"You think no one knew, but darling," she said, running her fingers through my hair now, "I would guess most people knew."

I let her words absorb into me. They came from a place of innocence and love. "I used to feel sorry for her one minute, and then a moment later I would start tossing her stuff all over the place, smashing her precious perfumes and ripping her binders full of notes about her dreams and goals she hoped to accomplish one day."

"I bet that felt really good." Her words crawled out to me, like a feline, arched and sensual, teasing me to draw nearer. "How did your family take it?"

"My family." I inhaled. "At first I thought, I'll just keep this whole mess hidden from them. I'll pretend she's away on some important venture, like building habitat homes for the poor up in the Appalachians somewhere."

"Judgmental folks, I take it?"

I shrugged. "Jessica has always been so good about not caring what people think about her. But I do."

"Is prison scary for you when you visit her?"

I paused and looked at Ross Simons on the Monopoly board. I ran my finger over the square wishing I could just sink into it and escape into some alternate reality where Ruby and I were walking hand-in-hand down a city street, wearing expensive clothes, chit-chatting about a Broadway play we had just seen and stopping into a cute, urban spot for some fancy drinks. Instead, I looked up into her waiting eyes. "Imagine being tossed into a gas chamber and having all of that noxious air, dead space, and stale smell trapped in there with you."

She pouted, offering me an empathetic sigh. Then, she climbed to her knees and crawled around my backside. She combed my hair with her fingers, massaging my scalp. She leaned in and whispered into my ear. "I'm listening."

"After we got through the whole bail, attorney meetings, and trial, she landed in jail. The judge sentenced her to two years in the state prison."

"That's it?"

"She was lucky she didn't do this in a different state with stricter minimum sentences."

"I'd say."

"I promised her I'd visit her that very next day. She walked away, crying, looking back at me over her shoulder. She looked so pathetic."

Ruby continued massaging my scalp. "Go on."

"So anyway, the next day was a Friday. I called the prison and asked about the visiting hours. They asked me if Jessica had placed me on her visitor list because if not I wouldn't be allowed to speak with her. I said, *of course she did. She's my wife.* So, the next day I braved all and headed to the Bridgewater Correctional Institute."

Ruby leaned in and caressed my neck. "You're trembling."

I continued. "When I entered and they asked me if she added me to her list, I once again said, *yes, I'm sure she did.*"

"She didn't, did she?"

"Nope. She failed to place me on her visitor list. I said to the clerk, *maybe she just didn't know she had to?* And she said to me as cocky as ever, *if she wanted you on her list, she would've placed you on it.*"

She traveled to my temples and circled them. "Tell me this gets better?"

"A few days later, I got a collect call from her telling me she added me to her list. She asked me to bring her some money and toiletries. It takes a couple of weeks for the visitor list updates to happen, so she had to wait. When I received notice that she added me to the list, I arranged to go in on a

Thursday. Well, Thursday came and a few hours before leaving to visit, Jessica's friend from the Burlesque club called me and invited me for lunch. I told her I planned to visit Jessica. And she said, oh when you see that clerk with the red hair and the big attitude, can you punch her in the face for me? She is beyond rude every time I go in there."

Ruby gasped and stopped massaging. She curled up around the front of me with a look of horror on her face. "Were they sleeping together?"

"No. I don't think so."

"So what happened when you finally went?"

"I didn't go that Thursday. I made her wait."

"Did you talk to her about her dancer friend?"

"When I finally walked into the prison, my fear superseded my memory. I forgot all about confronting her. I remember sitting there in my car thinking, I am going to walk in there holding my head up high even though I know everyone is going to be staring at me thinking *she married a loser.*

Ruby took my hands in hers. "You're still trembling." She rubbed my hands in hers.

Ruby listened to me in a way that no one ever did. She cared. She wanted to hear my story. No one ever wanted to hear my stories. I wanted to unload all of them to her. "I was a wreck that day. I had to be searched. The lady at the check-in counter growled like an angry tiger. She wore her dark hair in this tight bun. It shined blue under the fluorescent bulbs. She wrote my name in black marker on a visitor pass and flicked her finger to the right and told me to walk that way."

"Fuck this game of Monopoly," Ruby said. She swept it away from us and guided me backwards against the floor. She propped a pillow under my head and reached for a blanket on the couch. She covered me up, then held my hand. "Go on."

"That day was hell. The prison smelled like ammonia covered up in Pledge. I can still hear the way my heels clacked on the floor that first day. The walls closed in around me. As I walked towards the security guard, I swallowed nothing but dry air. My left eye twitched. I suddenly hated my friend Janie. I hated her for getting married and asking me to be her maid of honor. I hated hiring Jessica. I hated loving Jessica. I hated everything about Jessica at that point."

"Understandable." She squeezed my hand.

"When I approached the gray-haired man in uniform, he smiled at me and ushered me to a chair. I had to remove my shoes and jewelry just like at an airport. He treated me with dignity. My nerves shook every part of me, and he placed his gentle hand on my back and guided me to sit. I cried under his compassion. He had asked me if it was my first time. I couldn't even talk."

Ruby rubbed my arm, up and down, in long soothing strokes.

"He patted my shoulder blade and told me it wouldn't be so bad."

"Was it?"

"It was no massage, I can tell you that." I reached up for her hand. I laced my fingers in hers and admired their grace. I kissed them, one at a time with my trembling lips.

"Well, darling, nothing's going to be like my massage." She teased me with a wink. "Get to the part when you see her."

"Okay, so they take me to this room with Plexiglas, a row of chairs, and telephone receivers. I sat in the chair and waited. The room spun. I braced my hands on the counter, stood up, and contemplated just running and never looking back. Honestly, I was so angry. So incredibly angry that she did this to herself. Then, the door opened, and in she walked on the other side of the glass wearing an orange jumpsuit."

Ruby nodded, squirming. "I can't imagine."

"I just remember her eyes. They drooped. The life in them had vanished. The sparkle faded. Her jaw hung like a drug addict. She walked without swagger, without attitude. She didn't smile. She just sat down across from me and eyed her end of the receiver with gloom. I picked up my end first. I tried on a smile, but she didn't look. She just shook her head, exhaled, and stared up to the ceiling. I tapped on the glass, and the guard said *no tapping the glass, ma'am.*"

"Wow."

"Yeah." I blew out some air. "So, I sat there, studying her sullen face and lifeless body. Finally, she bowed her head and picked up the receiver. I said hi to her as sweetly as possible. She sat staring at the counter, not reciprocating. Her chin quivered and finally she burst into a crying fit. Tears flew. She choked on them. She hung her head in shame. She didn't once meet my eye. She just cried like a baby in an orange jumpsuit."

Ruby laid down beside me and curled up under the blanket.

"She did this for five minutes. I cradled the phone to my ear and prayed she would say something that I could walk away with that would offer me some peace. The guard stood in the corner staring straight ahead as if all too familiar with this scene. Then the guard told us to wrap up our visit. She pointed her eyes directly at me. "Don't come back," she whispered.

Ruby hugged me tightly.

"She hung up, and without looking at me, she walked out of the room."

"That's terrible."

"Well, so the next day I drove back to show her I would not abandon her, that we would get through this together. That's what we did. We got through things."

"Blend to mend."

"Yes," I said. "Blend to mend."

We shared a sigh.

"So, I walked up to the receptionist again, stated my name, and waited for her to hand me my name badge."

"The red headed bitch that the whore from the club told you about?" Ruby asked.

I hugged her, comforted by her spunk. "No. Just the same mean one with the tight bun. She said I wasn't on the list."

"She took you off the list?"

"She took me off of the list."

"So then what?"

"Dazed, I walked straight out of the door, straight past a mother tugging her two screaming toddlers by their tiny hands, and to my car. Then I sped away, numb. I didn't want to return home where her scent still lingered. I reached up to my dashboard and picked up the yellow duck she placed there a year ago. I opened my window and tossed it out. Then, I opened up the console and tore out her golf gloves. I tossed them out too. For the ten miles I drove, I left a trail of Jessica on the road."

"So how did you get back on the list?"

"My sister asked her."

"Your sister?"

We shared a laugh. "My sister to the rescue."

"Are you sad when you see her in there?"

"I feel very sad for her."

"Why are you with her? Why do you stay true to someone who has screwed up your life?"

I hinged on Ruby's question. "I'm holding out for the hope that when she comes back to me, she'll come back recharged and fun again. This new

Jessica, isn't really her. Jail is making her into this person. Once she's out of jail, we'll be able to get past all of this stuff. I'm sure of it."

She cupped my cheek in her hand. "Have you ever cheated on her?"

"I'm not that kind of person."

"Of course you're not," she whispered with a tease pulling on the corner of her moist lips.

Chapter Twelve
Ruby

My massage chair business grew quickly. I didn't have to, but I worked every lunch hour and every happy hour. Then later, Shawna and I would sit at the bar and talk about hair, makeup, and shoes. She loved shoes. She wore a different pair every night, and they ranged from flats, to sandals, to heels far too high to be comfortable behind a bar.

One night, after I closed up my massage chair, I went into the lounge for a drink. Shawna couldn't keep up with her orders. Customers filled every last seat. Her face flushed. She didn't even see me when I walked up to her. She rushed past and stuck a pencil behind her ear. So, I decided to step in and help her out. I walked behind the bar and took some guy's order for a shot of Sambuca. As I poured it, Shawna turned away from a trio of guys and locked eyes with me. She ran towards me, flinging her hands up. "Get out from back there."

She looked angry, like I'd just stolen her dog or her wallet or a great parking space at the mall at Christmas rush. She charged at me. I freaked out and hopped back over to the customer side of the bar. "Sorry." I slid out of her way as she tossed the empty tray on the bar.

"Please don't mess this up for me." Her eyes pleaded. Fear hung on each spoke.

"How would I mess this up for you?"

Despair leaked from her cheeks. "You're not supposed to be behind the counter. If you got caught, I could get myself and Nadia in a lot of trouble.

She went out on a limb here to hire me. Her brother-in-law can be a real asshole when he wants to be."

"I just wanted to help." My words fell out of my mouth. "I would never try to get you in trouble."

She sighed. "Not everybody is carefree like you, dear."

She walked away, shaking her head. For the first time, I felt out of place at the Gateway Suites Lounge. I sped out of there, through the back door and out into the dark parking lot. I climbed into my Camaro and sped away, cursing at the starless night for being so dark and dreary.

I turned on the radio, searching for a song. Every station played a commercial. So I drove all the way back to Jamestown in silence, fighting the deep gnawing in the pit of my stomach, blinking away the look of angst on Shawna's face.

I hated that I angered her. I hated even more that I cared.

Fuck friendships. What good were they anyway? The structure, expectations, and rules just complicated things. Yet, friendships depended on such details.

I didn't want to be counted on as a friend because I'd never be a good one. I would never be there in times of trouble. I would run away from dramatic, emotional phone calls in the middle of the night. I would never know what to advise someone if ever someone asked my opinion. I'd dish out the wrong advice, and next thing I'd be sitting in the front row of a funeral home staring at her casket because I, Ruby Clark, didn't tell her the right move.

I cried the rest of the drive home.

When I finally arrived at my place, I sat on my front porch and soothed myself by fantasizing about fun times with Nadia. She didn't infringe on my life. She didn't expect anything from me. She didn't set blind rules and get angry when I ignored them without even knowing. With Nadia, I was free. I would always remain free, because that would be the only way I'd ever fully live a life I could one day look back on and say, I played my cards as I saw fit.

Never would someone else get that ability to take over those cards or my life. I would never live as my mom did, wielding to a psychotic man, living like a little mouse pretending to enjoy the feast of old moldy cheese for the sake of keeping his spirits high so he wouldn't beat her with a belt. Never would I seek what the average person sought in life, marriage and undying love. That didn't exist. That was a façade. It ruined lust. It ruined passion. It killed a person, like Grace killed Grampa's spirit.

In my game plan, I would have fun. I would spend my days laughing, smiling, and playing. I would not owe anyone my commitment therefore no one could get upset with me or accuse me of crossing lines and not staying true.

Nadia didn't cling. She didn't need me. She wouldn't expect me to drop my life for hers because Jessica had already done that for her. For these reasons, she captivated me. Her mystery magnetized her to me. I wanted to always remain a mystery to each other. I wanted us guessing about the lives we spent outside our massages. I wanted to allow our personal lives to breathe so that when we came back together again, we'd always get high on the adrenaline and euphoria that circled us.

Thank God for Jessica.

Nadia's marriage actually saved us from future demise, standing in as a safety switch for my desire, saving me from falling where relationships crumbled and ended up broken at the bottom of an abyss.

I wanted to wonder about her when she traveled back to Connecticut. Not in a creepy sort of way, but rather a curious, simmering way. The more mystery, the less inclined I'd be to fly the nest that encapsulated our friendly moments together. I wanted that nest to be light and airy, a place to come to for affection, and a place to easily escape when the spark started to twitch and fade.

I wanted to crave her always.

Why didn't people offer the same flexibility in friendships? Why did Shawna carve out these unwritten rules and not explain them to me? How was I supposed to know I couldn't help her? Did I look like a mind reader?

I hated drama. I hated that an unsettled feeling brewed in me. I hated that I wasted the entire evening worrying.

I went back inside and fretted more over a bowl of cheese curls and a bottle of Budweiser. As I sipped the last of the beer, I heard a knock on my door. I opened it, and Shawna stood with a silly grin on her face holding my sweater. "You forgot something." Fresh lip gloss coated her lips and dramatic eye shadow deepened her eyes. "Have you been crying?"

I wiped under my swollen eyes.

"I don't believe anyone's ever cried for me before." She pulled in her bottom lip and tightened it, wobbling on the threat of a break down.

I fought to keep my trembling chin in order. "I would never compromise your job on purpose."

"I know." She handed my sweater to me. "But you could've."

"I'd never let a friend of mine get into trouble," I said.

A smile shined across her face. "You think of me as a friend?"

I folded the sweater over my arm. "Don't you think of me as a friend?"

She blinked extra slowly as if I'd just spoken to her in Russian.

"Do you not want me to be your friend?" I asked, annoyed now.

Again, a long extended blink. Then, a hand up to her mouth and a fresh batch of tears. She bit into her finger, and her shoulders started to buck. Soon she folded over at the waist and clung to her knees, crying.

I cradled her to me and let her have a good cry. I eventually joined in. The two of us clung to each other like pathetic, weepy fools, crying over friendship.

Mid-sniff she stood up. Her eyes were swollen and red. "Thank you."

"For?"

She backed away down to the steps of my porch and waved at me. "For being my friend." She ran off into the dark night, and I just stood there speechless, not sure how to digest her weird act of driving thirty miles to deliver my sweater in the middle of the night. Had she never been friends with someone before?

I sat on my couch, kicked my feet up and closed my eyes. Then my cell dinged. I read Shawna's message: "Thank you for being my friend."

My heart clenched. I allowed the drama to marinate within. I texted her back and told her how she honored me by calling me friend.

* *

Nadia and Shawna arrived at my grampa's apartment with blueberry muffins in hand. Grampa reached out to Nadia for the box. "Now, see there," he said to me. "She's a keeper." He nudged me.

"She's already taken." I hugged his shoulders and guided him to the side. "Let the poor girls enter. It's getting chilly outside."

We ate blueberry muffins while grampa showed off his story books to the girls. He handwrote each one over the years and drew stick figures in marker for the book covers. "It's not my art they come to see." He laughed. Bentley jumped on his lap, and he scratched the top of his head. Bentley purred.

Bentley always hated when I scratched his head.

The girls browsed his collection, and he glowed with their gushing.

By the time we left his apartment we had missed mass.

"How about we change it up for you a little this week with a different activity?" Nadia swung an arm around his neck and helped guide him into the front seat of her CRV.

"Thank you. By God. Yes, please," Grampa said, as if she just pulled him from the wreckage of a fiery car. Then, he rolled down the window and stuck his hand out like a little kid. "Take us somewhere fun."

She turned around to the backseat. "What do you say, pretty girl?"

I blew her a kiss, and she blinked extra heavily. I swallowed a moan and settled in for the ride.

Grampa turned around and offered a mint to Shawna. "You're sweet enough, but I'm offering one to you anyway."

"Oh, aren't you a cutie?" She took one from him.

"You think I'm cute now, just wait until I'm a few years older and have a little more gray hair on this head." He chuckled, and we all joined in.

I sat up and messed with his hair. "Grampa, always flirting."

"I see where you get it from now," Nadia said.

Shawna snuck me a smile and nudged my side with her elbow. When Nadia took off, Shawna mouthed, "You're all red."

I pushed her elbow away and turned to admire the pine trees rushing by us.

A few minutes later, Nadia pulled into the parking lot of a pottery café. My heart flipped. I gazed through the window at the adorable pieces displayed in the front window. "I love pottery."

Nadia glanced at me from the rearview window. We shared an extended stare, and she ended with a wink. This girl had some hold over me.

We climbed out of the car and walked into the pottery café. The place buzzed with people. Everything looked sunny and bright, from the yellow walls to the red flowered border to the speckled floor tiles. A lady wearing a polka dotted apron approached with a smile. Nadia stepped up. "I reserved a table for four."

The lady took my grampa's arm in the crook of hers. "Right this way."

My grampa swaggered alongside of her with a gigantic smile on his face.

Shawna followed a few close steps behind. I grabbed Nadia's hand and eased up to her side. "You have just made my grampa the happiest man in the world."

She pointed her gaze down to my lips and back up to my eyes. "It's just pottery."

I squeezed her hand. "Just pottery, huh?"

Her lips curved upwards. "Just pottery."

A few minutes later, we were playing with the clay like a group of kids. My grampa rolled his around forming a baseball. "I don't know how I ever got it so smooth," he said, admiring it.

I nudged Nadia's knee. She nudged mine back. Then, we just left them nestled up against each other under the privacy of the table.

"So, you're already taken, dear?" he asked Nadia.

She shrugged. "Yes, sir."

"How long?"

"We've been together for several years."

"Is he handsome like me?"

She shot me a look.

I nodded. "It's okay. Tell him."

"She, sir. I married a woman."

He rolled his perfect baseball around on the table. “Well, I guess I’ve got no shot, then, huh?”

“None of us have a shot.” I stole the ball from him. “I know you’re more creative than a baseball. Make a pretty mug for me.” I handed it back to him.

He kneaded the clay. “So, if you’re married, why are you always without her?”

Nadia looked at me again.

“Go on. Tell him.”

“She’s in jail, sir.” She twisted her clay, pulling on it, ripping it apart. “She killed someone in a drunk driving accident.”

The four of us pressed, rolled, and ripped at our clay.

“Have you forgiven her?” Grampa asked.

Nadia sighed. “It’s kind of hard when she hasn’t even forgiven herself, sir.”

He fixated on the stretch of table in front of Nadia. “You have to forgive her if you ever want to get on with your life.”

“You speak like you’re coming from experience,” Nadia said.

He nodded. “We’ve got some ugly baggage in our family too.”

Nadia cupped her clay ridden hand on his wrist. “Ruby told me about your daughter and her accident on the stairs. That must have been difficult.”

He licked his thin lips and shook off a bad memory. “We all have our problems in life. We survive them.” He pulled apart his clay. “Are you angry with her still?”

She pinched her clay. “That’s putting it mildly.”

“You’ve got to find a way to get rid of that. You’re far too young and sweet to carry that kind of bitterness around with you for the rest of your life.”

"I agree," Shawna said. "You have to let it go."

"You say that like it's something I can just toss aside and forget about." Nadia stretched out her clay, pressing it to the table with the palm of her hand.

"We'll help you figure out a way," Shawna said. "That's what friends are for."

* *

Later that day, Nadia and I took my grampa back to his apartment after we dropped off Shawna at the hotel. He fell asleep watching a hockey game. I closely followed. I peeked over at Nadia and she, too, had closed her eyes. I watched her sleep. Her silhouette breezed up and down in gentle whispers. I could've watched her breathe, listened to her gently snore, and fantasized about her curvy lips and velvety tongue forever.

She woke up and caught me staring at her. She rolled over, all lazy and beautiful, and touched my lips with her finger. "Your grampa told me something interesting today when you were talking with the owner of the pottery café."

"Did he tell you how much I nag him for not taking his meds?"

She circled her finger around my mouth and then down my jawline, to my throat and then dropped it to my arm. "He told me how proud he was of you with how you handled your mother's death."

I gulped. Nadia circled her fingers back to my throat. Their pressure mounted with each tough swallow. She stared at me with such sweetness, such concern, such love that I welled up. My chin quivered, and she started wiping my tears away with the back of her hand in gentle, sweeping motions. No one had ever taken care of me in this way. No one had ever asked me about my feelings.

"The day she died, I was supposed to fill the washing machine with the clothes. Tuesdays were my day to clean the house, do laundry and cook supper. Catherine, my best friend at the time, invited me to her Girl Scouts meeting. I had been begging her forever to let me go. Finally, her mother approved when I volunteered to watch their cat while they vacationed the following month. I was supposed to be home, but instead I sat in a circle with a bunch of girl scouts listening to some boring woman talk about life. Had this happened any other Tuesday, I could've helped my mother. She wouldn't have died."

Nadia pulled me into her arms and rocked me.

"Just goes to show you," I said. "You can't be everything to everyone."

She didn't respond with words. Instead, she cradled me until I fell asleep.

* *

We woke at six o'clock that night.

"I'm starved," Nadia said. "How about I go to the store and get us something to cook for dinner?"

"I could go for meatloaf," Grampa said.

"Meatloaf it is, then." Nadia climbed to her feet and stretched, exposing her taut belly. "I'll see what I can do about finding us a dessert, too."

When Nadia left, I looked at my grampa's messy hair. "You need a haircut."

"No better time than the present." He climbed to his feet and walked to the bathroom. "I'll grab the haircutting bag and meet you in the kitchen."

A minute later, he sat on a chair, and I began cutting.

"She's got big problems. She's going to need some help getting over that."

I combed his hair and chopped into it. "I have my doubts that this woman is even good for her."

"Well, love will prompt you to do funny things."

I shook my head, stuck between lying and surviving his statement. "Love is a funny word."

"Complicated word," he corrected.

"Yeah. People sacrifice themselves over it."

He pinched a smile on his face. "When you love someone, it's not a sacrifice."

I walked around to his back and chopped away at his long hair. Gray strands fell to his shoulders, taking up company on them while I tried to even out the mess in the back of his head.

"Do you think she'll stay married?"

I shrugged. "She'll stick it out. She has hope that things will go back to the way they were before. She's not like me. I would've walked away the minute I got the phone call about the accident."

"I doubt that." He bowed his head.

I chopped through his wiry hair, attacking it. "I'm not my mother."

"Where's this anger coming from?" he asked.

I chopped more of his hair. He loved his daughter, and I bit my tongue every time he spoke about her as though she reigned the world with angel wings to mother me. "I'm not angry. I just don't want to spend my life in a loveless marriage, that's all."

"Well, dear," he started, turning just as I chopped. I nicked my finger. Blood squirted. I screamed. He screamed. I ran to kitchen sink and stuck it under the faucet. "Son of a bitch," I yelled. The sting buckled my knees.

Grampa climbed to his feet and wobbled over to me, dragging his hair all over the kitchen floor. "You have to squeeze it." He tore off a paper towel and wrapped it around my finger. "Squeeze like this." My finger throbbed under the pressure.

I turned away from the bloody mess. "I can't look."

He wrapped my finger tightly and walked with me over to his kitchen table. I sat, and he dragged a chair to my side and sat down. He held my finger up in the air and squeezed it. I looked at the picture of Mother Mary on the wall next to the cloth wall calendar from nineteen eighty-two. A picture of The Rafters sat just below the year.

"I miss that place," I said, trying to wrap my mind around something, anything but my ravaged finger.

"Ah, that place glowed with magic. It had a healing quality to it. Guests would say it all the time. They'd come in there with their broken lives, broken marriages, and broken hearts and leave healed, strong and ready to forgive."

Yet, it couldn't heal him. The fact that he just up and packed away his life because of someone else never sat right with me. That's what commitments did to a person. They robbed people of the pleasure of pursuing their dreams. Nothing good ever came out of a relationship.

The room silenced as we both stared at this picture. We never spoke about that day we drove away. We never spoke about how life just turned gray afterwards. He never brought it up, and neither did I. I looked over at him. He looked sad. "I wish you would've stayed there."

"I wanted to move on," he said. He squeezed my finger, applying more pressure than it needed.

"One of these days we should take a trip there."

"I don't think so," he said.

He peeled away the paper towel and examined my injury.

"You said it, though. It's a place of healing."

His mouth hung open, and he looked perplexed. I got woozy and turned back to the calendar.

"No one needs any healing here."

"We could go fishing in our old pond."

"We've got plenty of ponds right here in Rhode Island."

I looked him squarely in the eye, into the eye of a man who walked away from his dreams. "What are you afraid of?"

He examined my finger. "Me afraid?" He scoffed. "The past should just stay in the past."

I pulled my finger away. "All of us could use a good dose of that place."

"All of us?" he asked.

"Me, you, Shawna, and Nadia. We could all use a change of scenery."

"I need to bandage this finger." He rose from his chair with a grunt and left me without an answer.

He bandaged my finger in silence. He never quieted for this long. I had put a thought in his head, and I prayed he'd come through on it. I wanted him to face his past so he could mend his broken spirit once and for all. Fear didn't sit right on his heart. It stole away the very essence of his dynamic character. He needed to mend this. Shawna needed to mend her frightful heart. Nadia needed to mend her restless feelings towards Jessica.

"I'd be so happy if you agree to take this trip."

He eyed me, kissed my bandaged finger, and walked back to the kitchen.

When Nadia returned, Grampa charged into the living room. "Nadia, would you be interested in taking a trip with us?"

I beamed and shot to my feet. "And Shawna, too."

"And Shawna, too," he corrected.

"Where to?" Nadia asked.

“To The Rafters, to the place where Ruby grew up.”

Her face blossomed into a smile. “When do we leave?”

He looked to me, waiting on a response. I imagined driving down the interstate en route to my old home, Grampa smiling away, his teeth shining, and Shawna, Nadia, and I singing Billy Joel at the top of our lungs while we crunched on Doritos.

“Let’s cook that meatloaf dinner and leave first thing in the morning. I’ll call and make reservations,” I said.

“Hell, yeah,” Nadia said.

Grampa hugged her. “God I love a girl who can shout out a good curse word without blinking.”

She kissed his cheek.

“I’ll call Shawna.” I pulled out my cell phone. “This is just what she needs.”

* *

The next morning, I arrived at my grampa’s apartment to find Shawna and Nadia already there scrambling eggs and burning toast.

I sat down with Grampa on the couch and stared at a picture of myself as a little girl. I was sitting on his lap. We were crafting a kite together. We were laughing. His smile stretched far and wide, and I looked like I was caught up in the moment, present, right there living that precious moment of time when nothing else in the world mattered but that kite.

“Do you remember when I got stung by all of those bees the day we flew this kite?” I asked him.

He chuckled. “I felt so bad for you. Your little legs could barely keep up with your fear that day. I thought for sure you’d break something. I’ve never seen anyone sprint down a hill.”

Grampa remembered the finest of details from the past.

"We had so much fun back then." I leaned against him admiring the memories that sat before us.

He cradled my wrist. "This trip is going to be good for me."

"It'll be good for us all."

I turned the photo album page and landed on a picture of him and my grandma on their wedding day. She wore a simple, cream dress with eyelets across the chest. Her hair swirled in finger waves and her lips straightened into a line. "Was grandma a happy lady?"

"Oh yes." He nodded. "Very happy, indeed. Well, except for when I forgot to wipe mud from my shoes. She'd lay into me for doing that."

"Do you think we would've gotten along?"

"She was just like your mother. Sweet, accommodating, always trying to please. You would've had a blast together."

I turned the page and landed on their wedding dance. "You loved her, huh?"

"Of course." He rubbed his finger on the worn photo album page. "She was my world until she died."

"Did you know right away?"

"Naturally."

His sureness with this word threw me off. "You weren't afraid to love her? Afraid she might not love you back? Or worse, love you and leave you later?"

"It's worth it."

I turned to another page and landed on The Rafters. I was about eight years old and skipping down the field where dandelions grew tall and abundantly. How many times had I tossed myself down that hill for a giggling tumble?

Grampa turned the next page, and we stared at a picture of me swinging over the creek with a rope that he had tied for me. Without looking up, he asked softly, "You love Nadia, don't you?"

"Shh." I turned towards the kitchen, and Nadia stood at the stove, humming and flipping eggs. "I'm never going to fall in love. It's not my style."

We both continued to gaze at the picture of free-spirited me. "I messed you up, didn't I?" he asked.

I snapped away from the picture. "Why would you say such a thing?"

"Look at you." He tossed his hand out in front of him, to the picture of me so happy. "You're afraid to love anyone." He exhaled and leaned back, turning from the photo album now and looking down at his frail hands. He wrestled his two fingers together, twitching his mouth side to side.

"You didn't do that to me, Grampa. My mother did."

"Don't say that, dear."

"She was weak. I don't know how you didn't see that." I stood up and walked away from my Grampa. "I need some air." I walked out of his apartment and to the waterfront across the street.

Moments later, Nadia found me pounding the sand with a stick. "He thinks she was such a perfect mother. I want to tell him the truth. I want to tell him how I had to endure listening to her fights, witness her bruises, and whisper whenever I spoke so my stepfather wouldn't get angry and take it out on my mother for having such a noisy daughter. Who am I to ruin his perception of her?"

Nadia wrapped her arm around me. I pulled away and stared at the waterfront. I watched a riverboat pass. A little girl on the boat waved at us. I dropped my sadness and waved back, honoring her youth and innocence. I closed my eyes and enjoyed the cool breeze wash over my face. I breathed in and held it there for a few long seconds before disengaging. "I never want to disappoint that man. It's just so hard to listen to him always say such great things about her. But, what good would it do now if I told him how ugly things turned?"

"No good at all."

I looked up at Nadia and found comfort in her smile. "We should get back before he gets worried."

I turned, and she followed.

* *

My grampa huddled over the photo album.

"I'm sorry," I said. "I don't know why I said all that."

A wave of relief crossed across his pale, grayish face. A fresh golden tone surfaced and brought him back to life. "Let's eat and get this road trip started already. What do you say?"

"Let's do it." I helped him up from the couch.

"You girls are going to love it there," he said. "You're going to just love it."

"I can't wait to stand on top of that hill again and sit by the creek with fishing rods," I said.

His smile brightened the space around us all. "Sounds like a slice of heaven is awaiting us."

Chapter Thirteen
Ruby

We knocked on the front door, and a familiar woman in her late seventies answered with a smile. “Welcome.”

“Do you remember this handsome guy?” I tilted my head in Grampa’s direction. He stood close by my side, beaming.

Recognition splayed on her face. “Mr. Clark!” She stretched out her arms to him. He folded into them like he’d been waiting to do this since the day he signed over the papers to her family.

“You still look beautiful as ever,” he said to her.

She pulled away and blushed. “You’re still a flirt.”

“Always,” he said, not even turning red.

She turned to me. “And you’re the young lady?”

“Yes, ma’am. That would be me.” I relaxed into a giggle.

She turned to Nadia and Shawna. “And who might these two lovelies be?”

Shawna blushed red.

“Great friends,” I answered. “They needed to see this place for themselves to understand how magical it is.”

“Well, come on in.” She waved us into the foyer. Nostalgia danced in my heart and swirled in my head. “I’ve got your rooms ready to go upstairs.”

I balanced a hand on the post of the staircase that led up to my old bedroom and the other eight guestrooms. Its slippery and smooth texture hadn’t changed in over a decade. The same carpet runner blanketed the steps, and I spotted the stain I had created back on Christmas day when I dropped a Dixie cup of pink oil paint. The foyer even smelled like home, like freshly baked bread and coffee.

"Wow, this is weird." I peeked around the planked floor and recognized the four divots I used to use as jumping points when I played hopscotch. "I feel like I just walked out the front door to get my grampa's *Providence Journal* and walked back in again."

The lady crossed her arms over her chest and nodded. "Yeah, I adored everything about this place. I've changed very little. Last summer I had to put a new heating system in, and the year before that we updated the carpeting in the bedrooms upstairs. For the most part, everything is still as charming as you all left it."

The air flowed, as fresh as ever.

Suddenly I heard a door close from up above, and a moment later a man and woman walked down the stairs holding hands and wearing easy smiles. The man tipped his head in my direction. "Hi there."

I smiled back. I morphed back into a young girl again with no troubles, no fears, just happiness floating around her greeting guests.

"Are you ready for some lunch?" The lady asked them.

"Of course. We're starved," the man said, sneaking past me with his hand draped across his lady's petite back.

"Why don't you join us for lunch?" she asked us. "Then, you can have a look around."

My mouth watered at the memory of a table filled with pretty casserole dishes overflowing with bacon, creamed sauces, loaf bread, pastries, and juices. "We'd love to."

"Do you still have that old, double-barrel woodstove in the basement?" Grampa asked.

"Oh yes. In fact, my beagle, Molly, loves it so much that she spends her nights down underneath it. Sometimes, she comes upstairs glowing." She giggled. "Would you like to see it while I'm cooking lunch?"

"You bet," he said, lighting up like a kid seeing his first airplane in the sky again.

"I have a better idea," I said. "Why don't we help start the lunch, and you two can go check out the stove?"

The lady looked from me to Grampa and shrugged. "That's a wonderful idea."

We whipped up bowtie pasta, marinara sauce, garlic bread, and salad while listening to James Taylor tunes on the old record player still working in the kitchen pantry. The kitchen smelled like a slice of heaven. This kitchen had always been the perfect one to cook in. The pans all hung from the ceiling right above a freestanding island. The lady had the best knives. They could cut through tin cans, I would guess.

The lady kept popping her head into the kitchen to see how she could help, and I kept brushing her away, waving my spatula in the air at her, and telling her to go keep my grampa engaged and happy.

The two of them laughed and chatted with each other in the living room in front of a roaring fire. A few other guests joined them, and they recommended great trails for hiking and great lakes for fishing. Then, my grampa told his famous story about the time he and I were on a hike and came across a cow giving birth. All that blood, the sac, and the mother licking the gooey slime were the grossest things I'd ever seen. Then, I saw that little calf stand up not more than five minutes later and wobble. It looked at its mother and walked to go stand by her side. My grampa hugged me, and I cried. I'd never witnessed anything as beautiful as that.

His voice rose higher. "I told her, sweetheart, you just witnessed a miracle." The guests oohed and ahhed, and this just kept Grampa going, telling more tales about fishing with sticks when no poles were around, about the time we got lost for nearly three hours in the back woods, and about the time a bear stood not more than fifteen feet in front of us and watched as we inched away. At one point, his voice animated so out of normality that I peeked in on him. I didn't need him passing out on us.

He sat on a chair waving his arms around telling the guests a story about the time we had a blizzard. It snowed for three days straight, and he had to shovel us out through a window.

My grampa went from a frail eighty-five year old man to a young, vigorous, jubilant man about twenty years younger. His face glowed, his eyes sparkled, his posture straightened. These people loved him. They smiled, nodded, and expressed pure joy from his excitement. I was fifteen years younger looking in on my grampa again, marveling at how he could stir a crowd.

I returned to the salad I had chopped and poured dressing over it. I wondered what kind of person he would be today if he hadn't sold out on himself.

A few minutes later, we called everyone to the dining table and enjoyed their compliments on the delicious-smelling lunch. We dug in and ate together, laughing and passing each other golden brown garlic bread and dressings and pasta dripping in tomato sauce. Being around people who were rested, peaceful, and excited to spend their day enjoying nature just did something to me that no neck rubbing, no beautiful ocean view, no wind-in-the-hair ride in my Camaro had ever been able to do. I belonged at this table. It grounded me in something beautiful. When I looked over at my grampa and saw him flirting with the pretty old lady with silver hair and laugh lines earned by a full life of smiling, my heart leapt. I was home. The peace and joy of my younger years returned like I had just gone out for a mail check and walked right back in. I tasted the pasta and its tangy flavor. I savored the garlic. I devoured the crisp salad and waited in fruitful anticipation for the tomatoes to squirt their flavor in me and fill me with that delicious homey warmth.

The room filled with laughter and chatter and buzzed with life. These were the good old days. I had forgotten all about this luxury of sitting in one spot for hours enjoying the stories of people from Great Britain and Germany and Colombia. I drank five cups of iced tea in that sitting, and even though I had to pee like no one's business, I stayed put in that seat because I didn't want to miss a syllable.

And then suddenly, the room quieted after the German couple finished telling their story about how they lived an entire year traveling in Japan, staying in bedrooms no bigger than broom closets.

The little old lady flirting with my grampa broke the stillness. "Why did you ever sell this place?"

My grampa dropped his smile and fiddled with his napkin a few too many times. I jumped to his rescue. "He wanted someone else to have some fun."

He looked to me. "That's right, sweetheart. I chose best." He turned back to the lady. "You've done a great job keeping up this place."

"It's a lot. My son-in-law and daughter help me out. And my granddaughter, Eloise, is a God-send."

"Yeah," my grampa said shaking his head side to side. "I get it. It's a lot of work. That's the reason I sold it. Isn't that right, dear?" He asked me.

I reassured him with a hand to his wrist. "Absolutely."

We broke into more idle chatter about farmlands in Colombia and how beautiful the mountains were during their summer seasons and how gigantic the insects grew in all of that open, undeveloped land.

Later that afternoon, Eloise arrived. She was a petite girl who looked about twelve, though we were told was twenty-three. She needed help getting some groceries out of the car. Shawna jumped to her rescue.

When they returned, Shawna popped into the living room. "I'm going to help Eloise with dinner. What do you say you girls go and get us some wine to go with it?"

It didn't take us long to agree to this marvelous idea. "On our way, I want to show you the apple orchard down the road. It's breathtaking." I handed Nadia her coat.

* *

Nadia and I enjoyed the fall afternoon strolling the open paths of the local apple orchard. We walked down a wide path, brushing hands every few feet each holding a basket for the apples. The trees reminded me of cranky old people when they first climbed out of bed in the morning, before they straightened their spines. The branches, knotty and crooked, stood against the backdrop of the perfect blue October sky. Big, red, shiny apples hung on the branches bringing beauty to the worn and battered-looking trees.

Nadia ran ahead of me to a tree. She dropped her basket and started to climb it, bracing her left foot in the crook of a branch and the tree trunk. She lifted herself up and onto the first branch.

A few people dotted the horizon, and a few more scampered around the main building paying us no mind. "I love it. A crazy girl just like me," I yelled up to her. "You'll probably get us kicked out before we can pick one of them."

She climbed up another branch and balanced her feet against two branches that didn't look strong enough to support her. "Stand right below me, and I'll toss some to you." She reached up, and her t-shirt scrunched up with her arms, exposing her tight tummy and her belly button. She picked an apple and tossed it to me. It landed by my foot.

"You're supposed to catch it," she said, narrowing her eyes at me.

"Try again," I said, readying myself for her pitch. She lobbed it down to me, and I hinged my eye on that apple not letting it bypass me this time. I caught it and leapt in the air.

"Good girl." Nadia winked at me, and we stared at each other, blocking out the rest of the orchard. She tossed apple after apple, and I caught them like a Gold Glove ballplayer each time.

Once my basket was filled, she climbed down and landed in my arms. Her hair hung wildly and blew around her face.

I couldn't help myself. I kissed her.

Our lips and tongues danced together under the apple tree, catapulting me to levels that opened up the gates to freedom, love, and beauty. "I shouldn't be kissing you, huh?"

Nadia placed her finger up to my lips. "Words get in the way."

I looked up at the tree. "She's a beauty, isn't she?"

"She sure is sweet."

"Let's call her Sweet Tree."

"Sweet Tree." Nadia eased into a smile. "What do you say we leave our baskets under Sweet Tree and just walk?" She reached for my hand. "Come on."

We strolled the orchard fields staring up at the blue sky and being present in the moment. Her hand softened in mine, warming my core, filling me with love and gratitude.

We circled the orchard three times, and I eventually led her back over to our Sweet Tree. We sat with our legs touching, our hands still entwined. "Something about fresh air brings back great childhood memories," I said.

"Tell me about your childhood." She scooted closer. "Tell me what excited little Ruby did when she was a young girl."

I stared off to the horizon. Nadia's eyes followed me. She feathered my hand. No one had ever asked me about my childhood. Up until that moment, I was happy about this. Now, I just wanted to tell her everything. She helped ease me into this state of safety that I didn't fear. It was the most beautiful feeling.

A smile sprung on my face. "I loved the fall. We'd get guests traveling in from all over the world to see the foliage. Each morning, the guests would gather out on the patio and huddle around the fire pit to drink their morning coffee and talk about how rested they felt and how comfortable the mattresses were. I loved this small talk. I loved seeing strangers come together to share stories and laughter. I would sit and sip my hot cocoa with marshmallows and giggle to myself over how some just looked so shackled to their rigid lives, and in a matter of moments, as the north wind blew in across the fields, their whole personas shifted. They became softer, flexible, and unrestricted from the heavy weight that they carried in just a day before. My grampa would call this first coffee morning the 'shedding period.' The next morning he named the 'bonding period.' That's when the same people came and picked up the same mug they used the day before and sat in the same spot they sat in the day before. They bonded by breaking the routine of the previous day by delving into questions. Before long, two hours passed, two or three cups of coffee were drunk, and these people were showing off photos of their kids, grandkids, dogs, neighbors, you name it."

Nadia kissed my neck and lingered a moment. "You smell so pretty."

"What are you doing?" I leaned into her.

Nadia pulled away and lay back on the grass, stretching her arms overhead, exposing her belly again. "Tell me the reason why you left this place."

I lay down too and extended my hands overhead so one would lie close to hers. I swaddled my hair to my neck, to the same spot she had just been kissing, and curled up my lashes to her. "Let's just enjoy this moment. We'll talk about that some other time."

"You're just going to leave me hanging?" She tapped her finger to my nose.

"Yup." I propped up on my knees and plucked an apple up from the basket and handed it to her. She bit into it and offered me a bite. We crunched into the juicy Macintosh until we bore down to its core. "I want more."

I reached in and plucked up another. We took turns feeding each other the apple, enjoying the warm sun and the romance of leaves blowing around. The leaves were just starting to peak with their shades of burnt orange and red. The air smelled like an old fashioned penny candy store, earthy and delicious. I fed her another bite. She crunched down hard. Juices squirted every which way. I started to wipe them away with the tip of my finger when her cell rang.

Nadia ignored it. "It's probably Jessica."

"Get it. I'll give you some privacy."

"She's not ruining this moment."

It stopped ringing.

We continued chomping and then it rang again. "I know you want to answer it. So go ahead."

She glanced at her cell. "It's not Jessica. Not sure who it is." She answered with a sigh. "Nadia Chase."

"Nadia. This is Robby," he said.

I could hear him, clear as day.

"Robby?" Nadia asked.

"I know. This is awkward."

"Yeah. A little."

"Listen, I'm calling about Jessica. She fell and twisted her ankle. She's at the hospital getting x-rays."

Nadia's face turned white. "How do you know?"

"They tried to call you, but you didn't pick up so they called me."

"Why would they call you?"

"I'm the next one listed as her emergency contact."

Nadia arched her face in pain. This tore at me too. My tongue swelled, and a series of prickles surfaced on my skin.

She paced in wide circles. "Have you been visiting her this whole time?"

"Yes. Of course I thought she might've told you by now."

I cringed for Nadia. I bowed my head pretending I couldn't hear a thing.

Nadia stood with her hand on her hip. "Is she okay?"

"She'll be fine. I'll have her call you when she knows for sure it's just a twisted ankle."

She hung up and held the cell to her chin. She turned to me. "She's totally having an affair on me with her ex."

"Well how do you know for sure?"

"Jessica never once mentioned that he visited or that he is her emergency contact after me. Who puts an ex as an emergency contact? And, I didn't even know she still spoke with him. What a fool I am. This whole time I stayed true to her. Meanwhile her ex-boyfriend steps in like a freaking superhero for her. Her ex is the one who calls me to tell me my wife is hurt?"

I walked over to her. "Do you want to head back to Connecticut tonight?"

She tossed her half-eaten apple into the nearby woods. "She just twisted her ankle. Robby can ice it for her."

We walked back to the checkout station carrying our baskets of apples. I should've consoled her by advising her not to jump to conclusions. Instead I joined the silence, seemingly consenting to the sentiment that her wife turned into a no-good cheater and she could do so much better without her.

"Don't mention this to anyone. I just want to enjoy the peace of this paradise before I have to deal with my future."

"Your secret is safe with me."

* *

We returned to The Rafters with several large bottles of wine. Shawna took them from me and raised her eyebrow in question. I rolled my eyes. "I was a perfect lady."

"Me too," Nadia said, winking and tilting her head over towards Eloise who stood before the big wash basin sink and scrubbed dishes.

"She's shy," Shawna said, "However, I'm getting her to open up a little."

"Oh really?" Nadia nudged her.

Shawna flushed red and headed over to her.

Grampa then walked into the room. "Let's take a walk you and I," he said.

Nadia brushed us off. "Go ahead. I'll be fine. I'll do some reading."

So, Grampa and I went for a walk to the top of our favorite hill. We sat together and picked at the dandelions.

"Can I ask you something?" he asked.

"Whatever you'd like, Grampa."

"Something's been bugging me since before we left on the trip. Something you said about your mother."

I don't want to talk about my mother right now." I would not ruin this trip by talking about her.

"You're angry with her, and I want to understand why."

I shifted and tore at a patch of weeds. I pulled out the roots and flung them down the hill. "There's no reason to bring that up."

"I'm bringing it up because I've never seen you so wound-up about her before. What happened?"

"Grampa, you loved her. I don't want to tarnish that with my opinion of her."

"You never talk to me about her. Never. Not even when you were little. Why? Why are you so hesitant to talk about her to me? Maybe I need to talk about her sometimes."

I stared into his eyes and saw hurt and sadness. "Your opinion and mine are far different. You think of her as sunshine and happiness." I hesitated. I figured I owed Grampa this conversation at some point. "I see rain and clouds. She feared her husband and allowed him to rule our world. She walked around with that spatula of hers singing folk songs, and then in the next breath, I'd catch her crying in the corner of the pantry. I could never understand why she didn't just pack our bags and leave. She was so weak. So pathetically weak. This pissed me off. Then I came to you, and you always spoke so highly of her. How could I ruin that impression now that she's dead?"

"Your mother was a wonderful person who ended up loving the wrong person." His voice shook.

"My mother lived as a desperate, scared, weak fool." I couldn't help snapping. "You always painted this picture of her as a martyr. I never wanted to ruin that for you, but maybe it's time I do. Maybe it's time you learn the truth that she kept us imprisoned in that house with a man who abused her. She allowed this like we deserved nothing better. She clung to this stupid love, and for what?"

"Do you think I never knew that?"

"Did you?" How could he just sit idle?

"Ruby, dear, you've got it wrong about your mother. She didn't cling like a desperate fool. She didn't settle. She fought. She planned. She strategized."

The air short-circuited between us. "How can you say that?"

"Your mother was just waiting for the right moment to safely exit. She planned your escape to The Rafters. She told me you were all excited about coming."

"She never told me we were going."

"She told me, 'Ruby can't wait to get there.'" The pockets under his eyes drooped.

"Well, she lied."

Grampa searched the horizon as if answers would come calling to him from the trees. "She must have been protecting you. Maybe she feared that you'd slip to your stepfather." Tears rolled down his cheeks.

My whole reality distorted. "She planned to take us here?"

"Yes. She just needed some time to figure it all out. She even mailed me your polka dotted bedspread and matching curtains and asked me to set it all up before you arrived."

A jolt surged through me with the image of my bare bed and windows. She had told me she was getting them cleaned.

I took it all in and let it marinate with all of the other memories I stored of her. We sat in silence, plucking blades of grass.

"I hated her. I thought she had settled and dragged me along with her."

"Your mother loved you. She was waiting on the right time to make her mark on life. You know, he threatened to kill her if she ever arrived home with divorce papers."

"Kill her?"

"Yes. Kill her."

This new information poked at my heart and sent me clamoring to understand more. "Did he push her down the stairs?"

"No, dear."

The man tortured her. "She must've been so scared."

He placed his hand on my arm. "She feared the situation. She wanted to plan everything carefully, to keep you both safe. She could've just ran away with you to The Rafters, but her mind clouded with fears about child abduction laws and truancy and her financial responsibilities. Things that didn't matter. But, when life is holding a knife to your throat, you can't think as straight. So, she freaked out a bit. I told her to just come, and we'd handle everything from here. She wasn't weak, dear. She was scared. Not weak. None of us knows how we would react under that pressure. The day he threatened her life about the divorce papers, though, her mind cleared. That very day she called me and told me you both would be arriving on the first day of spring."

"If only she had planned our escape for winter break instead."

"Life is full of what-ifs, dear." He squeezed my wrist, and tears dripped from his puffy eyes.

Chapter Fourteen
Nadia

When Ruby returned from outside with her grampa, she tapped my shoulder. "We should freshen up before dinner."

"Sounds like a great idea."

Ruby took my hand and led the way. We passed Grampa, who was already in the living room telling stories to a few guests. Their laughter bounced off of the walls and filled the house with the kind of joy big families produced at holidays.

We climbed the stairs to the third story landing. Our rooms sat opposite each other connected at the back by a shared bathroom. She directed me to the green bedroom. "This used to be my old room. It can be yours."

A soft light filtered in from the open shade, illuminating a path to a queen-sized bed. A chaise lounge holding a bathrobe and fluffy slippers sat under the window, which overlooked a beautiful, rolling, green field.

Ruby strolled up behind and wrapped her arms around me. "Are you going to be okay?"

I reached up for her hand. "I actually feel freer than ever."

She kissed my shoulder. "I love hearing that."

Ruby's breath tickled my skin. Mind-altering quivers shot through me.

"Make yourself at home," she said. "I'm going to jump in the shower."

She disappeared leaving me breathless.

I sat on the recliner's arm and scanned her old bedroom. Sage sticks, landscape books, essential oil bottles, and photos of The Rafters sat on the table beside me.

The shower started.

I sat back and took in the moment, picturing the hot, steamy water pouring down over her naked body.

"Nadia?" She called out from the steam.

I stared at the half-opened door. "Yes?"

"Would you mind grabbing a towel out of the closet in the hallway for me? They should hopefully still be in there."

I studied the moment. We were alone with an entire floor sandwiched between us and the rest of them.

"Did you hear me?"

"I heard you." I walked to the hallway closet and stared at a sea of fluffy towels. I chose the top one with tiny roses. I walked back in the bedroom and locked the door.

I tiptoed into the bathroom and planned to place it on the sink and walk out, then call out to her to tell her I had delivered it. As I entered the steam and saw Ruby's naked silhouette behind the clear shower curtain, my knees buckled, and my mind lost all sense of reason. Her long hair clung to her back, and she stood under the stream of water with her arms raised and her hands massaging her scalp. Her waist, taut and firm curved like a flower petal. I just stood there and stared, mesmerized by her beauty and elegance and complete innocence to the power she possessed.

Ruby opened the curtain and hid behind it. Speckles of water danced on her smooth cheeks. Her eyes glowed, and suds dripped from her golden hair. "You know, hot water does wonders for warming up the muscles prior to a massage."

I jumped at the opportunity. "I could use a massage."

Her eyes twinkled. We stood staring at each other with that line of reason between us. I wanted her. I needed her. This moment belonged to us. We deserved this moment.

My shirt and pants flew off before I could blink. I couldn't pass this up. I'd deal with the consequences after. I wanted to dig into this moment and live it in its full glory, in its beauty, in its truth of being perfect and necessary and point on with what the universe pushed to have happen.

I slid in under the water next to her.

Ruby squirted some strawberry twist bath gel on a loofa. "Turn around."

She rubbed the loofa around my back in tiny slow circles, steady over my shoulder blades. She cradled my naked hip with her other hand, pulling me closer to her. Soon we rocked our hips in the same sweet, sultry melody as she circled that loofa around my skin. Ruby dared on and traveled the outskirts of my back and over to my front. She cradled me even closer now, resting her chin on the crook of my neck, bathing my skin with her long wet hair. She circled around my tummy. I balanced against the shower wall, bracing against the breezes of ecstasy as she dared even lower and aptly tossed the loofa to the tub. She continued pampering me with her soft touch, her circular motions, and her soft kisses on my neck.

"Are you sure you're okay with this?" I whispered.

Ruby placed her lips on my ear. "Shh. Just enjoy the moment. Imagine yourself floating. We're flying high together, soaring above everything in this world. Just you and me, darling."

Ruby massaged me with increased pressure. I leaned harder against the wall, gaining footing under the whirlwind of this ride. My legs quivered against her hands. Water ran down my face. My heart lifted. My head swirled. Then, I floated. I floated on her tailwind, allowing her to guide me in her gentle wake as she steadied her massage and held me tightly, releasing me from the burdens of this world and taking me to a place where the steamy air encased us in a perpetual state of bliss and caressed us in a beauty so natural, so raw, so enlivening, even my eyelids tingled.

I wanted to please her too. I turned around and kissed her hard under the water. Ruby responded with a deep moan. I wrapped my arms around her waist and pulled her in close so our navels danced together under the spray of hot water.

I then soaped up the loofa and turned Ruby around this time. I massaged the loofa around her gentle skin and her beautiful tattoo of roots blooming into a tree of life on the back of her neck. I leaned in and kissed the branches and leaves spread across her skin, tickling it with my tongue, and enjoying her twitches as I licked her body. I turned her around and traveled down to her chest. When I landed at her breasts, I stayed for a while, flicking her nipples with the tip of my tongue and watching as she bucked and rolled under my tongue's caress. Ruby ran her fingers through her hair like a supermodel, stretching her torso. I cupped her breast in my hands and savored their softness, purity, fluidity. I knelt down against the tub's floor and went down on her. I pushed past the water and journeyed to the recesses of her soul, tasting her sweetness, reveling on her swollen wetness. She grabbed my hair and raked her hands through it as I fed a hunger too powerful to ignore. Her legs trembled, and before long she groaned and called out my name telling me to never stop. To never stop making her feel so fucking good.

* *

We took a nap under the fluffy comforter in her old bedroom. Our naked bodies entwined and became one, as we drifted off into a restful sleep. I dreamt of purple and yellow flowers dancing along a rolling green hill. We tumbled down the hill, giggling and kicking our feet out in front of us, stopping only at the bottom of the hill. I looked up and admired how fluffy the clouds hung against the brightest blue sky I'd ever seen. The air smelled like fresh cucumbers and watermelon. The fresh day, sprinkled in sunshine and bliss, bathed us in the kind of joy one could only find when clearheaded and supremely fulfilled.

When I drifted back to reality and stared at Ruby's pretty profile breathing ever so lightly, my heart leapt. I deserved this moment. We deserved this moment.

* *

Right before dinner, Robby called again to tell me he had dropped off Jessica at our home. "She's going to be just fine," he said.

"Well, I'm sure that thrills you."

"It's not like that," he said.

"Thanks for the update." I hung up without a trickle of remorse for what I'd just done with my sweet Ruby.

She and I shared a glance and then walked into the dining room to join the others. We ate dinner taking in the laughter and the new friendships brewing, all the while holding hands under the table.

Her grampa had us all in tears with his stories. The man was a natural storyteller and transformed from a feeble old man to a man of purpose. The more we laughed, the younger he looked.

By nine o'clock, his eyes were fluttering. "Time to get some shut eye," he said. He hugged us all. As soon as he left, all of the other guests decided to retire to their rooms, too.

"I'm pretty tired, too." I stood up and stretched.

Ruby followed suit. Shawna and Eloise remained seated on the couch. "Not interested in a game of Cribbage?" Shawna asked us.

"God no." Ruby yawned.

"I'll play," Eloise said.

Shawna lit up like a firecracker.

We left them alone and climbed to our third floor oasis.

We went to bed that night back in Ruby's old room, snuggled under that same soothing comforter with pretty flowers and lace. We listened to a cat purr on the rocking chair and admired the way the moon danced on the window.

* *

The next morning I woke to find Ruby lying supine on her bed. Her beautiful breasts were resting on the edge of a comforter softer than feathers and her long, curvy body was stretched and ready for pleasure. Caught up in the moment, comfortable under her own caress, she reached down to between her legs and gently massaged herself, climbing steadily to heated passion as I stared into her eyes.

"Roll over," Ruby commanded.

I rolled over and bore my back to her. She straddled me, and her wetness turned hot against the curve in my lower back. I stretched my arms above my head, and played with my hair as Ruby eased my shoulders with a light, soothing touch. I moaned under her caress, as she raised its intensity with each firm knead. Her skin, warm and tender, soothed me.

Ruby leaned in closer to increase the intensity of her touch. I moaned louder and swayed my hips, enjoying the feel of her wetness against my lower back. She kissed my neck, traveling to my ear and whispered, "This is so unprofessional of me right now."

"Who cares? Who wants professional? Did I say I wanted professional?"

"What do you want, darling?"

I moaned again, this time rolling over to face her. Ruby twirled my hair as I said in the sexiest manner I've ever talked to a woman before, "You. I want you."

Ruby cupped her hands around my face and placed her lips on mine, fervently kissing me. An intense heat pulsed between us, setting us on fire.

We rolled over so I now straddled Ruby and gazed into her eyes. She wrapped her legs around my waist and slipped her hands onto my ass, gripping it, pushing herself closer to me, gasping as she kissed me even harder.

Ruby rocked below me, and I responded by grazing her neck with my tongue, traveling from one freckle to another as I headed to her nipple. I opened up my lips and took it into my mouth, enjoying as it grew larger against my tongue. She clawed at my ass, squeezing it, leaving her mark. The more she clawed, the harder I sucked. Our movements turned symbiotic. I fed on her lust, her boldness, and her desires like a starved animal. She stroked me with the artistic touch of an artist, knowing when to feather, when to increase the pressure of her touch, when to stop and take in all she had created, a spent and relaxed woman with cheeks surely reddened and eyes hazed over in lust.

Ruby commanded the scene, taking me on a thrill ride that most anyone would envy. Her eyes only left mine to seek me out. This tingled my skin and sent my heart fluttering.

"I can't get enough of you," Ruby whispered.

I placed my finger over her lips. "Shh." Then, I slid off of her and pulled her up to her knees. I circled around to her backside and massaged her shoulders. I leaned in and blew hot breath on her neck. "I've wanted to massage you naked like this ever since that first night you massaged me." I guided her muscles to relax under my firm touch.

"I haven't had a massage since massage school." Ruby bowed her head and let me unwind her some more. I reached over to the bedside, poured massage oil into the palms of my hands and rubbed them together. Then, I slid my hands up and down her shoulders, to her arms and back up again. I guided her to lie back down and rest her head on the fluffy pillow. I continued to massage. She melted below me. I traveled down her back, reached around to her tummy, and traced her navel, breathing against her neck with soft, yet commanding, breaths.

"You're good at this," she said, rolling over to kiss me.

I moaned, kissed her back, and spread my hands up and over her breasts, cupping them in my hands, playing with her nipples. Hot moisture pooled between my legs. Ruby watched my fingers as I tugged on each nipple, massaging them into a state of complete and utter nirvana. I kept one hand on her left breast and reached down to her wetness with my free hand. I placed my fingers inside of her, and she screamed out in pleasure. I nibbled on her ear, and in less than ten seconds she melted in my hands. Wet, quivering, and high on an orgasm, she twisted below me. I cradled my body on top of hers and rocked her until our breathing paced down to quiet whispers.

* *

We spent the morning curled up in her bed under layers of blankets like two hibernating felines wanting no contact to the outside world. At moments, I'd wake up and watch Ruby breathe in and out in perfect harmonious rhythm. Her nose was petite and straight. Her eyelashes were long and curled. Her lips arched at just the right point, and reminded me of a clementine with their smooth and dewy texture. And her hair. God I loved her hair. I could spend my life wrapping strands around my finger, staring into her baby blue eyes and enjoying the view.

Why couldn't this be my life? I could so easily slip into this one as if my old one never existed. I could learn to fly around with her and enjoy new perspectives where life colored itself in rainbow hues instead of orange jumpsuits and gray prison walls, where my days wouldn't be spent hiding from the awkward silence that now sat between me and Jessica.

I sobered to her name. How would my life with Jessica pan out now? I married Jessica the Burlesque dancer, the fun one, the free one. That Jessica died along with the lady she killed. A cheater replaced her. What would I do with this new version of her?

I stared at Ruby's tattoo, envious of it, and scared that I wouldn't get to see it for much longer. It saddled her neck and hugged her. No matter what, that tattoo would always be able to call Ruby home. That pristine tattoo was hers.

I sat up and slid my finger down the vine of her tattoo. She didn't flinch. She bowed her head and allowed me to touch her. "I'm so sorry I've dragged you into this mess of mine."

"You're sorry this happened?"

"Are you?"

Ruby inhaled deeply and held onto the breath. It swirled in her, filling her lungs with life, traveling around her chest to her vital organs. Then, she exhaled and released the pressure, filtering out the stale with the revived.

I propped up on my knees and massaged Ruby's shoulders. She didn't move still. She didn't utter a word. She just bowed her head lower and continued drawing deep breaths and exhaling ever deeper ones, as if purging her system of everything messy and heavy that I dragged into her life.

I kneaded her soft skin falling prey to its beauty, its sun-kissed glow, its divinity. I massaged my apology for turning her into a mistress, focusing my thoughts on helping to cleanse her from me so she could go on innocently, untarnished by my sins.

She moaned, and I caressed her arms, sliding my hands up and down, attempting to soothe any coming angst. "Please say something."

Ruby rose, and my hands fell to my side. I remained propped up on my knees as if withstanding the pain of purgatory. She walked to the bathroom and stopped before entering. She pulled in her lower lip, squeezed her eyes closed, and then looked up at me. Her eyes housed compassion, not anger. Her dimples formed in the small smile that highlighted her forgiving face.

"What we have here together is perfect. Don't you think?" She blinked heavily, showing off her long lashes. "I wouldn't want to change a thing." She disappeared into the bathroom and started the shower.

God, how I loved everything about this girl.

* *

Ruby walked out of the steamy bathroom with a red face. She wore her hair in a fluffy white towel and waltzed towards me naked, her breasts perky, her nipples standing at attention. She stopped in front of me, offered me her hand. I accepted. She walked me to the bathroom, wiped steam off of the mirror, and then placed an arm around my shoulder. We faced each other in the mirror.

"Happy is the only way I know how to live," she said. "I don't allow in guilt, remorse, fear or anything that misaligns my sense of place in this world. I love being happy. I never want to give that up. I certainly don't want to get in the way of your marriage. So, we have a choice. We can view this as the perfect arrangement or not." She shrugged, arched her eye, and walked away.

I caught up to her and kissed her hard. I pushed us towards the bed and pressed against her, bearing all my weight and bearing no stops to my passion, to my desire for her, to this new intoxicating freedom to express myself without regret.

* *

The next morning, I drove us back to Rhode Island. Shawna sat shotgun and Grampa and Ruby sat in the backseat. When we crossed over to the Rhode Island border Grampa said to Ruby, "I'm glad we came."

"Me, too." She smiled and looked over at him.

A trace of serenity blanketed him.

"How are you feeling?" she asked him.

He stretched his gaze out over the trees edging the interstate. "I feel healed."

"Healed?" she asked.

He rolled his eyes down to his lap, scrunched up his mouth. "I didn't want to come. I vowed I would never return here. The place holds so many memories. First your grandma, and then Grace. I thought by leaving it all behind, I could find happiness elsewhere, beyond the wooden walls and the rolling fields. Then life just got dull. I feared going back and being stabbed with that fresh pain of them both leaving me again. Comfort swaddled me when I entered that warm foyer and ate that scrumptious breakfast and smelled the roaring fire. All of these years I ran away from the one source that could heal me, blaming it for my troubles."

He reflected on the trees again.

"That was beautiful," Ruby said. "I didn't think it was possible, but I admire you even more now."

"I missed out on a lot in life, because I refused to let go of these hurtful memories of losing Grace," Grampa said.

"You've lived such a rich life."

"I have. Though, I stopped just short of fantastic."

“How so?” she asked.

“I couldn’t bear to sit in that living room, to cook in that kitchen, to greet one more guest without her there by my side. It hurt to smile. It killed me to mow the grass that at one time we used to sit upon and stare out with love and dreams as we looked beyond the maple trees and to the deep blue sky behind them. I couldn’t stand to sleep alone in that big empty bedroom anymore or sit and read a book. She permeated everything. So, I ran. Of course, that just caused the bruises in my soul to deepen and worsen. Over time, it just scarred over, and every once in a while it still itches, hurts, and aches. It’s a constant reminder of what I’d sold out on and hadn’t ever regained back. Girls take it from me. Don’t do this to yourself. Don’t be afraid to live your lives.”

I looked back over to Shawna. She stared out the window and sniffled.

“Are you okay?”

She turned to me. “Just full of emotions right now,” she whispered.

Chapter Fifteen
Ruby

For the months that followed that special weekend, we had a blast together. We went hiking on the Cliff Walk in Newport, golfed at Fairlawn golf course, pigged out at Wright's Dairy Farm, and made love to each other in the most curious of places. One time we did it in a broom closet at a restaurant. Another time, we did it in the back row of the movie theater to the background noise of Will Ferrell acting goofy. Once we stopped alongside a busy interstate and did it right there in the backseat of her CRV.

We cemented down a good routine. Nadia spent two weeks in Rhode Island, then she'd go back to visit her wife for three days and come right back to me. On the days she'd leave for Connecticut, I'd take off work and go travel to escape routine and keep myself in this healthy mindset. Sometimes, I'd end up in the mountains of New Hampshire, climbing the Lafayette Trail, other times, I'd take a train to New York City for the day to go shopping at Barney's, and once in a while, I'd even venture to Canada and sit in a café in Quebec and listen to French Canadians speak with a pretty lisp to their voices. The nights before Nadia would return, I'd pace my condo searching for something to keep me occupied until the next day arrived when she would once again pull me into her arms under my warm blankets and tell me all about pottery and gardening and flowers. Her eyes would sparkle when she started telling me about the magic process of growing something out of nothing. She'd hold me tighter. She'd kiss my forehead more. She'd twirl her finger around my hair and talk about perennials and annuals and the power of plants in healing and well-being. Nadia was so smart.

I loved our arrangement. It worked. We indulged in a noncommittal relationship filled with sex and freedom. I dreamed up this girl. I asked the universe for someone just like her, down to the green eyes and smooth confidence at separation time.

She was unhappily married. I was single. We had great sex. Too perfect for words. Change any of that equation, and I'd end up a nauseous girl seeking an escape from the confines of what so many others spent their entire lives trying to force.

"Do you ever grow tired of hearing me speak?" Nadia asked one night after we just indulged in strawberry shortcakes and extra-large helpings of milk—the pure stuff, and not that watered-down skim crap.

I cuddled up to her bare chest and laid my head just above her breasts, resting my chin against her right nipple. "Sometimes words get in the way. But, not in your case. I could listen to you for years."

"Well, how about you?" She kissed the top of my head and ran her fingers through my tangled bedhead. "Tell me about your secret passion."

"I don't have secrets. I live life right out in the clear. What you see is what you get."

"Everyone has secrets."

"Not this girl anymore. Secrets just keep us from moving forward and enjoying life, like with not telling my grampa about my feelings towards my mother. Now that we spoke, everything is so much better for me."

Nadia kissed the tip of my nose. "Tell me what you loved most about growing up at The Rafters."

"I loved meeting the new guests. Some traveled in from different countries. I could sit there for hours listening to them tell me stories about their lives in faraway places. Maybe my passion is travel. Maybe I should become a world traveler, doing massages in Milan and Paris and Sicily. Then I could take naps in the afternoon while others slaved away at their desk jobs. I could eat all sorts of foods. Imagine? Hmmm. Pasta in Italy, arepas in Colombia, dal in India. I love culture."

"So we must travel one day."

Nadia's plan for a future we'd never have pricked me. "Yeah, definitely."

"Where would you like to go first?"

"You're such a dreamer." I circled her belly button, sucked into its supple swirl, suddenly wishing I could kiss it. I began to move towards it, and she stopped me.

"You know I wish that could happen, don't you?"

I continued on my journey around her skin. "Yeah, yeah. I told you, words get in the way. Let's just have this moment together."

Nadia pushed me away. "I have to tell you something."

Her tone scared me. I met her eyes. "You secretly hate to travel?"

She groaned. "I have to meet with the lawyer tomorrow. He has news on her parole."

I panicked. Neurons fired off in all directions. "It'll be fine," I said, being the supportive mistress. "Everything will be just fine."

* *

The next day, off she went to her wife. She didn't return for almost a week. When she did return, something had changed. She stiffened under my gaze.

"You're different," I said to her.

"I might've been wrong about Robby and Jessica."

"Why?"

"I found out that Robby's her AA sponsor. He's also married, and he and his wife are both on the visiting list."

Dread crawled around us. "Now you feel like what we did was wrong?"

Nadia tilted her head. "I thought she cheated on me."

The blood drained cold through my veins. I saw our moments fleeting, ebbing away. Ringing echoed in my head. "So was I just a return volley on that one?"

She shook her head. "Of course not."

I pined after her like a needy, whiny sap. "So what then?"

She gulped her Merlot. "I don't know."

I pulled at her. "Are you telling me we're over?"

Nadia hugged herself and looked away. "These past few months I lived in ignorance about whether she was cheating, and I enjoyed the bliss of it. Now that I know the truth, I feel guilty."

Her guilt caged me, backed into the corner. "I'm not here to complicate your life. I'd never do that to you."

Nadia raised up her glass. "I know you wouldn't." She gulped it back again. "We'll be fine. Don't worry."

Don't worry? How did I end up in this position? When did I allow her to turn me into someone who would worry? I gulped my Merlot, seeking its dark and mysterious power, willing it to come back to me. "You have to do what you have to do."

"She rested her hand on mine. "Thank you for being so supportive. You are something incredible. I hope you know that."

I just nodded.

We sat like two lost souls that night getting drunk at the lounge. I kissed her cheek and left her at the lobby entrance.

Nadia called me later on and apologized, citing the Merlot added to her sad mood. She promised the next day she'd be back to normal.

Normal didn't come again.

She distanced from me emotionally and withdrew from sex, stating the guilt consumed her. She seemed fine with falling back into our friendship status. But me? No way. Somewhere between falling in love with her and sipping Merlot, I had turned into a sap who couldn't tune into any other show but hers.

How did this happen?

I found myself suddenly waiting on her late night 'friendly' calls, and tossing and turning when they didn't come. I found myself asking her when she'd travel back to Rhode Island and whether she'd have time to visit with me for a 'friendly' chat. She would answer vague in her sultry manner, keeping me guessing until the very hour.

The loneliness in this new unsettling freedom Nadia tossed at me hurt like a stab to the chest.

I started to question her more about Jessica. I tossed out questions about their future and what that future meant for our 'friendship.' She flung flimsy answers back at me, like *let's not worry about that until it happens*.

I worried. I worried all the time. I feared the day she would stop calling, stop visiting, stop joining me, Shawna, and Grampa for pottery lessons, and stop being there for future overnight trips to The Rafters.

Then, one cold, snowy day, Nadia stopped by my massage oasis, popped her head in, and told me, "Jessica's parole was approved. She's coming home."

We both stood there, jaws dropped, pale skinned and sad.

Just like that, discomfort took over, replacing the freedom I pretended to enjoy. A silent mourning now wedged itself between us for a loss for what would never come. A sinking gloom hit me, the likes that dragged me to my knees and stomped on my back. "I hate that you're married."

"I have to go and pack." Nadia bowed her head and walked away.

I paced my massage room. Its potted-tree 'walls' closed in on me, clung to me, cut off my air. A man walked up and asked for a massage. I couldn't even respond. I tore off out of the oasis and charged towards the elevators. I couldn't let her go like this.

When Nadia opened her hotel door, I threw myself into her arms like some loving fool.

"Please don't do this," she whispered. "It's hard enough."

I looked up. Her eyes clenched onto mine and held me hostage. A sadness floated in them. The fine lines around them etched in an undeserved pain. I wanted her smiling, laughing, and enjoying herself.

I trailed the back of my hand down her cheek and jawline. She closed her eyes. Her lids fluttered. Her jaw loosened. Her shoulders relaxed. "What do you want?"

Nadia clasped her hand over mine and opened her eyes. "I want to be a good person."

"You are a good person."

She shook her head. "I wish things were different. I wish we would've met years ago. I wish I didn't live in Connecticut and you didn't live in Rhode Island."

I closed in on her. I brushed her lips with mine. And the dance began. The sweet dance of two girls enjoying each other for what they could in that moment.

On her drive to Connecticut, Nadia called me. "I care about you. I hope you know that."

I melted just like the first time she looked at me with love in her eyes. "So what happens now?"

Long pause. "Hmm," she said.

I closed my eyes, and a rush of panic coursed through me. "Nadia?"

"I just need some time to sort all of this out. Right now I need to be there for her."

"Yes," I said. "Yes, of course. I wouldn't expect anything less."

"So, you understand?" she asked.

I swallowed bitterness. "She needs you."

"She does." Nadia breathed heavily. "I'm so sorry."

"No. Don't apologize. I get it. I expected this day would come. I'm okay with it. You're married. You have to be there with her."

"I miss you terribly already," she said.

I let her words sink in and swaddle my heart. "You take care," I whispered and hung up. I spent the rest of the afternoon bawling in my massage oasis.

I hated this version of myself.

* *

Suddenly, I turned into an envious, snooping, ridiculous person, scrapping at anything that would save my future with her.

I snooped. I created a Facebook account for the first time just so I could gain access to her when I wanted to be in her arms. She friended me right away.

I snooped at every last picture of her. One of them of her at a bachelorette party dizzied me. She wore a white t-shirt, a black tie, and a garter belt. She was smoking a cigar, and her hair blew wildly as if she were sitting in front of a fan.

I refused to go into the photo album of her and Jessica. The one picture on the cover of the album freaked me out enough. Jessica was so fucking hot. They looked so happy together. Jessica's lips rested on her smiling cheek. Nadia glowed with a bright halo bathing her in pure joy.

She knew I'd see this, and this didn't faze her in the least bit.

I excelled at pretending that I didn't care about anything but being carefree and flirty, in only a friendly way now of course.

I craved more from her now. I wanted to cuddle. I wanted to kiss. I wanted her to twirl my hair. I wanted to please her. I wanted her to ask me about my life. I wanted her to confess that she hated her wife. That she didn't love her. That she was at least mad at her. But, she built her up to me, I surmised out of self-preservation, protecting her, falling victim to the very thing I had tried to avoid all of my life – a relationship.

I had become *that* girl.

I never thought I would be 'that girl.' You know, that girl who lived out of her car, borrowed money from her poor grampa, or fell in love with a married woman. Yet, here I was, all of that and more.

That first night when I lay in my old bedroom with her, staring at the back of her head, I should've walked. Her hair fell in gentle waves over her tanned shoulders, spilling onto the mattress. I should've run away. I should've torn myself from her, gotten dressed, picked up my pocketbook, and gone to the other room at the other end of the hallway. Instead, I swept my leg around hers and inhaled her alluring scent. My inner voice screamed at me to back away. I ignored it. I justified that we somehow both deserved this moment, that we could control our emotions, that it was just sex between two lonely women, and that we could fly away from this at any moment of our choosing, like two free birds in a wind tunnel.

This freedom caged me.

Chapter Sixteen
Nadia

Jessica sat on our couch for the first time in over a year and a half. She looked at me with apprehension, with sadness, with a desperate appeal to erase her mistakes so we could get back to living as we did before. Instinctively, I rushed to her side and comforted her. "You're home now. You're safe now. Everything's going to get better from here on out." I kissed the top of her head, and she fell into my embrace.

"Promise?"

I squeezed her tighter wanting to ease away her pain. "I promise."

For her first three days, I planted myself in a pot of sunshine and happiness for her. I cooked her favorite meals, rented her favorite movies, and bought her flowers. I did everything I could to renew her spirit to what it used to be before the accident.

She was broken.

I arranged one elaborate plan after the other, trying to recapture her spirit. We shopped at Neiman Marcus. We ate caviar on a rooftop restaurant in Manhattan. We spoiled ourselves by taking in two Broadway plays. Yet, still, when she laughed something was missing. When she flirted, it didn't seem sexy. When she passed people on the street, she didn't flip her hair or sway her hips in the same seductive way she had before. Jail sheared off a part of her essence.

I feared I'd never get her back.

Then, one morning as we sipped coffee in the living room together, she looked up at me with that special, adoring look that always sent tingles down my spine. For a blink of a moment, hope rested in the spokes of her eyes. A monumental tingle zoomed through me. "There you are."

The sparkle vanished. She cocked her head. "What do you mean?"

"Your old self."

"My old self?"

"The Jessica I fell in love with."

She feathered my cheek with the backside of her hand. "I don't think so, Butterfly. I don't know if I'll get back to that person again."

I cupped her hand to my face. "Sure you will."

"I'm not sure I can."

I pressed her hand against my face even harder. "Don't be silly. We'll get back to where we used to be."

She blinked heavily. "I've certainly missed this sweet side of you." Her eyes sunk lower than usual. I still tried to adjust to her dark circles from the stress and wear and tear of prison life. Her cheeks also sat sullen on her face like two sore pockets that once housed life. She no longer shined like the Burlesque star she used to be. Now in its former shiny place, sat a woman who looked older and more serious.

She folded her hands in her lap and looked around. She stopped on our wedding picture hanging above the fireplace mantle. She studied it, squinting at times and stretching one corner of her mouth up in a half smile. "I was definitely a wild person back then."

"Crazy wild." I cradled her wrist, and she shivered. "Are you cold?"

She shivered again. "I'm okay."

I plucked up the afghan behind us and curled it around her. "Better?"

"You're mothering me." She laid her head back against the suede and glanced at me with the lightest smile.

"I just want you to be comfortable." I patted her shoulders. "So what were you thinking of when looking at our wedding picture?" I cuddled in closer, forcing her arm to brush against mine.

She hugged herself, staring up at the portrait of us under an archway, smiling, dreamy-eyed, love pouring out of us and reflecting back at the camera. "Back then we had the whole world in front of us," she said.

"We still do." I nudged her. "We still have that great big world out there in front of us." A sinking truth of all I just gained and lost shrouded me. I fought past it, intent on staying true, on being a good wife again, on fixing her broken spirit. She needed me. "We can do anything with our life."

"You are such a good person," she said, admiring me. "I wish I could be the same for you again."

I softened my gaze, cupped her face in my hands, and spoon-fed love into her sad eyes. "What happened was a mistake. We're going to get past it. You are still a good person." I bore my eyes into hers. "Do you understand me? You are still a good person."

She gulped back tears and nodded.

I wiped them as they fell not taking my eyes off of her. In her eyes I saw fear. She needed me more than ever. I would heal her. I would help make her whole again.

Tears fell onto the afghan. "I'm not the same person."

"It's okay. We'll get you there again."

"I don't want to be, Nadia."

"Shh." I pulled her into my arms. "You have every right to be scared." We rocked back and forth amidst a weighty responsibility that shook my core.

She pulled away. "I've set up an appointment with the priest at the church around the corner for tomorrow. I'm going to start there and see if he can help me get rid of some of these bad feelings."

I poured more love into her desperate eyes, hungry to erase this grime from our lives and get back to laughing, sex, and pure Jessica-style fun. "Do you really need a priest?"

She leaned into me, rested her head against my chest. "He's already been to the prison to meet with me several times. I definitely know he can help me transition back to normal life."

Suddenly, as if the ground slipped away, I tumbled into unknown territory. How did I let her slip so far from my reach? I should've visited her more. I should've smiled more. I should've told her I loved her more. I shouldn't have been so selfish and scared. She needed me, and I turned away. And now she trusted a stranger of a priest more than her wife.

"Maybe I should be there with you."

She shook her head. "No. I need to do this part on my own."

The invisible cloak of reality tossed itself on top of us, dimming the light needed to sustain love, trust, and interdependence. I needed to stop thinking about Ruby, about The Rafters, about Rhode Island, and to start focusing back on this life that needed me, this life to which I had vowed my commitment.

* *

I insisted on going with her to see the priest. We sat before a tall, dark-haired man with a reserved smile and a softness to his cheeks that placed me in comfort.

He opened up the talk with a prayer. Jessica and he bowed their heads and surrendered to God. Meanwhile my cell buzzed, and I jumped to silence it. Ruby had texted me. "Just wanted to see how everything is going."

A smile sneaked onto my face, the likes of which should never be present during a solemn moment. I turned off my phone and bowed my head, reciting The Lord's Prayer along with them.

For the next thirty minutes, we sat there listening to Jessica confess her feelings. "I don't feel like I deserve good things to enter my life anymore."

"God has forgiven you already. You need to place your trust in Him, and do the same for yourself. If He has forgiven you, you can't question that by refusing to forgive yourself."

"I killed a woman. I robbed her of a lifetime. How do I forget that and pretend life is rosy?"

"Forgiving doesn't mean you forget. You must learn by this experience and be guided by this experience. God doesn't want you to live a life where you are inflicting resentment and guilt into the gift of each new day. He wants you to remember what happened and honor the experience by learning from it. He also wants you to pass these lessons onto others."

Jessica wobbled her head side-to-side. "This was so much easier to grasp in prison."

The priest nodded. "God is with you. He will get you through this."

Later on, I cooked us dinner. "Can you pass me the soy sauce from the cupboard?"

She opened it and rummaged through. "We need to reorganize this stuff." She picked up a jar of Thai red curry and squinted at the label. "This expired a year ago." She laughed and continued to search for the soy sauce. "Butterfly?"

I turned to her. She held up a bottle of Nyquil cold medicine. "We can't have this around anymore." Fear danced on her face again.

I stopped stirring my veggies. "Why not?"

"This contains alcohol."

"So? It's cold medicine."

"I'm an alcoholic."

The room spun around me, swallowing me up. Her words strung out in front of me, slapping me with a cold hard fist. "Don't say that."

"I am though."

It hurt to hear her admit defeat. My Jessica, the fun-loving, goofy woman who could turn a funeral into a party, needed to reclaim her strength. "You're too strong of a woman to label yourself that way."

She flung the expired bottle of curry sauce across the room. Red paste splattered across the cream granite. "Stop. Will you please just stop."

"Stop what?"

"Stop trying to save me from myself. I feel this pressure from you. Like if I don't snap back to the person I was before all of this, you're not going to love me. I'm okay with being an alcoholic. I'm okay with seeking outside help. I'm okay with having to change myself to better suit the condition. But you're not."

I flung the wooden spatula across the room now, too. "But you do need saving. Look at you." I waved my arms in the air. "You are walking around this place looking like you've got a death sentence hanging over your head. You haven't smiled in days. You've shown no signs of gratitude for everything I've put up with over the past two years. You look like you're about ready to burst into tears every other second. You need saving. And I'm at my wits end. I don't know how else to make you feel good. Everything I say you balk at."

Our chests heaved up and down. We panted like a couple of greyhound dogs at the end of a wild sprint.

"I'm weak right now. What can I say?" Her chin quivered. "I just need some time to find myself again, Nadia."

The instinct to save her pulled at me again. "You're not the weak one," I whispered.

She walked over to the splattered curry and knelt down. "We've got quite a mess here."

I joined her. I placed my hand on her thigh and stared at the mess. "Nothing we can't clean up."

* *

That night after I tucked Jessica into bed, I drew a hot bath. I sneaked in my bottle of white wine from the basement stash and turned on some classical music. I lay back against my bath pillow and thought of Ruby, of her long blonde hair, of her soft fingers on my skin, of her gentle smile. After drinking two glasses, I caved and called her.

"Hey, darling," she said.

Her voice wrapped itself around my heart and instantly melted me. "It's so good to hear your voice."

"Everything okay?" Ruby asked.

"It's okay, yes. I just missed hearing your voice," I said. "Are you doing okay?"

"I'm doing fantastic. How's the wifey?"

I hesitated. I didn't want to talk. I wanted to hear her soothing voice instead. "She's fine." God, I missed her. I missed everything about her. I missed her smell, her hair, the feel of her fingers on my skin, the passion in her eye, the tease on her lips. Like an addict myself, I reached out for a fix. "Do you miss me as much as I miss you right now?"

"Darling?" Ruby's tone carried the weight of many sandbags. "I really wish I could talk right now, but the truth is, I'm on a date, and we're getting ready to take off for a nighttime flight up to Maine."

My spirit burst, emptying the air from my lungs. "A date? Who is she?"

"She's a client." She lifted her voice in sing-song fashion. I could just picture her staring into the eyes of a beautiful woman, willing for me to hang up so she could get on with her exciting plans. "She flies a Cessna and wants to show me the nighttime sky. We're going to eat lobster and fly back. Isn't that so cool? Flying to Maine for lobster. Ha. Now that's a first for me."

My head buzzed. My heart ached. I gulped more wine. "Have a good time."

"Thanks, darling. I'll call you in a few days, and we'll catch up. Until then, take care of yourself and enjoy the time with your wife."

"Thanks. Will do."

"Bye!" she said.

The click echoed a finality that splintered me.

* *

I obsessed over Ruby all night long, imagining her forgetting all about me. Maybe this new woman would be the one to finally settle her. Maybe she'd travel across the interstate to western Massachusetts with Shawna and Grampa, singing Billy Joel tunes, and admiring the view of maple trees and the smell of hot apple cider. Maybe she'd be the lucky one who got to lay in bed under the comforters, hugging Ruby and cradling her curves. Maybe she'd be the one who got to massage Ruby under a stream of hot, steamy water as Ruby orgasmed in her arms.

I couldn't take it. I needed to see her. I needed to make sure she didn't forget me. I didn't want to blend into the background and fade away as that woman she once enjoyed time with and needed once upon a time.

The next morning, Jessica sneaked up behind me and nuzzled up to my neck. "You know what I could really go for right now?"

I sensed her need. "A latte from Starbucks?"

She moaned and rocked her hips against me. “What do you say?”

Jessica needed me. That should have been all that mattered. I needed Ruby out of my mind. So, I led her up the stairs to our bedroom and undressed her one button at a time. She peeled off my blouse. I dropped her pajama bottoms. She wrestled with my skirt. I wrangled with her hair, pushing it out of the way so I could kiss her neck.

I went through the motions, dragging my tongue along her skin, along her collar bone, down to her nipples. She swayed under my touch. I traveled down her belly to her vagina and nibbled on it the way she loved. She grabbed onto my shoulders and dug into them, groaning, urging me to suck on it. “Harder. Press harder.”

I did as told, feeding my wife something she hadn’t indulged in since the night before the accident. She moaned and bucked and screamed out in spastic grunts, digging into my shoulders and claiming me in her thrusts. “Oh Butterfly, you are incredible,” she yelled out. “You know just how to please me. I missed your tongue more than I could ever tell you.” She panted and tossed herself back on the bed. “No one can ever come close to what you just did.”

I rose and crawled up beside her. “So the women in jail couldn’t match me on this delivery?” I joked.

She reached down and fingered herself then placed her fingers in my mouth. “Not even close.”

I pulled her fingers away. “Wait? So, other women tried?”

Her eyes widened, recognition for her grave mistake splintered across her cheeks. She flung her arms out to the side. “I can’t even joke around correctly anymore.”

“You call that a joke?” I exhaled. “That is not a good joke.”

Her face wilted. “I’m sorry, I guess I just lost my timing a little.” She shrugged and looked down to the comforter. “I’m just full of disappointment.”

“What?” I lifted her chin. “Why would you say such a thing?”

Her eyes held defeat. Her confidence no longer there. She shook her head. “I don’t know. I just…” She fidgeted with a string. “I just don’t feel like the same person anymore. I honestly don’t know how you are going to love this new me.”

I stared into her weakened eyes. I wanted my confident, sexy Jessica to appear. “Seduce me. Come on. Just forget everything else and seduce me.”

She inhaled, rolled me over onto my back and straddled me. Then, she began her descent down on me. Each movement methodical and planned, mentally scrutinized. She planted kisses robotically on my inner thighs, ducking in between my legs as if performing a serious procedure. I lay back against our bed, imprisoned by her reluctance, gutted in thoughts of a gynecologic exam rather than a hot and steamy sexual encounter. Her tongue had lost its will, its pressure, and its power since the last time she’d gone down on me. I pushed her head harder against me, willing for her to return to her sexual roots and bring me to ecstasy. After five tiresome minutes of unsatisfied tongue flicks, I resorted to buck and grind and scream out a false pleasure. I faked my orgasm for the first time with her, offering her reprieve from what seemed like such hard work for her.

Ten minutes later, after a serious attempt to find comfort in her arms, I lied to her. “I’ve got to go to Rhode Island today for a meeting with the sales team. I’ll probably be away for several days.” I needed to get away.

An hour later, I drove to Rhode Island and straight to Ruby’s condo. I rang her bell at eight forty-five in the morning. The sun rose up over the horizon beyond the Jamestown Bridge. Seagulls were flying around squawking and dive-bombing to pluck up delicacies along the seashore. Early morning joggers blew white puffs of cool air as they sped past me. I stood on Ruby's doorstep taking this all in as I waited for her to answer.

Ruby never answered.

I peeked on the side of her condo for her car. Not there. She could be anywhere, and I had no right to know where. I called her cell. She didn't answer.

I left her a message. "Please call me as soon as you get this. I need to talk."

I sat on a swinging chair. It creaked. I wondered how many times she sat outside in this very spot and took in the view? Did I flood her mind, too? Every second of the day? Or had she already forgotten about me, her lover in between others.

Two hours later, I decided to walk on the beach. As I did, the water soothed me with peace. A strange swirling of tranquility mixed with the salt air and created a pocket of comfort. I'd only experienced this same level of comfort when I sat sandwiched between Ruby, Shawna and Grampa at the pottery cafe as we listened to Grampa tell stories to us about bonfires, sticks for fishing rods, and his days playing hockey on ponds that used to freeze but now just glazed over with algae.

I would miss that man.

I stared out at the open sea. I watched seagulls sink into the water and surface with a treat. I admired the majestic boats in the distance. I smiled at the shiny ripples on the crests of small waves and watched as they ran to shore and pushed back to the sea, to where they belonged. They had no doubt where they belonged.

I envied them.

* *

I sat in a small café and sipped some tea. I browsed *Rhode Island Monthly* magazine. My eyes fell upon an ad for Lifespan, a medical group. A young nurse was smiling, her chin raised, her eyes glowing, wearing her name badge, Trish. She'd probably spent years readying for that picture, a picture that showed off her hard work and dedication to something she loved, to something she stayed true to.

She probably married her childhood sweetheart and stayed loyal to him and their two intelligent and witty children. No doubt they enjoyed evening walks on the shores of Galilee and attended Sunday mass together each week. They probably even wore matching sweatshirts and spent their Saturdays doing fun things together like kayaking, not ever worrying that one of them would take off mid-relationship to tend to her alcoholic spouse who just got out of prison for killing someone.

* *

For two days I busied myself at the Rhode Island office waiting on Ruby to arrive at her massage chair. I imagined the worst during those days. I imagined her flying the skies with this new girlfriend of hers, forgetting all about me and all about her great gig at the hotel.

I dove headfirst into a pile of paperwork I needed to get through, when finally, Ruby called.

I answered before the first ring could finish. "Are you okay?"

"Of course," she said. "Are you?"

"Yes. Of course." I paused. "I'm in town. Any way I can see you?"

"You don't sound like you're okay."

"I want to see you," I said.

"I'm with Grampa. I'm sure he'd love to see you."

"And what about you?"

"We're at the pottery shop. We just started making mugs."

"You didn't answer me," I said.

"Is that really a good idea?"

"Probably not. I just want to see you."

"Then come," she said. "Just come."

Chapter Seventeen
Ruby

Nadia's CRV pulled into the parking lot of the pottery café.

"I'll be right back, Grampa." I stood up and met her outside.

Nadia walked with a bounce in her step, carrying a tray of coffee, gazing at me with her tiger eyes. Her hair fell like feathers upon her shoulders, and a side-swept bang flirted close to her right eye, just the way I liked it. She wore jeans that hugged her curvy hips and a fitted zipper jacket that showed off her toned abs. Under that zipper sat her navel, deep and erotic and last touched by my tongue just weeks ago.

"Hey you," she said with a friendly twist to her voice.

Why did she have to look so beautiful? I opened my arms and welcomed her into a hug. She fell into them and softened. Her hair smelled like she just stepped out of a salon. "You look gorgeous as ever," I whispered.

We stood outside the pottery cafe. Nadia offered me the coffee. I preferred tea, but never let on to this tiniest of facts. She did know, however, that I liked Mozart when I bathed and that I always brushed my teeth twice at night ever since having to get my first cavity filled at the age of twenty five. She also learned that I read the bible every night before going to sleep and that in the middle of the night, I ran to the bathroom because I still feared someone grabbing my ankles from under the bed.

We had so many more things to learn about each other that we'd never get a chance to, yet, here I stood breathing her soul, hungry for her kiss, delirious without her. Nothing freaked me out more.

Nadia carried all of the power. I flittered around her like a bird with clipped wings. All of the work I'd done to reestablish my balance in the wake of her sudden and painful exit from my life disappeared with the arrival of her sexy smile and magnetic energy.

We bantered back and forth about the weather and the spa and the hotel, nudging one another, and laughing like giddy girls. Not until I sipped the last of my coffee did I manage to toss out the question that would set me up as the independent, strong one, unaffected by the unfortunate reality that lay before us. "So, how's Jessica?"

"She's not handling the transition well," she said. "I feel sorry for her. I'm trying to empathize, but honestly, I have no idea what kind of thoughts must be tearing at her right now."

Jealousy ripped through me. I envisioned them curled up together in their bed, under a sea of comforting blankets warmed by their naked bodies, Nadia caressing her hair, her skin, her soul. I hated that she had this grip on my life. I hated that I could so easily turn to mush in her presence. "She's in good hands."

Nadia scrunched up a smile. "I don't know about that. I feel like I'm caught in between two worlds. You know?" Regret splayed out on her face.

"No need for that stress." I leaned against the wall like a strong, cool, and collected woman who was not succumbing to a riptide of hurt inside her tummy. "You love her. You'll work it out."

She gazed out over the trees lining the parking lot, struggling to inhale. "So how was your date?"

"Incredible. A hot woman who can fly an airplane. What more could a girl ask for, right?" My voice carried far too much angst in it. Fuck the hot girl who could fly. I wanted the one standing in front of me.

We dueled for balance. "I hate that I can't fix any of this."

"Fix what?"

"Fix the fact that I am caught up in these two worlds. I care so much for Jessica," she said. "I worry about her. I want her to be whole again. I want her to love life again. And at the same time, I hate that you went on a date. I hate that I can't be the girl who takes off in an airplane with you. I hate that I feel this way." She pulled in her lower lip and slowly released it on a seductive sigh.

I loved that she did. A spark of hope rested in that sigh, one that told me she'd be willing to stomp on her ideals for a temporary moment of passion. She could sneak into town, and Jessica would never have to know. The hunger growled in her eyes. The air sizzled between us. I adored her, and she adored me.

I stared at a married woman, though. She took vows. Her wife trusted those vows. She could so easily hurt me and leave me standing with my head bowed, alone, just like Grace did with Grampa.

Marriage stood in its rightful spot, front and center. I deserved no claim to her. The game had changed. She now stood before me just as eager for a temporary escape from the emptiness of our separation. A month, a year, a decade from now, I would hate for her to reflect back on me as that mistake.

I reached out for her hand and caressed it in mine. She stared down at it, then back up at me. Longing hung on each blink. "You're a good person," I said. "That's what I love so much about you."

"What we have is fun. It's pure. The purest I've experienced, ever," Nadia said. "I don't want to wrong her. But, at the same time, I don't want to wrong us either. You bring thrill into my life. I don't want to give that up."

I enjoyed the idea of fun-loving sex, but not like this, not with her. With her, I wanted more. "I don't think you're the type of person who can deal with having both. I also don't want to be a mistress to you."

"Please don't ever call yourself that."

I ran my fingers through Nadia's hair. "That's who I would be."

She bowed her head and wrestled with tears. They leaked from her eyes, and I did everything I could to stop them. I pulled her into my arms and consoled her. I rubbed her back, her hair, squeezed her tight, and buried my head along with hers, cheek to cheek.

She twisted towards my face, and I wouldn't let her. I pressed her head against me and rocked with her. I wanted to cave into this moment, to just pull her into my arms and hug her and tell her I wanted to continue being that source of pleasure.

One of us had to be strong. She loved two women. I only loved one. So, by default, I chose to be the strong one.

I cupped Nadia's face in my hands. "What do you say we just have fun right now and go in there and make my grampa smile a little bit today?"

"I'd say I would love to, Ruby."

I dropped my hands, reached out for her hand, and pushed open the door to the pottery café. "And I would say I love that you would love to, Nadia Chase."

* *

Nadia and I returned to my condo after dropping off my grampa. Marcy and Rachel were cleaning up in the kitchen. "You girls want to join us for drinks at the Beach House?" Marcy asked.

"I'm kind of tired," Nadia said. "I'm going to use the little girl's room and maybe head out in a few minutes."

Rachel passed by us and headed to her bedroom. “Suit yourself. They’re having dollar shot night.”

Nadia and I shared a private smirk before she headed into the bathroom.

A minute later, the girls swept out the door and wished me a good night.

I sat on my couch and flipped through the newspaper waiting for Nadia. She emerged looking gorgeous as ever with her caramel highlights and pink lip gloss.

She walked past me. I admired the way her jeans hugged her tight ass.

She leaned up against the pole that separated the kitchen from living room areas. Her eyes swept over me. “Just one more time. Please.”

I melted when she cocked her head and smiled at me. “Stop that.” My tummy rolled.

“Come on. Just one last time.” With coy eyes, she placed the tip of her finger in between her rosy lips and nibbled on it.

“I thought we settled this.”

Nadia pouted.

My heart raced. I stood up. “Darling,” I said, all breathy, braving closer. “Once you turn on this spigot, there’s no turning it off.”

She swept me over with that seductive glance again. “I don’t want to turn it off.”

I moved in close, unable to resist her advance. “I don’t want you to either.” I feathered her lips with my fingers. She nibbled on it, never taking her eyes off of mine.

I closed my eyes and enjoyed the coolness of her teeth against my finger, the softness of her lips as they hugged my skin. I pulsed and moistened, hungry for her touch. She needed this. I needed this. We were two girls with needs that only we could fulfill and satisfy.

Nadia's eyes flickered and she bit down a little harder. Her chest rose and fell with great breadth, begging me to take her away from her misery and bring her to sheer pleasure. "Kiss me," she whispered. "Please, kiss me."

I couldn't contain my passion another moment. I lost my sense of resolve and strength as I pulled Nadia in close to me and kissed her hard. Then she spun me around and pushed me against the pole and tore off my top. I reciprocated and tore off hers. Panting, and clawing at each other's clothes, we wrestled out of them and stood, skin-to-skin trembling.

We kissed as we both caressed each other, traveling to those parts that only we knew how to bring to life. Nadia began her descent down on me. I raked my hands through her hair and prompted her to keep blowing her warm breath on my most delicate skin. She knelt on the ground, her luscious lips a mere inch from serving me ecstasy. I pulled her back, and she stared up at me with desire.

"I love you, Nadia," I whispered.

She rose to her feet and kissed me. "I love you." She pressed harder against me. "Too much."

I caught my breath. "Is there really such a thing?"

She rolled her tongue against mine, wedging her leg up in between mine. "Don't you think so under the circumstances?"

I stiffened. "I suppose so."

"We should stop, shouldn't we?" Her breath blew hot in my mouth.

I pulsed. "If you have to ask, then yes, we should." I clawed her back, unable to match my words with my actions. I failed to contain my euphoric release induced by her hot breath.

Nadia traveled down my neck. "I need you. I need this." She sucked on my skin, traveling lower towards the curve of my breast, hungry, animalistic, like she would implode if I stopped her. I turned into her life source, leaning ready for the tap in, for my call to action, for my elixir to save her from her newly-troubled life.

I was the other woman, the mistress, the one with no claim, no fringe benefits, and no commitment.

I pushed away from her advances. "We should stop before someone gets hurt."

"Please don't push me away. Please just let's have this moment." Nadia moved in closer, placing her lips back on me, as if weakened by my weakness for her. In a day or two I'd be right back to the foolish person snooping around her Facebook profile for clues on her whereabouts. I'd wonder how much love she poured into Jessica. I'd stress about their future, their happiness, their investments, their laughter, and their quiet moments together. I couldn't go through this torture.

I shoved off of her. "I don't want to be this to you."

She draped her hands over my shoulders. "Be what to me?"

"Be regret."

"I could never regret you."

I pulled away and hugged myself. "Then leave her. Just leave her."

Nadia dropped her hands. "Why are you doing this?"

I shrugged unable to find the right words.

"You know I can't just leave her."

"Well then you should stay true to her." I regretted the words as soon as they tumbled out of my mouth.

"You're making me sound like some kind of whore."

"Well, you're not exactly acting like a married woman. Are you?" I dissed out one regrettable word after another.

Nadia scoffed, pulled on her clothes, then flew out of my front door and down onto the landing. Then, she ran across the two lane road straight towards the beach. I followed suit. I bolted towards her, away from the pigeons, away from their hungry snappy beaks.

"This is so unfair what you're doing to me," she said.

"What I'm doing to you?"

"You're a freedom-lover, remember? You want to fly up somewhere in the clouds where no one else goes. You want to have fun. You want to remain unsettled. You want to travel around and massage people's necks. You don't want to commit. You are okay with me being married. Remember?"

"So I'm supposed to just be your little fuck buddy?" I tripped over the sand, following her sprint to the seashore.

"I don't want to leave her. She needs me. Don't you understand?"

Nadia's words stung me like a slap. "Well, I can't do this anymore." I stammered away, embarrassed, humiliated and heartbroken.

She ran after me. "You wouldn't know what to do with me if I left her. You'd feel smothered in less than a month. You'd be so bored."

"You should just go back to her. You can obviously trust her more than me with your future."

"That's not fair," she said.

"I'd rather be alone and hopeful, than with someone and lonely. So, I am choosing right now to stay alone."

Nadia tossed her arms up in the air. "When it matters, you can't even put aside your fears of commitment and face the truth."

I just stared at her, at the straightness of her spine, at her soft shoulders, at her brown flowing hair. "I told you I loved you. How much more truth can I tell you?"

She sighed. "I want to be with you. I do. I can't give you more than this, though." She closed in on me, cupped her hands around my face. "You are on my mind always. I don't want to ruin this good thing we have going on together. I don't want to leave you behind. I can't rise out of bed in the morning without first thinking of you. I can't go to sleep at night before imagining your arms wrapping around me. I care about you Ruby Clark."

"Prove it then."

"I can't."

"You can't or you don't want to?"

"I don't want to," she said much too quickly.

"Well, there we have it. Question answered."

We stared at each other, two broken women with exposed regrets.

"I just want things to stay the way they are." Nadia leaned over the edge of desperation, and I pictured her losing her footing and slipping, then tumbling down into an abyss way out of my reach to help. "I want you to be you, that special willowy girl who I adore. I want to share romantic moments with you without regret. I want to sip wine and massage each other and enjoy expressing ourselves without fear of hurting the other."

"You want two worlds."

"I want what we've always had. Fun. Intoxicating sex. Friendship. A safe haven to be happy together. What we have is perfect as-is. We have fun. We enjoy each other. It's fresh and spirited. If we change these elements, it could ruin everything."

"So, in other words, you want freedom from guilt."

"Yes," Nadia whispered. "Love should never cause guilt."

I didn't want to be that safe place for her. I wanted to be her only place. "I don't want to be your source of guilt one day."

She flinched.

"Unless you leave her, you'll feel guilt."

Nadia's forehead creased under the pressure. "I can't leave her."

"You love the way she needs you. You love being the saving grace. This defines you. You are so afraid of removing that from your life and standing on your own for once."

She cupped her hands to her face and squeezed her eyes. "Why shouldn't I be? Who wants to be alone? There is purpose in helping people."

"Somewhere along the way, you broke down. You claim you blend to mend, like with your sister, but that's bullshit. Way back when, she hit a nerve and you've been trying to put yourself back together ever since. You seek out people with problems and try to fix them to make yourself feel whole. What you need is time to mend yourself. You're the broken one here, Nadia." The words landed in a thud at our feet.

Tears streamed down her face now. "Don't do that," she pointed. "I'm not broken. I help those who are. There's a big difference."

"You assumed I was broken. So you swooped in like the saving grace and tried to fix me by giving me a job and getting me to open up to you."

Nadia nodded. "When I first met you, I saw you sleeping in your car in the parking lot. You were massaging strangers in a dark lounge. You had no plan. You were broken, and of course I wanted to help you."

"I don't need your help. I am not broken. I love my life. I am a survivor. I am strong-willed. I can live in a car, shower in a YMCA, eat at a homeless shelter and still smile. I don't need a helping hand. I've proven that. You, on the other hand, would never be able to survive some of the things I did. So, let's stop the martyrdom here."

"Martyrdom? Give me a fucking break. Without me, you'd be in deep financial trouble. Admit it."

Fuck her. "Even if you left your wife now, we'd be done. I could never be with someone who views me as weak and broken. I'm done with this conversation."

"Stop," she said. "Stop being ridiculous. Just because you need someone doesn't make you weak. You're talking out of fear now."

"When you're unattached like me, you are spared fear."

Nadia rolled her eyes. "You think you're this free-spirited, willowy princess who can land in the streams and wade under the sparkle of the sun and then fly up to mountaintops and gaze out over the land like you're some kind of elusive being who is better than the rest of us mere mortals who have responsibilities and commitments." She rolled her eyes and scoffed.

"You're afraid to not have anyone at all," I said. "You wouldn't know how to stand up without someone by your side. You've always had someone by your side. If it wasn't Jessica, it was your sister. When Jessica ended up in jail, you found me. You always need to be needed."

"Better to be like that than to be afraid of settling down in life. Actually, I think you're incapable of settling down." She tightened her face. "Incapable."

"I am not incapable. Don't ever tell me I'm incapable."

"You were a traveling masseuse with no clients before I met you. I helped you."

"Helped me." I winced. "There you go again, jumping in headfirst to the rescue."

"You needed help. I helped."

"I will never need someone. Never. I am self-reliant. I don't need saving," I said.

"Everyone needs someone at some point," Nadia said. "The fact that you think you're so perfect as-is will only hold you back further in life. I feel bad for you. I really do."

"You go around trying to save everyone like you're the perfect host to some model life we should all strive to live. It's you who needs to be saved from your enormous ego."

She backed up as if I'd just slapped her. She ran off, past the pigeons, past the docks, past the toddlers tossing bread, past the park bench we sat on just a few weeks earlier, past it all.

Chapter Eighteen
Nadia

I drove back to Connecticut replaying our fight. I'm the one who needs to be saved?

And, how could she worry that I viewed her as my "little fuck buddy"?

Ruby had seduced me.

How fucked up. Ruby couldn't even admit that she needed help. She worked so hard to keep up the façade of being this free spirit. When the end of the day came, however, did she not realize she needed money to put shelter over her head, food in her stomach, and gas in her car? I saved her from having to sacrifice any of those things. What was wrong with that?

I helped my sister, Jessica, Shawna, and Ruby because I liked to help them. Everyone liked to be needed. Didn't they? This had nothing to do with an inflated ego.

Broken? Me?

I punched my steering wheel. Fuck that.

I would request a transfer immediately.

I didn't need this crap in my life. I would stay focused on the woman who needed me.

A transfer would sever the tie between us. Ruby didn't need me? Fine. I'd like to see how far she would get without my help.

I punched the steering wheel again. Why did I have to flip out the way I did? I could've kept quiet and let her vent. Now, she'd certainly never take my calls.

In thirty short minutes, I had screwed up my whole life. Now I'd lose touch with Shawna. Our friendship would fizzle. I'd no longer be able to monitor people at the lounge. She'd be forced to deal with idiots on her own.

And what about Ruby's grampa? Would he still create pottery? He loved molding clay. He loved painting his finished piece. Would that all go away for him now? Would Ruby and Shawna bring him back there? Or would he be forced back into his routine of Sunday breakfast and stale conversation with the old ladies at the senior center?

No more Ruby. No more flirty phone calls. No more surprise cards delivered to me in the middle of the day. A lump formed in my throat. How would I ever enjoy a work day without looking down from my office and seeing her beautiful, long hair flapping around her toned shoulders as she leaned over strangers and massaged them? Would I ever be able to eat an apple again without reminiscing about our Sweet Tree? What if my neck knotted up again? Could I have another masseuse touch me without the stab of heartbreak interfering with recovery?

Fuck no.

I punched the wheel even harder.

No way.

Impossible.

I couldn't.

My heart hurt. It ached, like someone had jumped on it and flattened it, emptying it of all its oxygen, its life.

I missed her already.

The sobs piled up in the back of my throat and unleashed. I bawled for miles, singing sad songs and reminiscing over our shared memories. She loved me. Of course she couldn't stand to hang around pining for our time together while I catered to my marriage on the side. Ruby deserved greater than that. She deserved a full time lover who would commit to her and help her to see that needing each other was healthy. I thought of the pilot. They could fly around the skies enjoying the lightness of air and unlimited escapes to lands beyond the reach of Interstate ninety-five. She deserved this freedom, not the confines of being a mistress. I loved her. Wasn't I supposed to want her happiness above my own? Was it supposed to hurt like this?

Ruby would never admit to needing me. How could I ever be with someone who feared my support? What kind of relationship would that be?

It wouldn't be one.

I sped up, wanting to outrun the past and get started on the future. Maybe if I put enough miles between us, I'd get over her quicker.

I called Jessica about one hundred and thirty miles north of our home. "I'm on my way home. I should get there in two hours if traffic cooperates."

"I've got some good news."

"What's that?"

"I got a great job."

My heart should've twirled at this news. Life already took a better turn. "Doing what?"

"Dancing again."

"Dancing?" Dancing meant temptation. Dancing meant busy schedules. Dancing meant booze. "How did that come about?"

"I answered a job in the paper and the guy at first said no way, he doesn't hire people with a criminal record. So, I told him I'd show him my abilities by working one day for free. He agreed. I impressed him I guess. Of course, I was the only sober dancer on the stage."

My new Jessica, Mrs. Industrious. Mrs. Clean and Sober. "How will you deal with the pressures?"

"I'm a changed woman. I'll rely on the goodness of God to help me through."

"You don't have to rush into getting a job."

"I need to work. I'm driving myself nuts hanging around here all day."

"Is dancing the answer?"

She chuckled. "Hey, Butterfly?"

"Yes, sweetheart."

"Just hurry up and get home. I can't wait to give you a big hug."

* *

When I got home, I unlocked the front door and Jessica was lounging on the couch watching television. She hopped right up from the couch and ran over to me. Before I could even drop my luggage, she took it from me and walked it into the living room. "Come on. Let me order us a pizza. We'll nibble on it and hang out together."

"Like old times?" My words dripped with hope.

"Just like old times. Sans the beer."

I hugged her and she smelled like a cigarette. "Have you been smoking?"

She pulled away. "I'm sorry. It was just one cigarette."

I braced her at arms' length. "Really? Smoking?"

She lowered her eyes like a child. "I know I shouldn't. I picked up the habit in prison and with all the stress of trying to get back to normal living, it helps."

"I don't want you to be a smoker. Promise me you'll quit."

She looked up at me. "I promise. I've just got a couple more in the pack, and I promise never to buy another one."

"Why not just toss them now?"

She tilted her head. "I'd rather not. It's a mental thing. You know like starting a workout mid-week wouldn't work as well as starting on a Monday."

"Okay." I dropped my hands from her. I was too tired to argue. I'd deal with it later. "I'm just going to go refresh before we eat."

I climbed the stairs and inhaled deeply, reassuring myself that everything would fall back into place as it was before. I would see to it.

In the month that followed, I focused on my marriage, working harder than ever to build Jessica back up to her prime position. The dancing gig lasted all of two days. She quit when her fellow dancers pressured her to drink with them. She refused and came home smelling of cigarettes again. "Yes, I've been smoking. I'm stressed." She stormed up the stairs. "Is it too much to ask that I just want to work?" She slammed our bedroom door.

By the second week, her stress exploded when Sasha told her that Keith would not be able to hire her to work in the hotel. "That was my last resort." She lit a cigarette on the patio, pacing feverishly back and forth, shaking. "She actually told me Keith didn't want to hire an ex-con. She actually called me an ex-con." She drew long and hard on her cigarette. "If family can't give me a break, who will?" Smoke streamed from her nostrils.

"Just calm down." I stared at the tip of her dangling cigarette. I had no idea how to make her quit. "I'll have a talk with her."

"I know what you're thinking. You're thinking I'm weak and pathetic because I traded one bad habit for another. I need you to ease up on me here."

I tossed my hands in the air. "I didn't say anything."

"No, but you've got that stern look about you."

I needed to soften her. I needed her to listen to me. I couldn't help her in this frazzled state. "I'm not your enemy," I whispered.

She flung her head back. "I know." She clung to herself. I'd never seen her so distraught, not even when she had entered prison. I needed to prove I was on her side. As much as I dreaded it, I picked up her pack from the table and lit one for myself. I inhaled deeply. "See," I said, coughing. "I'm right by your side. If this is what you need to get you through, then we'll smoke." I inhaled again. The smoke stung my eyes. "We'll get through this together."

"I love you so much," she said, pulling me into her arms.

"I love you, too."

We clung to each other dragging on our cigarettes like a couple of rough and tough women. First build the trust. Then, remold and redefine. Blend to mend.

As the days passed, I lifted her mood by spoiling her with things like digital montages of our vacation photos and new pillows for the bed. She responded with brighter smiles and a fresh perspective on her situation. "Maybe it's time I do something totally different with my life."

"This is a great opportunity for you to break away from what you've always done."

Within three weeks, Jessica got a job landscaping. She came home happy and smiling, humming tunes while preparing chicken and fish dinners. "I can see myself opening up my own landscaping company one day. It's seriously so simple. Most of the clients already told me they'd hire me in a heartbeat." She breaded chicken cutlets, and a smile danced on her face.

* *

A week later, I trekked up to the Rhode Island office to check on things. I sneaked in the back door so I wouldn't have to walk past Ruby's massage oasis.

Shawna tended the bar, wiping up remnants of someone's lunch. "It's about freaking time."

"I'm sorry I haven't had a chance to call you back." I sat down. "I've been busy."

She arched her eye. "Did corporate tell you?"

"Tell me what?"

"Ruby quit."

My body numbed. "No one told me."

"Yup, she's not even massaging anymore. She's walking dogs."

I poured salt from the shaker in front of me and twirled my finger around in it. "She's so freaking stubborn."

"Why are you making a mess of my bar?"

I stopped twirling, surprised at her authority. "I'm sorry."

Shawna braced against the bar, easing her command over my salt pile. "Are you doing okay?"

"I'm fine." I lifted my face to meet her eye. "I miss her. But, I want her to be happy."

"She's dating that pilot woman. She's actually very sweet. But she's no you."

The truth jerked at my heart. "Well, I'm glad to see she's getting on with her life." I swallowed the bitter lie. "How about you? Are things going okay here for you? Any problems that I should know about?"

"I fired someone." A proud twinkle danced in her eye.

"What happened?"

"He couldn't handle me. He said my lipstick disturbed him. So, I told him his face disturbed me and kicked him out."

I laughed. I could just see the scene playing out with Shawna standing tall, challenging the guy to give her more attitude and he backing down and running away. "Good for you." I swirled my salt some more. "Have you seen her grampa?"

"That's another reason I was trying to call you. He's having some trouble with his eyes. He's got that macular degenerative disease and it's serving him up some trouble. I feel bad for him. So, I've been reading to him almost every day." She wiped away my salt. "He's always asking about pretty Nadia."

"That man brings a smile to my face. He's a true spirit, isn't he?"

She nodded. "I'm heading over there after my lunch shift if you want to go."

"Will Ruby be there?"

"Not today. She can only get there a few days a week with her dog walking schedule."

"She's on a schedule?"

"Our girl is on a schedule." She laughed. "Imagine that?"

* *

A few hours later, Shawna and I walked into his apartment. He slurped Jell-O while watching *Days of Our Lives*. He looked up at me and smiled. "There's my pretty girl." He lifted his Jell-O cup. "Hey, want some?"

"No." I sat down on the couch. "You enjoy it."

He smiled and continued to slurp. He looked like a child swishing the Jell-O around his cup. "So Ruby tells me you got a big promotion. Is that why you haven't been around?"

I nodded, admiring Ruby's compassion. "It's been a little hectic, yes, sir."

"Where's Ruby? She didn't come with you?"

"She's out walking dogs," Shawna said.

He nodded. "Oh yes. That's right." His wrinkles looked deeper since the last time I saw him. His face drooped more. "She's wild just like her mother was. You know," he leaned in and whispered. "You can't cage those two. They're like those feral cats that used to wander around my barn. They just want to roam on their terms."

"I suppose you're right."

"That's why they sparkle with such beauty." He winked.

I reached out and placed my hand over his wrist ready to change the tone. "How's life treating you?"

He craned his head. "My eyes are giving me a bit of some trouble. I can barely read the large print anymore."

"Do you want me to read to you?"

"No." He straightened his lips. "I just want to talk. Do you want to hear some fascinating stories?"

I scooted in closer. "You bet."

We spent an hour with him listening to stories about his days working the farm and how the great flood of thirty-eight nearly swept away his whole town. He enlightened us about how lucky we had it these days now that we could enjoy indoor plumbing and electricity and town water. He circled around some of his childhood memories with a laugh, and then he plowed through some facts about immigrating to America from Canada. He explained how tough of a time he had learning to speak English. As he finished telling us about a joke he played on some neighborhood punks who used to make fun of him for talking with a French Canadian accent, he started to nod off. We took the cue and stood. I leaned down and kissed his cheek and whispered, "Next time I'll bring a book."

Shawna and I walked out of his home saddened. "Does the guy ever get to leave his apartment?" I asked.

"Every Sunday. We've been taking him out to that Rafters place. He turns into a light bulb there. He just brightens to life. Ruby does too. It's like all the burdens of life just drop off onto the front stoop and allow those two to enjoy quality time together."

I envied Shawna. How badly I wanted to spend my weekends tumbling down the rolling hills, building massive bonfires and cooking bacon and pancakes on the old-fashioned stove instead of waking to boring bowls of Cheerios and the morning news. "Do you like it there?"

"I do." She blushed.

"Why are you blushing?"

She fanned herself, reddening even more. "I'm not blushing."

"Doesn't have anything to do with Eloise, does it?" I nudged her.

Her face broke out into blotches. "Oh stop." She brushed my comment away with a flick of her wrist.

I latched onto her. "Tell me more."

She licked her lips, twisted her mouth, and blinked heavily.

"I've got a lot of time, if you have something to tell me." I squeezed her arm in mine.

She stopped, drew a deep breath, and exhaled. "How about if we just go to the pottery shop and make a mug or something?"

I released her arm. "Last one to the car buys the coffee."

I sped off leaving her in my dust.

* *

We sat molding clay. She formed a ridiculous mug. "Do you like it?"

"Keep working it." We pinched and tucked and smoothed our clay as she dodged questions about Eloise.

"Come on. Tell me something."

"She's much younger than I am."

"Like how much?"

"Thirteen years younger."

I laughed. "So does she adore you as much as you adore her?"

"Not in the least bit." She lifted up her mug.

"That is getting worse by the minute," I laughed. Shawna arched her eye in agreement.

"Does she know you adore her?"

"I turn into a silly, giggly fool whenever she enters the room. I get worse each visit."

"So you've got no game?"

"None."

"Have you tried to let her know you're interested?"

She shook her head. "I won't. I couldn't. I mean how would I start such a conversation with someone?"

"Don't use words." I smiled.

She flushed. "You have no idea what it's like for me."

"You don't give people enough credit. Everyone is not out to get you."

"Boss, there are some sick bastards out there," she said.

"I hardly doubt Eloise is one of them."

"She's sweet. She's shy. She can't even look me in the eye."

"Invite her out for a walk by the river. Just let nature take its course."

"I'm not going to take her out by the river and start putting the moves on her. She'd freak out."

"Give me a break!"

"It's always awkward when a girl discovers my penis." She tilted her head and examined the base of her mug. "The girls I want aren't interested in it. So, you tell me, how am I supposed to entice a girl who expects something far different between my legs?"

"People don't fall in love because of your gender."

"Give *me* a fucking break."

"Love knows nothing about gender. Souls fall in love. We might be more physically aroused by certain body parts, but that's just sex. That's not love."

"Maybe in your world."

My cell rang. It was Jessica. I let it continue ringing.

"I miss Ruby." I didn't look up. "It's like I've got this hole in my heart right now. Every time I take a breath it hurts."

"Why are you still with Jessica?"

Because like a romantic fool, I hinged on the hope that she would've remained the old Jessica forever. "Who the fuck knows."

"Do you love her?"

I rested on her question for a moment. "I do… I did… I love solving her problems."

Shawna tossed her clay down. "Ladies and gentlemen, she finally admits it."

I stood up from the table and punched my clay. It felt amazing. So, I punched it again.

"Go ahead and punch the shit out of it. That's what you need to do. Get mad. Get mad about something that belongs to you. Fuck everyone else's shit. Get mad because you want to get mad."

I punched that clay over and over again, fueled by an insatiable tolerance for pain that rose in me. I owned this anger. No one else did. I punched it harder with each blow until Shawna grabbed me from behind and pulled me away from it.

"Easy does it there. I didn't mean for you to break your knuckles."

I wrestled out of her grip and grabbed my clay and tore at it, shredding it piece by piece with my fingers like an angry tiger clawing at its prey. I tossed wads of clay all over the table, feeding this anger in me, this relentless anger for wasting so much of my time on trying to be the right person for everyone. "I'm so tired," I said, firing the shreds at the table. "So tired of putting myself last all of these years and letting people ruin the things I deserve out of life. Where does it get me?"

Shawna picked up her ugly mug and squished it between her hands, stretching and pulling at it. She grunted and dropped the clay to the table and rubbed it back and forth. "We're in control of our lives. Just like this clay, you see, we're in control. We're reshaping it to what we want it to be. I say what it turns into. Nobody gets to choose that for me. It molds after me, not the other way around."

I gathered all of my shredded clay and starting rolling it together, forming a long, snakelike shape. The cool, earthy clay soothed my hands, and I rolled it like I meant to roll it. It would become what I wanted it to become. I grunted as I worked it and pounded it, conforming it to my standards, my ideal, and my vision.

Shawna cheered me on, coached me to keep going, to keep pruning, and refining. "Make it yours."

I swirled my snakelike coil into a circular shape, rolling it in on itself until I formed a round hotplate. Each curve smoothed. The top surface flattened. It reminded me of a braided area rug, so perfect and equal.

We both sat down and stared at my hotplate. "Why a hotplate?" she asked.

"Because that's what I wanted it to be."

She patted my back, leaned her head against my shoulder and continued staring at it with me. "Good enough reason for me, friend."

* *

I returned home not more than two weeks later to find a used pickup truck in my driveway with a trailer attached. In it sat several lawn mowers, rakes, trimmers and other landscaping equipment. The truck's decal read Jessica's Landscaping.

I entered the living room and Jessica was sitting in front of a massive pile of paperwork wearing glasses. "Hey, you," she said without rising, without looking away from her paperwork.

"What's going on here?"

"I told you, I wanted to start my own company. So I did." She finally looked up at me. "Cool right?"

"Shouldn't we have discussed this first?" I stood holding my suitcase still. She eyed it.

"It's done. There really was nothing to discuss. If prison taught me anything, it's to work smarter, not harder. I just went for it."

"So that's it. You're in business?"

"Yes. I got a CPA to draw up the LLC paperwork."

She looked too much like a woman in charge. "How did you afford this?"

"Crystal from the club invested in it for me. She gets a percentage of profits and owns part of the shares to the company."

She sounded like she was speaking a different language. How did she know how to do all of this? Why hadn't she asked me to do this for her? "Am I part of this LLC, too?"

She tapped her cheek with a ballpoint pen. "We can add your name, sure."

"Add my name? This isn't an electronic flyer that you can just edit."

She calmly placed her glasses down on her lap. "You're mad?"

"Well, yes. I'm mad. This is absurd. I go away for a few weeks and suddenly you turn into Jessica, owner of a company?"

She stared me down. "I thought you'd be happy for me."

I fumed. How dare she change our lives like this without even considering my opinion? I never would've chosen that ugly font for the decal and I certainly never would've bought a Nissan. I couldn't get over that she met with a CPA and ironed out the details of her company name, investors, and equipment purchases without me. "I could've helped."

She softened. "I know. I just needed to do this on my own."

I nodded and broke the stare. "Okay." I headed towards the stairs with my suitcase. "I get it."

For the next several weeks I watched as Jessica morphed into Ms. Entrepreneur. She worked long days, and by the time she returned home, she barely had the energy to say goodnight, let alone kiss me. When we did speak, we did so in snippets. *How was your day? Good. How was yours? Excellent? Any new clients? Yep. How many? So many.*

At night, while she sneaked in full of grass stains and smelling of mulch, I sat on the patio and cried. I hated our routine. I hated not having a role. I hated not being included. She ran her business and thrived. Meanwhile, I worked out of the boring corporate office of The Gateway Suites and wanted to bury myself in a hole and suffocate. She bloomed to life, and every time I saw the twinkle of satisfaction in her eye, I cringed. She found life in the same spot where I found death, the death of us, of our future.

I turned into a weed, nourished only from her occasional request to pay a bill or call a client for her to let them know her crew was running late. Soon, I hated everything landscaping. I hated the pungent smell of gasoline, the relentless stains of grass, and the endless streams of mud that found its way into my foyer.

Somewhere in between exiting prison as an ex-con and wielding corporate paperwork, Jessica distanced herself from me, from us. "I just need to do something bigger than the old me," she said one rare night as she joined me on the patio after dinner.

"I just want to be included. That's all I'm asking," I said, tossing out one last Hail Mary pass.

"I've got it covered. You need to just trust that."

I stared up at a woman who I didn't even know anymore. I didn't recognize the serious tone of her voice, the cocky attitude, the confident stance. A stranger stood before me. She wedged this business in between us and allowed it to take my spot as her partner, her companion, the thing to which she turned.

One blink she clung to my every word, the next she spoke over me. We had nothing in common suddenly, other than enjoying a nightly cigarette together now. And, I hated smoking. So go figure. I bent to meet her needs and in the process I became addicted to nicotine and suffered serious mending withdrawals.

She was fixed, and I had no idea what to do with her mended soul.

This truth slapped me.

I was the broken one.

I was the fucked-up one.

I was the one craving to mend still.

I willed for her to stand before me, dangling her problems and broken spirit in my face like a tease. I wanted her to need me because that would land me in the sweet spot where purpose and direction merged and offered me something I could wrap my brain around and mold into something full of purpose again.

I craved the older version of Jessica, the worst of her.

I looked into her red eyes and allowed the silence to fill our space. Then, I took my first brave step out on the ledge. “You don’t need me anymore.”

She squeezed her eyes shut and inhaled. “We live two different lives now. And I carry around this enormous amount of guilt for my success.”

“Please don’t.”

“I do. You need me to be someone you can save. I can’t be that for you anymore.”

I bowed my head ashamed that I would want her to be any less.

“Now that I’m sober it’s even harder for me to play weak for you.”

“Play weak?”

“I loved how you used to take care of me before all of this happened. I leaned on you, and you were always there to pick up my pieces.”

“I loved being there to pick up your pieces.”

“That defined us. Now, we don’t have that anymore. I have no desire to have that anymore,” she said.

“Me either.” I kicked the dirt. “I care about you. I hope you know that.”

“You prefer me broken, though.”

We stared at each other. I did. I absolutely did. And like a freight train, it hit me that this wasn’t about Jessica. It was about me.

She exhaled. “I had these dreams of when I got home we’d start right back off where we left. No matter what I tried, nothing worked. I felt like you were waiting for me to crack. When I didn't, I could see the boredom set in. You have no interests in my interests, any more than I have in yours."

"You hate pottery," I said.

"You hate discussing lawn equipment and shrubbery."

"We have zero in common," I said, flatly.

"Zero."

We stood amongst the silent remnants of our tattered marriage, neither mad nor shocked.

"Knowing what you absolutely don't want out of life is more powerful than knowing what you do want," she said with surprising confidence. "At least in my case. I don't want to be a drunk. All I want to do is stay on this upward path, where I can find myself, my true self, my best self."

I exhaled. "Me too."

* *

I packed up my belongings and drove up to Rhode Island to live with Shawna until my house sold.

I knocked on Shawna's door. She answered wearing pink pajamas and hot rollers. "I am so glad to see you." She shuffled me in and proceeded down her hallway to the guest room. "Just toss your stuff in there and we'll settle you in later. Right now, I need your help." She started pulling out the hot rollers as we headed back to her kitchen. She turned around. "Gosh, where are my manners? Tell me how you are, gorgeous."

"I feel amazing."

She stopped walking and tugging at her rollers. "You look amazing."

"So what's going on here?" I asked, taking in the living room. It looked like something out of a designer magazine with its fluffy pillows, lacy curtains, and wicker basket filled with yarns and knitting needles. A total chick room.

"She called me." Her eyes sparkled. "Like thirty minutes ago! She invited me to go with her to tour Sakonnet Vineyards. She'll be here in half an hour. I'm nowhere near ready."

"What can I do?"

"Iron." She spun around, biting on her nails. "Get the iron from the closet and iron my skirt while I fix my hair and makeup."

"I've never seen you look so nervous." I laughed. Her hair waved up all over and bounced along with her walk.

She pointed to the closet on her way by. "Closet. Iron. Go."

Thirty minutes later, exactly, Eloise knocked on the door.

Shawna's eyes popped. She ran towards the bathroom. "You answer."

"My God, you're acting like this is the first time you've ever met her."

"For a date it is!" She ran down the hallway and slammed the door.

I stood alone to face the welcome. I opened the door to Eloise. She wore her dirty blonde hair in a French braid and wore a light shade of lipstick to match her fair, freckled complexion. "Hey I remember you from The Rafters," she said with a low, sweet voice. "Nadia, right?"

"Yes. That's right. Come on in." I invited her into my new temporary home.

A moment later, Shawna emerged. Her eyes erupted into a smile as soon as they landed on Eloise. "You look so pretty."

Eloise blushed equally as red.

Love definitely floated in the air.

* *

Our house sold within a month. At the signing over of the paperwork, we acted like two professionals completing a project. Then, when we said goodbye, we hugged and she cradled my head the way I used to do for her. "Take care of yourself, my little Butterfly."

A lump formed in my throat. “You too,” I managed to say.

“Don’t be a stranger,” she said.

I smiled and waved goodbye.

* *

I sat on a good down payment for a place of my own, but decided at the pleadings of Shawna to take my time and stay on as her roommate for a little while longer. Eloise visited often and the three of us would cook up these gourmet spreads and pig out until our stomachs hurt.

Every once in a while they’d slip about Ruby and her pilot girlfriend, and I’d mentally ball up in pain. I attempted to call her a few times, but failed to hit send. Her life had taken off, and I didn’t wait to screw it up for her.

So instead, I focused on something I could positively affect. I visited with her grampa every day that I knew Shawna or Ruby could not. I begged him to promise me not to tell Ruby.

“Our little secret,” he’d whisper.

“Yes,” I said. “Our little secret.”

I’d sit on his couch and talk to him about his younger days. He would talk about the farming and the mill work he did, about his younger brother dying from pneumonia, about his mother falling sick to heart disease, and how his older sister had to quit school to take care of the kids after that. He loved talking about school, and how he only managed to get to eighth grade because he too had to quit and work the farm.

He laughed when he talked about his old house, about how they lived on a hill and their house sat below the well, and about how the outhouse sat above the well. We laughed so loud at this I feared he’d choke.

The man lived a fascinating life. He used to brew his own moonshine. Sew his own clothes. Grow his own food. Raise chicken and cattle. “There were no grocery stores around us," he would say, gazing off as if looking out over those beautiful fields again. "We'd race to see who picked the most corn or tomatoes, and the winner would always get to hand off a chore the very next day. Life was simple back then. You know?"

"It sounds hard to me." I laughed. "I'm tortured when I have to go to the grocery store and buy produce."

"It was tough. Tough was good. Tough forced a person to get strong. We got to horse around out in the fields and get all that fresh air. Nowadays all the younger ones do is sit in front of the television. Kids don't know how to play."

Each time I visited, his fragility got worse. He'd have a hard time seeing me. We'd spend much of my visit going over the same memories. Each time I arrived, his spirit came alive. I enjoyed seeing the smile and color return to his cheeks when he'd talk about young Ruby, about his wife, and about his beloved Grace.

Each visit ended with at least one point of recognition where he'd look at me and smile like a little boy.

Shawna accused me of using him as a crutch, as that next person to mend and fix. Maybe at first I needed him that way. Yet, as my visits grew, I started to realize I couldn't mend a man who wasn't broken.

My visits became less about trying to find something to fix and more about learning to just let be.

We sipped tea. We slurped Jell-O. We read books. We sat in silence staring at the tree outside of his window. We prayed. We reminisced. We developed a trust and a friendship, one rooted in the present moment, and not ugly past failures, hurts, or expectations.

When he would go into his foggy moments, I'd ramble on about work and about the weather. Sometimes, I'd even indulge in the trust he provided and tell him how much I missed Ruby and how I had no idea how to get back into her life. I confessed to him, staring straight into his hazy eyes, that I wanted to call her several times but chickened out. "I lost a good one," I said on my latest visit. He stared straight ahead, completely in his own world. "I just want to know if she's okay. I've completely failed by not calling her."

Grampa looked over at me finally and said, "Sometimes you just got to let them go so they can learn to fly on their own. When they learn, if they come back, you've got someone who will always return and land on your heart like a whisper."

I stared at a glass of ginger ale on his bedside and admired the way the bubbles floated to the top. When they reached the air, they popped, freeing themselves. The bubbles aided one another, lifting each other to this freedom.

It dawned on me, suddenly. Just like these bubbles, Ruby lifted me up and pushed me out of the way. She set me free so I could learn to fly.

"Ruby is special," he said.

"Yes, sir, I know that."

"She's unconventional and can't be trapped. You can't clip her wings. She'll fall flat. She needs room and plenty of air under those wings. Watch out, because when she starts to soar, she gets up there really high and just whoosh, takes off like a bat out of hell." He laughed so hard he started to choke.

"What's to say she won't just keep on flying?"

"In time, I have faith that my Ruby will land where she needs."

I took a deep breath.

"I hurt her feelings."

He squinted at me. "How badly?"

"Very badly. I told her she was incapable."

He turned serious. "Do you think she is?"

"At times she's been a little reckless with her life."

"Does she laugh while being reckless?"

"She's always smiling."

"Are others laughing along with her?"

"Always."

"Then you must let her be."

"I already have. I backed out of her life months ago. She told me back then that she thinks I'm controlling because I like to help mend people."

"Are you a therapist?"

I laughed. "Hell no."

"Then, stop mending."

I nodded.

He stared off to the television. "Why do you come visit me?"

"Because I like you."

"Are you trying to mend me?"

"More like you're mending me," I said.

He looked back at me and smiled. "An old man like me?"

I nodded. "More than you'll ever know."

He sighed and labored for a breath. "Promise me something, dear."

"Anything."

"Well two things. One, don't trap her. Two, take care of her."

"Sir," I said, leaning in. "Those two things can't be compatible. You said so yourself. She's got wings, and those wings need to fly."

"Those wings also need air to lift them up. So promise me."

"I promise."

"Now listen carefully. Ruby doesn't trust easily."

"I know. I doubt she'd ever take my call again, if I'm even brave enough to press send."

"I'm going to ensure that one day she will take your call. She'll take it, because you're going to tell her I told you a secret."

"You've got a secret?"

"I'm going to tell you my secret, because I trust you."

I leaned in closer. "You've got my word."

"I'm not going to last much longer."

"Stop." I tapped his hand.

"When I die, I want you to show her something for me. Can you do that?"

"Stop talking like this."

"I buried a time capsule treasure for her back when I sold The Rafters. It's got a bunch of sentimental things that we shared over the years. I was feeling nostalgic back then. I wanted her to get back there one day. So, I planted the time capsule and told my lawyer about it. Of course, after I met Mrs. Green, I asked her to tell Ruby instead. I called my lawyer the next day and told him this change of plan. And now, guess what?"

"What?"

"Now, I want you to be the one to tell her. I want you to be there when she goes through it."

I swallowed back the strain of tears. "Wow. That's the sweetest thing ever."

"It's in the barn of The Rafters underneath the granite stone in the left corner."

"I'll see to it that she finds it many, many years from now." I winked.

He smiled. "I'm tired right now."

"Get some rest." I rose and smoothed his hair. "I'll be back in a few days, and we'll start on the next story."

He closed his eyes, and I walked out of his apartment.

Chapter Nineteen
Ruby

I never took my grampa back to the pottery café.

I never read to him again.

I would never get to hear another one of his stories.

I would never get to watch the silly grin pop on his face as the wind brushed past his hand sticking out of the window on our weekly trips to The Rafters.

My grampa, my role model, my saving grace, fell asleep and never woke up again.

The moment I walked into his living room and spotted him in his recliner, my heart clenched. His chest didn't rise or fall. His eyes didn't flutter. His hands didn't tremble.

A peaceful smile blanketed his face and wrapped me in comfort.

I sat down on the couch beside the recliner and cradled his hand with mine. I didn't cry. I just rested in peace alongside of him for a while, knowing that's exactly what he would've wanted from me.

* *

Later on that day, I returned to my condo with some of his photo albums and boxes of personal belongings. I sat on my bed and scanned over pictures of us through the years. He laughed and smiled in all of them. He never let on to the loneliness he carried. He loved me. He took me in his arms and led me through some of the strangest, funniest, and most memorable paths in life.

I pulled out the shoebox. It contained his expired driver's license, some dental floss, a copy of his birth certificate, an old *Time* magazine with a model T Ford on the cover. Underneath all of this laid a picture of him and Nadia sitting on his couch. She swept her arm around his shoulders. He smiled like he was the king of the prom, proud to be showing off his pretty date. In the photo, the daily calendar on his recliner's end table read just two months prior.

My heart swelled.

I stared at it for a long time. She adored my grampa. She hung onto his words the way a student hung onto a favorite teacher's. She asked him questions, involving him in conversation that brought life to his eyes. I admired this most about Nadia.

They both wore relaxed, peaceful smiles on their faces.

She needed him just as much as he needed her.

A strange envy stirred. I witnessed the true reflection of freedom in the lift on their cheeks and in the sparkles that shined in their eyes. The true freedom for them was not the absence of needing each other, but rather in needing each other.

I'd never get to sit and take a photo like this one with him.

A lump formed in my throat.

Nadia was the only one who would know just what to say to me to ease my pain.

I needed her.

I wanted her there with me, hugging me, telling me all would be okay. I wanted her to nurture my broken heart. I wanted her there with me looking through his things, helping me to remember him in his greatest light.

I stared long and hard at the image of them smiling, then picked up the phone and called her.

When I heard her delicate, soothing, familiar voice call out my name, peace blanketed me and I fell into her virtual embrace.

"Nadia," I whispered.

"Is everything okay?" she asked, her voice soft as a lullaby.

I folded over myself.

"Ruby?

I cried, whimpering in soft successions.

"Why are you crying?" Panic edged on her voice.

"Grampa died this morning."

"Oh," she moaned. "No." Her cry caught on, and she wailed into the phone along with me. We just cried. We couldn't stop. The cries grew louder and echoed each other. Her sorrow and pain comforted me in a way too deep for words.

* *

The procession from the funeral home to the church stretched for at least eighty cars. My heart swelled with pride as we drove past the library that he cherished so much. Outside the library, his friends—the children and their parents who shared his passion and love for stories—created an honor guard that spread across the front lawn and spanned down on either end of the sidewalk leading to the library's parking lot entrance. Nadia and Shawna sat with me in the limousine and wept along with me.

We celebrated his life in a Christian funeral mass at our church. We sat in the front row in my grampa's favorite spot. Nadia held my hand and offered me tissues and comforted me through his beloved church hymns.

Later, Shawna, Eloise, Rachel, and Marcy joined me for a catered lunch at the pottery café where his closest friends paid tribute to him by reading his stories aloud. Chuckles replaced tears as friends shared fond memories of a man who lived to tell stories and make people smile.

After the celebration of his life ended, Nadia walked with me around the park across the street from the pottery café. The sun shone, and the birds chirped in the trees above. We passed a group of families picnicking on a series of checkered blankets, giggling and enjoying life. The air smelled sweet and caressed me in nostalgia.

"You were right about me, you know," Nadia said, reaching for my hand. "I didn't know I had it in me to stand up without someone by my side. Since I separated from Jessica, I've gotten to know myself so much better. Your grampa helped me a lot with that."

I stopped walking and smoothed over the top of her hand, circling my fingers over her soft skin. "Do you miss her?"

"The old version of me misses the old version of her. It's best that those girls are never coming back, because they didn't live lives where they brought out the best in anyone, not even themselves."

"And how is the 'new you'? Are you happy?" I asked.

"This, right here," she said tightening her hand in mine, "Is the happiest I've been in a long time. Just being around you makes me feel alive."

I gazed into her loving eyes. "It's as if the air is easier to breathe."

We both inhaled.

"Where's your pilot girlfriend?"

I winced. "That didn't end well. She flew me to Block Island and refused to fly me back when I asked, because there was this party she wanted to attend. So, I hopped a ferry instead."

Relief washed over Nadia's smooth complexion. "I'm sorry that I called you incapable," she whispered. "You're far from that."

"You were right, though. I'm afraid to get hurt. I don't want to be anymore."

"You don't need to be."

"I'm learning that."

She swung our arms and cocked her head.

"I'm so glad you called me."

"I'm so glad you could be here for me."

"I love being there for you," she said. She opened her sweet smile to me, and I shed all of my fears right there in that park when I leaned in and kissed her. Her lips sheltered me from all I resisted and opened up a brand new path that sparkled with hope and radiated love in its most rarest and precious of forms.

* *

My grampa left me with over one hundred thousand dollars from the sale of The Rafters all those years ago. He never spent it on himself. He left a note for me telling me to spoil myself with it. All of this time I worried about paying him back five hundred dollars. Even as an adult, he guided me to focus on what mattered in life, which had nothing to do with money and everything to do with love of life. If he had handed me the money earlier on in life, I never would've met Nadia or Shawna.

A reason existed for everything under the sun.

As Nadia and I drove out to The Rafters to pay one last homage to my grampa, I stared out at the trees whizzing past us and mulled over what I'd do with all of that money.

I could rent a trendy beach condo. I could open up my very own massage studio. Nadia and I could take a month long vacation to Hawaii if we wanted. I could hire a maid service to clean my new condo. I could buy a new car and rest my beloved Camaro so she stayed nice and pristine for many years to come. I had so many choices; I didn't know which to choose.

"Thank you for coming with me, darling." I laid my hand on her wrist.

She raised my hand up to her lips and kissed it. "I'm honored that you'd ask me to come with you. I know this is not going to be easy."

"It's what he would've wanted."

A few hours later, we stood on top of the grassy field together. I held his ashes against my chest. "We used to race down this hill together, and just when we'd get to the bottom, he'd let me roll by him and win."

Nadia wiped her eyes but the tears still rolled down.

"This is where he'd want to be. Right here."

She braced her hand against my lower back. "Go ahead. Let him fly."

I opened the urn. The breeze took him in her graces, giving him the air he needed to lift up and fly away.

We watched him dance in the air, twirling along with the whispers of the wild and free energy that brought life to the trees, to the hills, to the grass, to the butterflies, to the birds, to all who breathed in its majestic power. We stood together and watched as he blended with his favorite place on Earth. When he disappeared into the fields, and I gasped, Nadia mended my soul with her loving embrace.

She held me for a long time as the sun faded in and out behind the white, fluffy clouds. I felt at peace and as one with the universe on top of that hillside.

This was home.

We spent the afternoon snuggled together on top of that hill. Then, as the sun started to set over the tree line, Nadia feathered my cheek with her lips. "Ruby, your grampa told me a secret."

"He doesn't tell many people secrets."

"He left something for you here, in the barn."

I placed my hand on my heart. "He did?" Fresh tears stung my cheeks.

"He feared you wouldn't trust me again, so he told me this secret in the hopes you would see he trusted me."

I felt my grampa's spirit all around us, enveloping us in a truth so clearly defined for us in this moment. "He always knew what was best for me." I stared out over the backdrop of our hill, the hill that defined me, and now would forever define us.

She cradled my arms and looked me in the eye. "I love you, Ruby Clark."

I kissed her with a new sense of freedom, opening myself up to her, and letting her in to feel my vulnerability, my tremble, and most of all, my love.

"Are you ready to see his secret?" she asked, kissing the tip of my nose.

I nuzzled up against her. "More ready than ever."

She took my hand in hers and lifted me up to my feet and led me down the hill, towards the barn. She led me over to a granite piece and picked it up. Together we dropped to our knees and bowed our heads. We held hands at this point and steadied our breathing. We stared into each other's eyes. Then, together, like a couple of mad women, we dug the earth with our fingertips, scratching and tossing dirt aside until we reached the plastic case.

I pulled it up and stared at it for a few long seconds.

"Open it."

I unlatched the top and smiled when I saw the plastic horse. I pulled it out. "Oh my God. This was his favorite toy as a kid." I handed it to Nadia. She cradled it in her hands.

A note sat on top of the rest of the items that read: *Dear Ruby, I got you to come back here, didn't I?! This place was magical and built us both into the people we've become. I am sad on this day because I am leaving The Rafters behind, but it is time to move on for me. This place just isn't the same without you in it, my precious free bird. Never forget this place, okay?*

Never forget the happiness that we shared. The memories we created. The lives we affected through my (INGENIOUS) stories (HAHA) and your sweet smile. May these tokens from our past years here together bring you joy as you continue on to make this world a better place. Keep smiling and living life to its fullest. I will love you always, your Grampa. P.S. Thank you for filling my life with joy.

"Wow." I stared at his messy handwriting. "This man sure had a way with words." I handed Nadia the note and started pulling out the token items one by one.

I pulled out my favorite childhood doll that he gave to me on my tenth birthday. Her red lips had faded to a soft pink and her blonde hair still hung in its side ponytail. "He would sit this doll on his lap while he read stories to his guests, because I worried she'd miss out somehow if she wasn't right next to him."

Nadia took her and chuckled. "So cute."

The box overflowed with things that brought back so many happy memories of dinners, walks, fishing trips, birthdays, Christmases, and story times. My entire childhood sat on the floor beside me, reminding me how great The Rafters was. It healed my broken childhood heart. It grew a trusting bond between Grampa and me. It taught me the value of friendship, of freedom, and now of love.

At the bottom of the box sat a handmade book.

"He wrote me a story."

"Read it."

I read his story about a bird named Ruby who witnessed one too many of her family and friends falling mid-flight. So this little bird, despite sneaking longing peeks up to the sky, stayed grounded. She spent her days wandering around the ground pecking at droppings and looking up to the sky, wishing she could fly. As her friends all began their flight lessons, she hung back, pulled by a fear too big to tackle. She denied this fear and blamed a broken wing. Soon, everyone she knew flew by day and left her alone to wander the open hillsides alone. She longed to be a part of the sky, so she wandered to the mountain's edge day after day just to feel the breeze rustle through the feathers on her wings. She dreamed of flying up to where the clouds danced above. But, the fear of falling weighed heavier. So, she sat alone on the mountainside day after day. Then one day, this beautiful yellow bird came to her side and nudged her off the edge of the mountain side. When she flapped her wings, and they failed, the yellow bird dove under her and guided her, giving her the support and confidence to flap her wings again and fly.

He ended with a personal note to me.

Fly, beautiful Ruby. Fly like the free bird you are. Never fear life, for you've got an angel watching over you.

My grampa stood right there with us, caressing us in his warm spirit. "Now I've got two angels."

Nadia pulled me into her embrace. I curled up against her and wept. She smoothed my hair and rocked with me.

"I want to honor him and make him proud."

"Of course you do," she said kissing the top of my head.

Many months later

Nadia and I purchased The Rafters back from Mrs. Green. I asked her to stay on and help. She agreed without blinking, as Eloise was moving to Providence with Shawna.

I stood in the center of the naked room that used to be decorated in dark, rustic furniture. My heart fluttered with a joy I could only describe as the feeling of wings flapping against my inner walls. My soul snapped alive. I scanned the bare, green walls, the laminated floors, and the baseboards with their crackling paint, and the elation mounted to surreal levels. I spotted an ant crawling across the floor in a mad dash to clear the room and make it to the corner. It danced across the laminate, eager to meet up with its destiny under the baseboard. This beautiful ant lived in my house. My house. I spun, arms wide-open taking in this moment when I finally owned something other than a portable massage chair. And what a room the chair would embrace finally.

The silence tickled my ears as if a thousand trumpets blew. I'd never heard anything quite as beautiful. In its wake, the echo of possibility rang and lifted me to a level where I could finally take in the full-scale view of life's beauty.

I walked up to the wall and ran my fingers down its smooth surface. A layer of dust trailed behind on my fingertip. I massaged it, stared at it, and got this jolt of excitement for what was to come.

I pictured a fresh coat of whisper yellow, embellished by beautiful artwork of mountain landscapes. I saw oversized chairs with matching ottomans and glass accent tables adorned with vases filled to the rim with polished rocks. Accent lighting would cozy up the space and elicit conversation from guests returning from a day's adventure walking under the canopy of colorful trees. Their faces would be kissed by the sun, their breathing methodically slow and steady, their gingerly laughter rising as they retold their funny accounts of the day spent enjoying one of the country's hidden treasures.

Couples would sit together in the oversized chairs, ankles draped over each other's, holding hands, kissing the tips of each other's noses, relishing in the inviting home that would become a sweet memory and possible tradition. And in the kitchen, I would bake cookies and brew tea. I'd deliver them on my grampa's silver tray.

Nadia, Shawna, Eloise, and Nadia's sister Sasha walked in carrying boxes. They dropped them in the corner where the ant had just crawled.

"Actually those are going up to the massage parlor room," I said.

Nadia dug into a tote bag. "Sweetheart, we should have a toast first." She broke out a bottle of champagne and glasses.

"Here, let me help," Sasha jumped in to the rescue.

Nadia handed her the champagne bottle. "Thanks for being here, sis."

Sasha busied herself with popping the cork, swallowing a smile, and turning red. "Don't be silly. It's nothing."

Nadia sneaked me an eye roll and half smile—a secret look we'd surely continue enjoying for years to come. She handed each of us a glass, and Sasha poured the bubbly. We held them up, and Nadia toasted.

"To Grampa Clark, the greatest man I've ever met," she said. "He dazzled. He joked. He laughed. He lit up the room with his smile. More importantly, he brought us all here to this moment in time. Without him, this moment, and all future moments together, would never exist. May we all live with such intensity, such character, such integrity, and such true freedom."

We clinked glasses and sipped our champagne.

I breathed in this moment.

I never thought I would be 'that girl.' You know, that girl who grew roots, employed others, and fell in love with a beautiful woman who needed her.

Yet, here I was, all of that and more.

I was finally *that* girl.

NOTE FROM THE AUTHOR

As with all of my books, I enjoy giving a portion of proceeds back to the community by donating to the NOH8 Campaign www.noh8campaign.com and Hearts United for Animals: www.hua.org. Thank you for being a part of this special contribution.

A SPECIAL REQUEST

If you enjoyed reading this story, I'd be so grateful for your favorable review of it. Just a sentence or two saying what you liked about *Staying True* will help others discover it and help me to serve you better with future books! (www.amazon.com/author/suziecarr)

Made in the USA
Lexington, KY
10 July 2013